TITUS

By
Keith Yocum

ISBN-10: 1482691213

EAN-13: 9781482691214

Library of Congress Control Number: 2013904688

CreateSpace Independent Publishing Platform

North Charleston, South Carolina

GLOSSARY

Amputation: Surgeons in both the Union and Confederate Armies employed amputation as a treatment for wounds to limbs that resulted in fractured bones. The soft lead composition of Minié balls often caused soldiers' bones to shatter on impact, necessitating amputation before infection and gangrene set in. There were an estimated 30,000 amputations by Union Army surgeons during the war.

Army of Northern Virginia: The primary Confederate Army that fought the Union Army of the Potomac in the East. It was led for most of the war by Gen. Robert E. Lee.

Army of the Potomac: The primary Union Army that fought the Confederate Army of Northern Virginia in Virginia, Maryland, and Pennsylvania.

Blue Mass: A pharmaceutical product of the era used to treat a wide variety of illnesses. While pharmacists could customize the concoction, it always included mercury, a toxic heavy metal.

Brigade: This military grouping or organization consisted of three to four regiments and was part of a division, with three divisions typically organized into a corps.

Busthead: Popular slang for alcoholic beverages.

Butternut: Name given to the medium-brown or tan-brown color of some Confederate uniforms. Also slang for Southern soldiers and civilians.

Enfield: A British-manufactured rifle used by both the North and South during the Civil War.

Foraging: The act of searching for food or provisions.

Gum blanket: Rubberized ground cloth used by Union and Confederate troops as either a poncho or ground cover.

Hard tack: A staple food item for Union and Confederate soldiers, it was a three-inch square cracker or biscuit made from water, flour, and often salt.

Laudanum: An opium-based narcotic that was mixed with alcohol into a tincture used before, during, and after the Civil War. It was used to treat a variety of illnesses including severe diarrhea and pain, and as a cough suppressant. It was highly addictive, though not known to be at the time, and many Americans of the era used it excessively, including Mary Todd Lincoln, wife of the President.

Limber: The short, two-wheeled portion of an artillery piece that housed ammunition and fuses.

Minié ball: The primary rifle bullet used by both armies in the Civil War. Co-invented by Frenchman Claude-Étienne Minié, the bullet was initially used in the Crimean War but was most effectively employed in the US Civil War. Its primary features were that it was conically shaped, had circular grooves around its circumference and featured a concave bottom. When fired the lead bullet expanded slightly and acquired spin from the rifling grooves in the barrel that dramatically improved its accuracy. While it was called a "ball," it was in fact bullet shaped, and it was popularly referred to as a "minnie."

Napoleons: Name given to the most common field artillery piece used on both sides during the Civil War. It fired a twelve-pound projectile and had a range of approximately sixteen hundred yards.

Parole: In the early years of the Civil War, both armies employed the European method of dealing with prisoners of war. Captured troops were released under the promise that they would not take up arms again during the war unless they were exchanged for a soldier on the opposite side. Late in the war, the Union restricted the process of parole to deny returning troops to the less-populated South.

Provost Marshal: During the Civil War the Union and Confederate armies concentrated police and judicial responsibilities under the provost marshal. These units exercised broad responsibility over many aspects of military and civilian life, including policing stragglers and deserters, preventing gambling, maintaining discipline, and interacting with civilians. While most provost marshals acted appropriately, some were criticized as overzealous, arbitrary, and even corrupt.

Regiment: A military unit that was often commanded by a colonel and consisted usually of ten companies. These companies were in turn led by officers and noncommissioned officers. Most companies were given sequential alphabetical designations starting with A. Companies consisted, at full strength, of approximately one hundred soldiers. Due to illness, desertions, and injury, companies were rarely at full strength.

Shelter half tent: Each Union soldier was given a half of a tent that was five feet long and could be buttoned to another half to make a full, two-soldier tent sometimes called a "dog tent."

Skedaddle: Slang used during the Civil War for running away or desertion.

Solid Shot: Artillery rounds could be fused to explode shortly after hitting an object or were timed to explode above the heads of the enemy, but some were also designed to remain intact, or solid. Solid shot was often in the form of cannonballs used against structures, fortifications, or ships.

Sutler: An independent merchant who followed the armies and sold a wide variety of items including writing supplies, newspapers, combs, playing cards, and any other product of value to soldiers in the field, usually at highly inflated prices.

"Though I have been trained as a soldier
and participated in many battles,
there never was a time when, in my opinion,
some way could not be found to
prevent the drawing of the sword."

—Ulysses S. Grant

*For Brenda, whose fascination with the Civil War sparked my own interest;
and for Denise, who has sustained me throughout.*

CHAPTER 1

They found the first one on Tuesday.

He was discovered slumped over the horizontal carcass of a hundred-foot loblolly pine tree that had fallen from the twin tugs of age and gravity.

The tree had been given a second, more pragmatic life as a latrine. Soldiers in the field typically sought out a sitting toilet, whether it was a sanctioned latrine or not.

It was Pvt. Buster Sturger from Huntingdon County, Pennsylvania, who found the first one.

Buster had taken off at a spirited trot from camp at the first sounds of the disagreement in his stomach. Long familiar with what those sounds presaged, he found the forlorn pine tree he had used the day before and took up position.

Buster grunted loudly as he did his business, feeling the sharp edges of the pine bark digging into his thighs.

It was only after standing up, cinching his belt and re-arranging his privates in the way that soldiers did when completing their toilet that he noticed the other soldier nearly thirty feet away from him at the other end of the log.

Perhaps it was the severe forward angle of the man's head and shoulders—his head was lodged between his knees—that captured Buster's attention. Or maybe it was the strange tilt of his body, but Buster had a notion that his latrine mate was in some form of distress. The soldier's exposed paper-white buttocks stood out in sharp relief from his dark-blue field jacket.

"Hey," Buster yelled in greeting.

The soldier did not move.

"Hey there," Buster said. "How yer doin'"?

The only sound Buster could hear was the chatter of two soldiers walking through the undergrowth toward the makeshift latrine. One of the two soldiers laughed and Buster recognized the high-pitched giggle as emanating from Nate Blute, one of his Company I comrades.

"Hey, Blute," Buster yelled as the two soldiers came closer.

"Hey, Buster," Nate replied. "It sure smells something bad over this way. I wished they'd had chosen another place for their defecations. I swear I can smell this stench in camp."

"No you cain't," the other soldier said.

"Yes I can," Nate said. "It about makes me sick to my stomach."

"Nate," Buster said, "what do you reckon ails our friend down there? He ain't as much as made a peep since I been here. I hardly know'd he was there till I stood up. He might be in a sick way, do you reckon?"

The three soldiers stood in the mottled light of the forest and stared at the man bent sharply forward.

"Hey!" Buster yelled. "You feelin' all right there, fellar?"

The only sound came from a mob of horseflies that had discovered hundreds of pounds of waste in the trench on the other side of the pine log.

"Hey," yelled Nate.

In the distance they could hear a soldier in camp yelling, his voice muffled through the trees.

"I reckon he ain't feelin' his best," Buster said. The three men walked slowly toward the sitting man. They stood looking at him and Buster noticed immediately that, while the soldier's face was hidden between his knees, a fair amount of blood had soaked into the brown leaves and black soil around his shoes. A fly could be seen crawling on the back of the man's neck.

"That's a might bit of blood, wouldn't you say, Buster?" Nate said carefully, seemingly measuring each word as if it were a pound of salt on a balance scale. "You think he might have spit that up?"

"Not to my thinkin'," Buster said. "I ain't seen nobody spit that much blood up. I think our good fellar here might have perished, sittin' here doin' his business."

"Well, that would be a sad state of affairs," the other soldier said.

"Hey," Nate said feebly to the prostrate figure.

Nate put his hand lightly on top of the black, greasy, matted hair of the man on the log and shoved him slightly but nothing happened. Then he shoved him harder and the figure toppled onto the ground, his arched back against the log.

"Oh," Buster said, as he and the other two stepped back.

The downed man's predicament was plain to see and they grimaced reflexively. The dead soldier's throat had been sliced open. A gap of at least an inch could be seen between the cut edges of flesh, showing the pink-and-white vertebrae in the man's neck and exposing the larynx as if it were an object about to fall out of its pocket.

SECOND LT. CLIVE RHYS HAD A HABIT OF whistling to himself when he was busy with a task that required concentration. He was not unaware that some of the other junior officers found the whistling irksome—some called it childish, even—but he was not deterred. It was an old habit, and truth be told, it was the only tool he could summon to distract himself from the drudgery and petty tasks that were given to a very junior officer.

Mind you, Rhys's status as a second lieutenant was not given much credibility by his fellow officers. The only reason young Rhys had a do-nothing officer's position was because his uncle, Third Division Commander Gen. Sylvester Paxton, had directed the Second Brigade commander Col. Stanley Rittenhouse to take his nephew under his wing.

But Col. Rittenhouse already had a full complement of brigade staff officers and he in turn directed his aide-de-camp, a fine soldier named Capt. Caleb Lynch, to take young Second Lt. Rhys under *his* wing.

Some men would have taken on this demeaning task with displeasure and hostility.

Capt. Lynch, though, took this assignment with quiet acceptance. The War of Secession had been going on for more than two years and had not really shown its ugly face to the 239th Pennsylvania Volunteers. The regiment had not tasted battle yet but its turn was coming soon. Lynch had a notion that the 239th would soon "see the elephant." And if what Lynch heard was true, the regiment would likely need a young Lt. Rhys sooner than even Lt. Rhys knew.

May 1, 1863, found clean-shaven, curly-haired Lt. Rhys whistling a spirited rendition of "The Battle Hymn of the Republic." Though the tune was well known as "John Brown's Body," there were new lyrics written by a woman named Julia Howe that stirred Rhys's patriotic blood like nothing else. He could only remember a few lines but they were his favorite:

He has sounded forth the trumpet that shall never call retreat;
He is sifting out the hearts of men before His judgment-seat:
Oh, be swift, my soul, to answer Him! Be jubilant, my feet!
Our God is marching on.

Glory, glory, hallelujah!
Glory, glory, hallelujah!
Glory, glory, hallelujah!
Our God is marching on.

Still, he was a far better whistler than a singer, so he dutifully polished his boots in his tent, absorbed in the task and oblivious to the muddy, chaotic assembly of 130,000 Union troops spread over many miles of Virginia countryside on the hunt for Bobby Lee's Secessionist army of traitors.

The rhythmic clanking of a sword announced the appearance of an important visitor, and Rhys stopped his incessant polishing and self-absorbed whistle.

"Lt. Rhys," a voice called from outside the tent.

"Yes, Capt. Lynch," Rhys said standing up and stooping past the low flap in his bare feet.

Lynch, a short, black-haired man with high cheekbones and graceful, handsome features, stood outside and looked down at Rhys's feet.

"Sorry, sir," Rhys said quickly. "I was polishing my boots. They were in need of cleaning, sir."

"I see," Lynch said. "Lieutenant, we are in the field at this stage and may be seeing the enemy any day now. You need not worry about the condition of your boots. I believe no one will notice nor remark on their condition."

"Of course, sir."

"I'd like you to look into something for me, please," Lynch said.

"Anything, sir."

"There was a soldier found dead near the sinks," he said, absently brushing a fly away from his face. "Please notify Capt. Fetzer of Company I. It was one of his men who found the body. I'd like to know whether we have some of these Virginia locals killing our men, or whether it's Jeb Stuart's men in our proximity. Please report back to me as soon as possible. Thank you."

Lynch turned, his sword clanking lightly, and he walked briskly away, his boots squishing in the soft mud.

"YOU RECKON WE'RE BEING STALKED BY SOME MURDEROUS Injuns that are workin' for the Secessionists?" Buster said, sitting on a small log and toying with an eight-inch strip of birch. At five foot seven inches, Buster sported thick black hair and a drooping mustache that he sometimes sucked absently into the corners of his mouth. A thin, one-inch scar running diagonally on his cheekbone under his left eye gave him a rakish air, especially when he flashed his hazel-tinted eyes in mischief.

"Stop talking about Injuns, for God's sake," Pvt. Titus Mott said. "There's no Injuns here. We kilt most of them years ago and run off what's left to somewhere out west."

"I'm tellin' you that no Rebel soldier is going to sneak up on a man who's emptyin' his bowels, in a defenseless position, and near cut his head off," Buster said, sucking the edges of his moustache. "He might take him prisoner, or if he had to, he might just stab him, but he wouldn't have sliced him that way. That weren't no Rebel."

"Buster, you got too much going on inside that head of yours," Titus said. "Stop talkin' gibberish."

"Well, you didn't see the poor fellar. He had his head nearly took off. It was bothersome to look at."

Titus toyed with the fire absently, pushing an oak twig against a glowing charcoal slab. Combined with the hundred other small fire pits in the temporary camp, the heavy blue-gray layers of smoke stratified into the air. The soldiers in the 239th had recently moved out of their winter quarters in Warrenton, and had already grown that brownish, sooty pallor of men exposed relentlessly to the sun, dust, and wood smoke.

Titus's sandy brown hair sat in two waves parted down the middle, turning up slightly at the edges. His light blue eyes, tanned face, and thin frame gave him a handsome but serious look.

"I promise you it won't be the most bothersome thing you'll see in this damned war," Titus said. "I guarantee you that."

THE RAIN HAD ENDED TWO DAYS BEFORE, SATURATING the fertile countryside near the Rapidan and Rappahannock Rivers. The moisture complemented the cool spring days, keeping the soldiers comfortable. But it turned the roads into rivers of reddish-brown mud and the thick parts of the forest into sponge carpets of decaying leaves. As Lt. Rhys walked through the trees and pine scrub, his freshly polished boots made almost no sound. The pitch pine and eastern hemlock trees gave off a sharp medicinal smell that he found pleasing, while the isolated huge black oak, and boxelder trees crowded out the light from above.

Again, for perhaps the hundredth time, he wondered how such a beautiful and gentle countryside could house several hundred thousand soldiers whose purpose was to kill and maim each other.

"Whew, that's quite a smell," Rhys said.

"Yep, well, it's a latrine. And there sure are a lot of men who need a place to relieve themselves," Capt. Fetzer said.

The two officers could now see the temporary pine-tree latrine through the brush. Two soldiers sat fifteen feet apart talking animatedly as the men approached. Rhys was aware of the disdain Capt. Fetzer had for him and his special position as a second lieutenant attached to the Brigade command. When it came time for the 239th to see action, it would be officers like Fetzer who would stand with his company and bear the brunt of the lead balls from the Rebel army, while Rhys would be riding around following Capt. Lynch as he delivered messages.

The two soldiers on the log stopped talking as Fetzer and Rhys approached.

"Cap'n," one of them said. "Is it true a man was kilt here at the latrine?"

"Seems to be the case," Fetzer said. "You boys watch yourselves out here. Orders are at least two at a time when you visit. Stick by those rules, please."

"Is it true he was stabbed by an Injun?" the second soldier asked, wiping his pale buttocks with a piece of newspaper.

"Good Lord, son, who told you that?" Fetzer said.

"I just heard it, that's all Cap'n," he said. "Cain't remember who done told me."

"No it is not true," Fetzer said. "For your information we're fightin' Secessionists here in Virginia. Keep an eye out for them before you go looking for heathens."

The two soldiers mumbled a few words to each other, quickly finished, and took off back to camp.

Fetzer walked over to a spot on the log.

"That's where he was found," he said.

"Why do those men think it was an Indian that killed the poor fellow?" Rhys asked.

"Well, he had his throat slit from ear to ear," Fetzer said running the upturned thumb of his right hand underneath his neck. His thumbnail coursing against a three-day stubble gave the gesture a loud, raspy sound. "Some of these boys think only an Indian kills a man that way and that's how the rumor started. At least that's my guess."

"Capt. Lynch asked me to check on whether Stuart's men were responsible for the killing," Rhys said looking around the forest.

"We've had no reports of Rebels in our area at all," Fetzer said. "We haven't seen anyone, to be honest."

"Any locals here? Farmers?"

"Haven't seen a soul," Fetzer said. "Just an unlucky cow."

"An unlucky cow?"

"Well, lucky for us, unlucky for her. She's already been eaten. Wasn't half bad at that."

"What was the dead soldier's name?"

"Pvt. Seymour Hesh, of Company H."

"What's your opinion of what happened to the dead soldier?" Rhys asked.

"He got his throat slit, that's what happened to him."

Rhys could feel the reproach rising from the senior officer, and he decided to end the meeting as quickly as possible. "Thank you, Captain," he said turning away to camp.

"There was one thing that was peculiar, I suppose," Fetzer said.

Rhys stopped. "There was?" he said, turning to face Fetzer.

"Well, it seemed that way," Fetzer said. "I'm sure it's nothing."

"Can you share that with me and Capt. Lynch perhaps?"

"I'm not trying to make more out of it than it seemed," Fetzer said, defensively.

"Don't worry," Rhys said, shifting his six-foot frame and looking down at the smaller Fetzer. "I'll make sure to downplay it. You won't be called to headquarters to give an accounting, if that's what you're worried about."

Fetzer took a moment and idly scanned the cool and damp forest. "Well, the poor fellow had a cross on his forehead," Fetzer said. "Or maybe it was an 'X.' It was small, maybe an inch or two. Seemed like someone put the tip of their finger in the fellow's blood and made the mark on his forehead."

Rhys and Fetzer looked at each other for several seconds without speaking. In the distance a dog barked several times. And from even farther away a muffled bugle call twisted its way through the undergrowth.

"On his forehead?" Rhys asked.

"Yep."

"Might someone else besides the killer have made the mark after he died?"

"Maybe, but most of the fellars were petrified to even approach the body," Fetzer said.

"You said it was a cross or an 'X?' on his forehead?"

"Yep."

CHAPTER 2

Capt. Lynch stood in the rear of the brigade's assembly of officers. He preferred to remain at the periphery of these huge conclaves. His primary responsibility was to understand the broad outlines of particular troop movements for the corps and to serve the communications needs of brigade commander Col. Rittenhouse.

The Army of the Potomac had fallen in love with a technology called the telegraph service, and they had strung long rubber-coated wires up in trees all the way back to Washington. The War Department could now send messages almost instantaneously to the army's Major Gen. Joseph Hooker using some kind of code. Lynch and several other aides-de-camp were deeply suspicious of this communications tool, which seemed like more meddling from Washington. But when it came to the give-and-take of battle, it would require messengers like Lynch to ride between regiments and corps headquarters to deliver orders of battle.

That's if the regimental and divisional officers could remain calm and sober. Rittenhouse was probably a good man and capable of inspired leadership, but like many senior officers, Lynch knew that the Colonel drank too much and was often visibly drunk during the day. It was the scourge of too many fine officers in the Union Army, he felt, but the abundance of army-issue whiskey was too much temptation for some.

"Well, it seems that Hooker wants to use First Corps here as a bit of flank protection and a reserve to the main forces," Rittenhouse said to spirited boos and hisses.

"Now, now, men," he said raising his hand to quiet them. "They'll be plenty of battles in this war for us and our time will certainly come. And let's not forget that as a reserve unit in this battle we could be thrown in at any time."

Rittenhouse stood up from the table and wobbled a bit under the combined effect of too little sleep and too much whiskey.

"Come round here, men, and let's review the plan of battle," he said pointing at a large map on the table. "I think we might have got those Rebels in a fix and it's going to be hard for them to keep Richmond out of our hands this time, by God."

BUSTER STOOD MOTIONLESS AND STRUGGLED TO CONTROL HIS breathing, both surprised and shocked at his good fortune. Holding the firewood tight against his chest, he could hear the other men on firewood detail spread out to his left, and he was hoping none of them would cut back to disrupt the scene playing out before him.

About thirty yards in front of Buster, in a small clearing, stood the mangiest mule he'd ever seen. The beast pawed at the thin undergrowth and busied itself with searching out what few morsels it could nose from the soil.

Gently and with as much stealth as he could muster, Buster slowly tiptoed backward until he was far enough away from the animal to turn and run back to camp to dump his load. He rushed up to Master Sergeant McVickers and dropped the pile.

"What the hell do you think that is, Sturger?" McVickers said.

"That's my wood," he said, hurriedly backing away.

"You scoundrel, that's barely half a load. You get your ass out there now and bring back another load."

"I cain't, sergeant," he said feebly over his shoulder. "I need to attend to somethin' mighty important. It's vital."

"Goddamn you, Sturger, get back here!"

But he was already running back to his tent, set as he was on his mission. After rummaging through his shared tent, he found two four-foot lengths of rope that he quickly tied together and before he knew it, Buster was back where he had stood fifteen minutes earlier, looking for the abandoned or runaway mule.

But the mule had disappeared.

"Damn," he said in a whisper. He scanned the area in a 360-degree arc.

His prey had most certainly moved on, and Buster debated whether to continue the hunt or return to camp. He worried that if he wandered too far away from Union lines he might find himself in a Rebel camp sooner than he found his runaway mule.

A throttled kind of whinny to his right startled Buster. He turned to see the black mule staring at him from forty feet away.

The animal's short, spiked ears twitched as it considered Buster.

"Hey there," Buster said softly. "I got somethin' fer ya."

He reached into his pocket and pulled out a hardtack biscuit square, holding it forward in the palm of his hand.

The mule snorted, shifted its front legs slightly, and focused on the proffered food.

"Come on," Buster said softly. "This is fer ya, but yer goin' to have to come and git it fer yerself."

The animal stared at Buster intently but made no move to advance.

The stare down continued for several more seconds, until Buster raised the biscuit to his mouth and took a bite out of the corner. "Darn, that is so good," he said. "Mmmm."

Buster took a single step backward. "Come on," he repeated, holding out the biscuit again.

The mule seemed to consider its options for a few moments, whinnied again, and then made a tentative step forward, its appetite overcoming any innate suspicion.

Buster took another bite, chewing loudly and with exaggerated gusto. He held out the biscuit again.

The mule took several steps closer, stopped, and then continued its tentative advance toward the biscuit. Now he was only about ten feet away. Buster knew that it was unlikely he could snare the animal even at that distance.

He broke off a small chunk of the hardtack and threw it at the front hooves of the animal. The mule quickly covered the piece with its lips and absorbed it along with several accompanying tree leaves.

Buster held out the remaining piece in his hand. The animal, with the taste fresh in its memory, now had a burning desire for more. It stepped forward and enveloped Buster's hand in its sloppy lips, pulling the piece away in one swipe. The mule chewed the hardtack with enormous enthusiasm and dropped his snout as he became absorbed in the pleasure of consuming the biscuit.

Buster quickly put the noose over the mule's head and tightened it only slightly around its neck. "Well, darn, that wasn't so hard," he said out loud.

After chewing the hardtack the mule pushed its nose against Buster's pants pocket looking for more food.

"Hold on there, fellar," Buster chuckled. "I ain't got no more. You just come with me and everything is goin' to be fine."

He led the docile animal the two hundred yards or so back to camp and made his way to the commissary tent.

"Hello there Sgt. Knoll," Buster said leading his charge to a halt in front of the commissary tent.

"What have you got there, Buster?" Knoll said, pushing his hat back off his forehead with his right thumb and scratching his stomach with his left hand.

"It be a mule, Sgt. Knoll."

"I can see that with my own tired eyes, Buster," he said. "Where did you come upon this creature? He's got a Union brand on him."

"Found him in the woods all by he self, just munchin'," Buster said. "Was goin' to take him to the mule master but thought you might have a need for an extra mule."

"We always have a need for an extra mule," Knoll said, scratching his stomach again. Walking over to the animal he slapped its neck several times. "What kind of disposition does this animal have?"

"He's as cuddly as a house cat," Buster said.

"A house cat, you say?"

"Yes, sir."

"Does he meow like a house cat?" Knoll asked.

"Cain't say I heard him do that, Sgt. Knoll," Buster said.

The two men and the mule took turns staring at each other, each shifting their feet from time to time.

"What do you reckon a mule like this would cost me?" Knoll said at last.

"Some bacon," Buster said. "And some coffee. And maybe some beans."

"Even a scoundrel like you, Buster, is aware that robbery is a crime in this army. You can take that animal to the mule master for all I care."

Buster turned slowly and led the animal away but stopped when Knoll said, "Damn you, Buster. I know you have some redeeming qualities, but I just cannot for the moment conjure them up. Bring that pitiful beast over here and collect your ill-gotten gains."

Pvt. Joseph Meir of Company D was pleased to be on guard duty, since there was no threat of rain and the night was pleasantly cool. The ring of night pickets was strung out over a wide arc facing southwest and situated approximately two hundred yards from the sleeping members of the 239th.

What Meir and nearly every infantryman in the Union Army liked most about guard duty was the fact that they were instantly immune to the aggravating travails of camp life, including inspection, drills, firewood patrols, and the like. The typical guard schedule called for twenty-four hours of duty, with two hours on and four hours off, so that in twenty-four hours, a guard would be on duty for eight hours.

But Meir had been told to sit for a double shift this night, because his replacement, a seventeen-year-old from Harrisburg, Pennsylvania, had come down sick. Ordinarily he would have complained bitterly, but night attacks were so rare that he knew he could probably sleep while simultaneously gaining some favor with that irksome sergeant of the guard.

Sitting on his gum blanket to insulate himself from the damp forest soil, Meir pulled his wool blanket over his shoulders and nestled into the pile of soft and medicinal-smelling needles of a large black pine tree. Placing his Enfield rifle across his knees, he stared out into the blackness of the forest and tried to remain vigilant. The nearest guards were hunkered down twenty yards away from him on either side. He reasoned that his neighbors were too far away to notice him sleeping if, in fact, he succumbed to that siren song. But any intruder to their front would certainly rouse at least one of the nearby guards and get some hot lead to discourage their approach.

So Meir snuggled his back up to the tree trunk and closed his eyes, listening to the sounds of vociferous insects on the prowl after their winter slumber. Every now and then he heard the mournful hooting of an owl.

He had struggled through a lengthy period of disturbed half-sleep when he was alerted by the sounds of footsteps behind him.

Damn sergeant of the guard better not be checkin' up on us, he thought. *I swear he is an irksome man.*

The visitor stood in front of Meir and said softly, "Hello."

"Hey" Meir said, confused about the presence of his visitor.

"Can you let me see your bayonet?" the visitor said.

"My bayonet?" Meir said. "I guess so." He leaned over and pulled his bayonet out of its scabbard, handing it up.

The visitor took the bayonet in his right hand, readjusted it so that he held it at the base just above the ring, and said softly, "Wait just a moment before you get up."

With one swift motion the man took a step toward Meir using all of his momentum to ram the eighteen-inch tapered blade into the area near Meir's heart. The attacker had also reached out with his left hand and covered Meir's mouth, pressing the startled man's head hard against the tree trunk.

The blade had been driven with such force that it easily slid between two front ribs, punctured the top of Meir's heart and exited an inch beyond his back, impaling itself into the bark of the tree.

Stunned, Meir felt a nauseating wave of pain wash over him and he reflexively grabbed the wrist of his attacker as the man continued to thrust the bayonet with all his might. Meir tried to cry out but his punctured lung made it difficult to muster the wind.

His attacker, now on one knee in front of Meir, whispered softly to him to "Shhhh. Quiet there. You can sleep now."

And just as suddenly as the attack had begun, Meir felt a calm pervade his body and he stopped struggling.

The last sound he heard as he fell unconscious was the cry of an owl in the Virginia countryside.

There were five soldiers surrounding a small fire trying to fight off the early morning chill. The camp was filled with many other small fires, and the dampness and still air kept the smoke close to the ground, creating a palpable fog that clung to clothes and skin.

Titus had finished grinding a handful of coffee beans with his jury-rigged pestle and was emptying them into his small tin cup when Buster said, "I told you them Injuns was near us. I cain't believe I just walked out there to catch me a wayward mule. I could have been murdered by one of them savages."

"Oh, stop yer talk about Injuns," Titus said, carefully adding water from his canteen to the tin cup. The crushed coffee beans floated to the top while he used a Y-shaped stick to hold the cup over the fire.

"Titus, I'm tellin' you, they found another one last night, or at least that's what I been told," Buster said.

"I heard it too, Titus," said Pvt. James Baltz. "Cain't say it was an Injun, but fellar in Company C was stabbed to death on guard duty."

"I ain't saying the poor fellow *wasn't* killed, I'm just tryin' to keep Buster here from saying it was Injuns," Titus said.

"Well, who else sneaks up and stabs a man like that?" Buster said, sopping up bacon grease with hardtack on his tin plate. "That's not how Jeb Stuart takes to battle—one Yankee soldier at a time with a knife. Don't make no sense."

"Sometimes you just hurt my brain," Titus said shaking his cup as it began to boil over the fire.

"Well, until somebody has a better idea, I'm stickin' to Injuns," Buster said.

The only dead person Lt. Rhys had seen in his life was his Aunt Martha. She had been in her seventies when she passed away. His family had attended the wake and funeral. For the wake, Aunt Martha was laid out in her best Sunday clothes in the living room of his uncle's house, but besides looking more pale than usual, she appeared normal.

So he was expecting more or less the same as he stood in front of Pvt. Meir's body as it sat impaled against the pine tree.

But Meir did not look normal in death. The front of his field jacket was saturated with a huge black-red stain; his mouth was contorted in a kind of snarl, and his eyes were partly open, as if they were trying to focus on some distant object. His field cap was several feet away on the ground.

"Well, I wouldn't have bothered to show the body to you," Capt. Fetzer said. "Except for the forehead."

Rhys swallowed nervously as he tried to focus on the forehead of the dead man. He bent down and could see a two-inch X or cross smeared in blood on Meir's forehead.

"What do you think the mark means?" Rhys asked standing up.

"Faintest idea," Fetzer replied.

"Did you say he was stabbed with his own bayonet?" Rhys asked.

"Appears that way," he said. "Can't for the life of me comprehend why a man on guard duty would turn over his bayonet to someone standing in front of him in the middle of the night, and then just sit as the attacker rammed the damn thing through him."

"Could the bayonet be the attacker's?" Rhys asked.

"Well, it's a federal-issue bayonet. And you can see Meir's missing his bayonet, so my conclusion would be that he handed it over to this attacker," Fetzer said.

Rhys stared into the distance. He did not want to appear confused. It was far better to look uninterested or distracted. He had seen his mentor, Capt. Lynch, affect this behavior many times and thought it a useful lesson.

"Why do you think Meir would give up his bayonet?" Rhys asked.

"Like I said," Fetzer said, "I cannot fathom a reasonable answer to this question. Except..."

"Except what?"

"Except if Meir knew the man he was handing it to and trusted him," Fetzer said quickly.

"Pardon me?" Rhys said.

"Pardon you, what?" Fetzer said.

"Are you suggesting a federal soldier stabbed this man?"

"It's one option, I reckon," he said.

"And the X or cross seems to be the same thing that you found on that other fellar at the latrine?" Rhys asked.

"Yep," Fetzer said.

CHAPTER 3

Dr. Grayson Morse had finished his meager breakfast of coffee, hard-tack, and fried bacon and was trying to steel himself for the morning sick call. He heard the drum call rumble throughout camp and knew that within twenty minutes he would be assaulted by a long line of soldiers for sick call exhibiting myriad symptoms from dysentery, nervous exhaustion and, most especially, malingering. As the regiment had moved farther from its winter quarters and closer to battle the number of daily sick-call soldiers had grown.

Capt. Morse, a small, thin man with touches of gray at the temples and a clean-shaven chin, was growing apprehensive about the 239th's expected brush with the enemy. Like many of his physician peers, Morse had not at-tended medical school but served as an apprentice during his training. He had been a country doctor for ten years prior to the war and had not been sufficiently trained to manage the volume of his patients nor the rigors and complexity of attending to battle wounds.

The only training for field surgery he had received was a single day in Washington, DC, when a military surgeon had demonstrated the finer points of amputation to a group of thirty or so country doctors in his group.

First, the surgeon stated, chloroform was given to the wounded patient. Ether was not available in sufficient quantities, the surgeon reported, so they should plan to administer chloroform as the anesthesia. It was poured onto a small sponge inside a copper funnel that was placed over the nose and mouth of the patient. If the funnel was not available, a simple piece of cotton cloth could be saturated with the anesthesia and placed over the patient's mouth and nose. The patient was to be asked to breathe deeply and count down from fifty.

If too much chloroform was administered, the soldier could die, the military surgeon told the doctors in training as an afterthought.

"How much is too much?" an older physician had asked.

"Just a couple of drops should do it," the surgeon had responded, "and perhaps a few more drops for a larger man."

"And how would you know if you did *not* administer enough chloroform?" another physician asked.

"Oh, you'll know that soon enough," the military surgeon said. "Your patient will grab your throat with his remaining hand and squeeze it until you, too, feel like sleeping."

This comment caused a smattering of chuckles, and the teacher pressed on.

In the case of an amputation, a tourniquet was to be applied above the closest major joint from the damaged extremities. So a wound to the calf or shin would call for a tourniquet slightly above the knee; a wound to the forearm would mean a tourniquet should be applied above the elbow. If the wound was above the major joint, then the tourniquet should be applied as close as possible to either the shoulder or hip joint.

Once the tourniquet stopped the flow of blood, and the patient was unconscious, then a long surgeon's knife was used to cut away the skin completely around the appendage with allowance made for extra skin to cover the stump at the end. A smaller scalpel was used to cut the muscles and tendons. Finally a capital saw was used to cut through the bone. To tie off the arteries and blood vessels the physician was to use a delicate hooked tool called a tenaculum to grab the vessels that might have retracted into the stump. Nippers or a bone file could be used to clean up the ends of the bone and finally silk or horsehair sutures were used to close up the stump.

Capt. Morse thought it sounded easy enough, but he had heard stories of surgeons in field hospitals amputating a hundred limbs at a stretch until their arms were useless from fatigue.

But that was what he expected *after* battle; he could barely keep up with the soldiers who showed up each day complaining of some minor malady long *before* battle.

"Let's get ready," Morse said to his assistant Pvt. Peter Sandler. "The sheep are surely on their way over." The two men maintained a shared joke about the men of sick call being a "flock of sheep" and exhibiting all the qualities of such a mob: skittishness at being singled out, a tendency to pack together tightly when stressed, and the ability to repeat the exact behavior of the other sheep until the group appeared massed into a single unit.

"Baaaaa," Sandler said, eliciting a short but deep chuckle from Morse.

The first soldier in line stood in front of Morse. He was about five feet eight inches tall, thin, and sported a dirty blond mop of hair and a scrawny beard. Morse thought the soldier looked ill, with dark circles around his eyes. He also made a slight wheezing sound when he breathed.

"What's ailing you, Private?" Morse asked.

"My bowels feel something awful," the soldier said. "Food runs right through me and I spend most of my day at the latrine. I need something to calm my bowels."

"Sandler, give this man some quinine," Morse said to his aide.

"Doc, you gave that to me three days ago and that medicine did nothin' for my bowels," the soldier said, his face strained. "Got any other kind of medicine for the belly? I'm feelin' mighty sick these days."

"I'm sorry for your suffering, son, but we only have a limited supply of medicine," Morse said. "And quinine is the best we have."

"I'm feelin' so weak that I just don't think I could fight off one of them Injuns if they come after me," the soldier said, wiping his nose with the back of his right hand.

"Pardon me?" Morse said shooting a sideways glance at Sandler. "Did you say *Indians?* Are you feverish too, son?"

"Heck, ain't feelin' feverish," the man said. "It's my bowels that's burnin' up."

"Then what was it you said about Indians?"

"Injuns are killin' soldiers, didn't you know? Them Rebs got Injuns sneakin' into camp and killin' boys. Two already been kilt. And I don't plan to be the third one. No, sir."

"Pvt. Sandler, you hear anything about Indians sneaking into camp?"

"Can't say that I have," Sandler said.

"Well, give this poor fellow some quinine and a shot of whiskey."

"Now yer talkin', Doc," the soldier said, absently rubbing his stomach with the palm of his left hand.

It was Company I's turn and Titus Mott inched his way forward in the long snaking line of soldiers. He was never a big talker, but he was even quieter than usual as he shuffled ahead to pick up his rations. The company was being given three days' rations and that could only mean one thing— they were going into battle.

Titus was not frightened of battle; they had trained long and hard, and he was confident that he and the other members of the regiment would acquit themselves well. But he worried about the battalion and corps planners. So many battles had gone against the Union due to poor planning, and this was not lost on the men who would have to do the fighting.

There were already several hundred thousand Union and Rebel soldiers facing each other in the Virginia countryside near the Rapidan River this very day. Titus was confident that he would do *his* duty, even though he was a very small cog in the machinery of war. Still, he fretted that he might forfeit his life due to another tactical mistake or bout of cowardice by a Union general.

When it was his turn in line, Titus stooped down on one knee and picked up his allotment that was grouped into small individual piles on a large canvas sheet set on the ground. Each soldier grabbed his three-day ration of bacon, hard tack, and coffee beans and returned to his tent to pack away the food.

As he stood up off the canvas he heard Buster yell from back in the line, "Hey there, Titus, leave us some victuals. How about some Christian charity?"

There were guffaws of laughter.

Titus turned and said, "Don't you worry none. I know'd it's yer third time through the line, so the quartermaster here said I could have yer whiskey for the next month."

More laughter followed, some of which was directed at Buster and some of which was the nervous release of men worried about the looming battle.

Already they could hear a desultory artillery duel taking place miles away, the booms rumbling across the freshly plowed fields and lush foothills.

A welcome chill had settled on the camp in the late afternoon and the sun cast long, sharp shadows across every structure. Titus packed away his food into his knapsack, wrapped the bacon in some newspaper, and then wrapped all the food in a small piece of canvas and tied it with a piece of string.

After a while he was joined by his tentmate.

"Hey, Titus," Buster said, pulling his knapsack out of the tent, "you got any extra bacon you don't want? I could sure use some extra."

"Nope," Titus said, "afraid I got no extras."

The two men sorted their belongings in silence and set aside their dinner rations for that evening.

"I heard one of the sergeants tellin' that we're going to be breakin' camp in the wee hours of the mornin'," Buster said. "Did you hear that?"

"I don't pay no attention to that stuff, I just go where they tell me to go and fight when they tell me to fight."

Buster settled into a cross-legged position in front of the tent and toyed with a small piece of wood he had whittled earlier.

"Titus, I got some vexin' thoughts," Buster said, using his pen knife to sharpen a dried branch from a locust tree.

"What thoughts?"

"I got some thoughts that are botherin' me," Buster said.

"Don't reckon I know'd what you're talking about," Titus said.

The early spring chill accelerated as the sun fell farther behind the tree line and Buster buttoned the top of his field jacket and crossed his arms to keep the warmth in.

"Well, I was just thinking about tomorrow."

"What about tomorrow?" Titus asked.

"You know what I'm sayin'," Buster said.

"No I don't. You got to speak so as I can understand you, fer God's sake."

"I got a bad feelin' about tomorrow. I'm tryin' not to think about it, but it keeps pressin' on my brain."

"Cain't say I got any idea what yer talkin' about, Buster. You eat something bad today?"

"Hell no, that's not what I'm talkin' about. I'm talkin' about tomorrow. When we line up against them Rebs out there. That's what I'm talkin' about."

"What about it?"

"I'm just sayin' that I have half a mind to skedaddle if the lead starts flyin' 'round me too tight."

Titus took a long look at Buster, whose face was now covered with an ink-black shadow. Soldiers throughout the camp were sitting in small groups cooking, writing letters, or talking quietly. Every now and then a peal of laughter could be heard cutting through the dense campfire smoke.

"I don't take you for someone who will skedaddle," Titus said. "You don't seem that type, and if I were you I would just put that thought out of yer mind."

"But I got the feelin' that I might just turn and walk," Buster said. "I ain't sayin' I *want* to skedaddle, it's just that I might not have control of what my legs do."

"Look at me, Buster. No, you ain't lookin' at me. Look right here at my eyes. Good. Listen to me: you are not goin' to skedaddle tomorrow or any such day. It ain't in you. It might be in those other idiots, but it just ain't in you to do that. Stop wastin' your time thinkin' about somethin' that just ain't going to happen. You got that?"

"I'd like to believe you, Titus, but I got them feelin's that makes my belly feel like it's full of hornets."

"Let's get something to eat," Titus said. "You jest need some food in yer belly to chase those damned hornets away."

Col. Rittenhouse cut into his slab of beefsteak, took a bite, chewed for several seconds, and then turned to his servant.

"Sam, this is terrific piece of meat and cooked to perfection," he said. "I can't believe how lucky I am to have someone like you looking out for me. And I'm sure my dinner companions tonight will vouch for that."

"A fine meal, Sam," Dr. Morse said.

"My compliments," Lt. Rhys said, raising his fork.

"Excellent," Capt. Lynch said.

Sam, a former slave from Virginia, nodded in appreciation. "Thank you. Thank you kindly."

As was the fashion in camp, Rittenhouse and other senior officers routinely invited small groups of officers to share in a meal if their servants were able to land a particularly nice piece of beef, pork, or even a whole chicken. In some circumstances officers' wives accompanied their men in camp, but neither of these men had their wives with them.

This evening, with a soothing chill in the air, Sam set up a small table in front of Rittenhouse's wall tent. Sam had cooked four small steaks on a large skillet and had boiled some beans, adding some salt pork and chopped onion to the beans.

Dr. Morse had brought along some medicinal whiskey and the men sipped and ate their meals. Even Lynch, who barely drank alcohol, found himself sipping the whiskey. Although he prided himself on his aplomb and steadiness, he was noticeably nervous about what was in store the following day and thought that a bracing drink might provide a calming effect.

Gen. Paxton had made it clear that I Corps was going to play a secondary role in the next day's battle, but there was really no accounting for how the battle would unfold, Rittenhouse knew. Two years into the War of Secession, the level of chaos and confusion during battle was all too obvious to him and the other officers of the Army of the Potomac.

And the potential for carnage was staggering. Rittenhouse had seen the stunning casualty figures from a single day's battle the previous September in Maryland near a creek called Antietam. That battle tallied twelve thousand Union soldiers killed, wounded, or captured, he was told confidentially. Confederate casualties were said to be just as high.

Dr. Morse finished his meal quickly, since it was his habit to eat fast so that he could enjoy the discourse and the whiskey. He particularly enjoyed

Rittenhouse's company—a learned man with modest behaviors and good manners. And like Morse, the Colonel was fond of whiskey.

"So, tomorrow is a big day," Dr. Morse said. "We will see the elephant, no doubt."

"Well, perhaps not the whole elephant," Lynch said. "Maybe just the trunk or one or more tusks of that ungodly pachyderm. But probably not the whole beast."

"So it's true that we'll be in reserve?" Rhys asked.

"Most likely," Rittenhouse said, taking a large sip of whiskey.

"Well, I for one am just as happy with that turn of events," Dr. Morse said. "I'm not anxious to tend to all those poor fellows misfortunate enough to be maimed, as brave and fearless as they are."

"And heavens knows they are fearless and bucking for a fight," Lynch said.

"Well, many are, but each day at sick call I see my fair share of malingerers," Dr. Morse said. "As we've come closer to actual battle, the proportion of men reporting some form of illness has grown."

"Ah, well, there will always be a few that cannot stand up to the pressures," Rittenhouse said. "These are the weak ones that must be weeded out."

"Some are mightily frightened, I'll tell you," Dr. Morse said taking a long pull of his whiskey. "And what is all this talk of Indians in our midst? I had two men tell me today that they're more frightened of being killed by natives during the night than Rebels. What kind of preposterous silliness is that?"

"Lt. Rhys," Lynch said, "why don't you enlighten the good doctor here about the mystery of our dead soldiers?"

"Well, Dr. Morse," the lieutenant said, "in fact, two soldiers were killed in the last couple of days, and some of the men think it was an Indian who did it."

"An Indian?" Dr. Morse said. "Here, on the banks of the Rapidan in Virginia? You must be trying to tease an old man."

"No, sir, it's the truth. That's what some of the men are talking about," Rhys said, putting down his knife and fork to address the issue. "Mind you, most officers don't believe it's anything like an Indian that is killing these men. It's just how these soldiers get to talking and all. They've worked up quite a lather about it."

"Now wait just a minute," said Dr. Morse, affecting a troubled countenance and turning to face the young lieutenant. "If it is *not* an Indian killing these men, then who by God *is* killing them?"

"Well, again, Dr. Morse, that is the crux of the issue," Rhys said.

"Col. Rittenhouse," the doctor said turning to face him, "what in heaven's name is going on here? Surely you've reported this up the chain of command and something is being done about it?"

"Of course I reported to Gen. Paxton's staff," he said a little defensively. "But Major Johnston just laughed and said, 'Rittenhouse, we lose five men a day to accidents and disease in First Corps and you're telling me that you just lost two men to some marauder in your midst? Damnit, man, get that Rebel who's sneaking into your lines. Don't you dare bother the general with such trivial concerns."

"Did he direct you to the provost marshal then?" Morse asked.

"Gen. Paxton hates our provost, as you know," Rittenhouse said. "If I approached the provost I'd find myself commanding a company of mule drivers."

"Well, have you caught the Rebel bastard yet?" Dr. Morse asked, looking at Rhys.

"No," said Rhys. "The issue is somewhat complicated."

"How could it be complicated?" asked the doctor.

"Well, the killer could be a Union soldier," Rhys said.

"What?" the doctor said, dropping his empty glass onto the small table for emphasis. "The killer is a Union soldier? I'm hard pressed to believe that."

CHAPTER 4

Pvt. George Aldridge of Company B tried to put the growing discomfort out of his mind by turning onto his left side. Several acres were filled with two-man tents and he could hear snoring and the nonsensical babbling of soldiers talking in their sleep. It was perhaps one of the oddest aspects of camp life, but he could wake up at any time of night and hear someone talking in his sleep. Sometimes he could understand the sentences clearly, as if it were one side of a conversation. At other times men would babble words that made no sense at all. The worst were the screamers, soldiers who suddenly yelled, "Watch out!" or "Get away from me! Get!"

In those circumstances the screamer would be hit across the head by his tentmate or loudly threatened by nearby sleepers. Sometimes the threats were bloodcurdling in their vehemence, especially if the regiment had just come off a long march.

This night Aldridge's tentmate, Pvt. Charles Cuddy, was snoring very loudly, creating a kind of kind of gurgling-drowning sound. He considered shoving Cuddy to wake him.

But Cuddy, a large man who stood six feet, one inch and weighed over two hundred pounds, was about as good a tentmate as any soldier of the Army of the Potomac could have. Cuddy shared his food rations with Aldridge, was big enough to protect the smaller Aldridge from the ever-present camp bullies, and was a gentle fellow to boot.

Aldridge turned onto his other side but it was no help. The nagging *urge* to urinate was now turning into the ungodly all-powerful *need* to urinate.

"Damn," he whispered to himself.

Sitting up in the tent he kicked off his blanket, reached around blindly for his shoes and pulled them on. He debated briefly whether to put on his field jacket, since the air was cool, but decided to just make a run for it.

During daylight hours while in camp soldiers were encouraged to urinate at the latrines but at night it was a different matter and men stumbled far enough away from the tent areas to avoid waking their comrades before relieving themselves. But it had to be far enough away from the tents that the stream of urine onto a pile of dead leaves could not be heard. Tired soldiers were capable of turning viciously on anyone who woke them.

Aldridge poked his head outside the tent flap and saw that there was no moon to navigate by. The camp had an eerie quality to it during the early morning hours, as if a powerful miasma had fallen over the area suppressing all forms of life. Instead of men laughing around fire pits, or arguing over card games, there was nothing but snoring, occasional babblings from dreamers, and the neighing of a horse that was in all probability also dreaming.

He stood up, arched his back, rubbed his stomach absently and then made his way quietly past at least a half-dozen tents to the periphery of the camp. Aldridge was careful not to trip over a tent guy-wire or any other impediment.

Finally into the underbrush Aldridge pushed forward, his face brushing past the harsh fingers of swamp maples and scrub oak. He was hampered somewhat by the lack of moonlight to guide him, but he eventually stopped to do his business.

And even though he was safely near a full regiment of armed soldiers, Aldridge was uneasy. The camp was overcome with rumors about the recent deaths of two soldiers, and he was not immune to the wild speculations of who was doing the killing.

He started to urinate against the base of what he took to be a medium-sized oak tree and he could plainly hear the gushing torrent hitting the bark of the tree and streaming down to the base. He stood back several steps from the tree so that his shoes would not fall victim to the pooling liquid.

Just as he finished squeezing the last few drops, he heard a strange noise several steps behind him. He froze. He turned abruptly and tried to see into the impenetrable darkness, but he felt completely blind.

What was that noise, he thought? Damn if it didn't sound like someone was right behind me.

He listened. The only sounds were the wild thumping of his heart and the braying of a mule somewhere on the other side of camp.

After pausing for a few moments to get his bearings, Aldridge rushed back to camp, clumsily pushing branches away from his face with both arms as if swimming in a deep pond.

At one point he missed a branch with his outstretched left arm and it slapped him sharply across the forehead.

Irritated and embarrassed by his panic-stricken return to camp he continued to force his way through the remaining ten yards of brush until he nearly fell into the camp clearing. Panting slightly, he tiptoed to his tent, kicked off his shoes, and pulled the blanket over his body as he turned away from Cuddy and faced the descending tent half only inches from where it met the ground.

He was relieved that Cuddy, a heavy snorer, had grown silent and he readjusted himself several times so as to avoid a tree root that pressed against his ribs. After several attempts at this Aldridge noticed that the heels of his feet were wet.

Damn, he thought, now I ended up peein' on my own shoes. What a godforsaken night this is turnin' out to be.

After several minutes he finally slid into a fitful sleep that took him through to the sound of the morning wake-up drums. He rested on his back and covered his eyes with his left arm and lay there, listening to the curses of men waking to what might be their first real day of battle.

Aldridge noticed, almost as an afterthought, that his right elbow was now wet and he pulled it off the ground and reached over with his right hand and felt the dampness around his elbow.

"What the hell, Cuddy?" he said as he complained to his tentmate.

———

BUSTER WAS STANDING UP OUTSIDE HIS TENT STRETCHING when he heard it. The sound was unnatural, as if coming from a large wounded animal.

"Titus," he said leaning into the tent. "What do you figure that noise was? Sounds like a stuck pig or somethin.'"

———

THE REGIMENT WAS BREAKING CAMP IN A MORE subdued manner than when they first set up. There was little talking after a hurried breakfast; tents came down quickly and knapsacks were assembled with soldiers' personal belongings.

The camp fires were stamped out and many were left smoldering as the companies assembled. Officers raced by on horseback to attend meetings or pass along orders for movement. The campfire smoke seemed to gather in the low-lying swales and hollows, and combined with a cool morning mist it enshrouded the thousands of men in what seemed like a porous steel wool.

Lt. Rhys stood in front of Pvt. Aldridge and could not seem to get the soldier's attention. The young man kept moaning and swaying back and forth. While all the other tents of the 239th were unbuttoned and packed away, Aldridge's tent remained standing. Out of the entrance of the tent poked the stocking feet of his tentmate, a private named Cuddy.

"Pvt. Aldridge, how long did you say you were away from your tent last night?" Rhys asked. "Pvt. Aldridge please answer me. Pvt. Aldridge…!"

Rhys turned to Sgt. Samuel Wheeler in desperation. "Sergeant, how am I to question this poor sod when he's babbling? I need to get him to answer a few questions before we break camp."

Sgt. Wheeler, a short, stout man with a long, droopy coal-black mustache, took a step toward Aldridge and slapped him across his left cheek with such force that Aldridge fell onto his backside in a puff of dust. The meaty sound of the slap could be heard fifty yards away.

Aldridge sat on the ground and rubbed his cheek that was now bright pink.

"Stand up there private before I give you another cup," Wheeler said. "I said get up. Now!"

Aldridge stood up and fought to control himself by wrapping his arms across his chest. His eyes were sunken, and the whites of eyes were a red smear.

"Aldridge, please tell me—how long you were out of your tent last night when you relieved yourself?" Rhys asked.

"I already told you," he said straining with emotion. "Maybe ten minutes, maybe twelve minutes. But no more than that."

"And when you came back into your tent you didn't notice anything strange?"

"No, like I said, I just tried to get back to sleep. And I did, after a time."

"Did you get along with Cuddy? Did you have a gripe with him for anything?" Rhys said.

"No! He was my best friend. Sgt. Wheeler, you know about Cuddy and me. We was the best of friends and stuck together all the time. He was just a real big ol' bear of a fellow that everyone liked."

Rhys looked at Wheeler, and the sergeant nodded in confirmation.

"Hello there, Lieutenant," came a voice from behind and Rhys turned to see Dr. Morse walking toward the small gathering.

"Thank you for joining me this morning," Rhys said. "I know we're breaking camp on a very important day for the 239th, but I wondered if you'd take a look at something for me. You remember we were talking about those recent deaths of soldiers in and around camp?"

"Of course I do," Morse said. "The Indian scoundrels killing our soldiers? How could I forget that bit of silliness?"

"We may have another similar death," Rhys said.

"Really?" Morse said, clearly intrigued. "Where?"

Rhys pointed his chin at the protruding socked feet from the tent.

"Our latest victim?" Morse asked.

"'Fraid so," Rhys said. "Can you have a look at the body for me please?"

Aldridge suddenly started to moan and sway again, clutching his chest tightly.

"Damn you, I swear I'll knock you all the way to Centreville if you don't stop that," Wheeler said taking a step toward Aldridge.

The young soldier stepped backward and used both hands to cover his mouth to muffle his moaning.

Morse kneeled down and crawled into the tent on Aldridge's vacated half. Rhys crawled in behind him.

"Well now," Morse said. "This fellow sure gave up a lot of blood." Rhys grimaced slightly at the amount of black coagulated blood that lay pooled over Cuddy's chest and the blanket that came up to his chest.

Morse pushed, pulled, and turned the body, every now and then making small clucking sounds as if in confirmation of some fact or point of reference.

The doctor paid close attention to Cuddy's forehead and put his face within six inches of the dead man's face, adjusting his spectacles in the process.

"I'd say that the mark that you spoke about on this man's forehead is a 'cross,'" and not an 'X,'" he said. "Or at least that's how it looks to me. The man who killed Cuddy here stuck his finger in the man's blood and made this mark. You can actually make out the fingerprint. Amazing really."

"Tell me," Rhys said, "how could someone sneak into this tent and stab a big man like Cuddy here without a loud fight? Just doesn't make sense. No one heard a thing."

"Ah, good question," Morse said. "The answer is right here." He turned Cuddy's large head away from Rhys and pointed to a deep gash at the base of the dead man's neck. "Our killer took one mighty stab at the base of Cuddy's neck and drove the knife—I presume it was a very hefty blade, and he might have used a hammer or large stone—into his spine, severing it. That would paralyze the poor man while he slept and he would be unable to protect himself. Then it appears our invader slit the man's throat from ear to ear and he bled to death fairly rapidly."

The two men backed out of the tent and stood up, brushing dust off their knees and elbows. Rhys noticed that his left knee had absorbed a little blood, and he tried furiously to brush it off.

"And some soldiers here think this is the work of a renegade Indian on the loose in Virginia in the middle of 240,000 Union soldiers?" Morse asked. "I wouldn't countenance that theory. We've either got a Rebel-loving spy in our midst or something else entirely."

"What are you suggesting?" Rhys asked.

"Well, from the looks of it, we just might have someone who likes killing," Morse said.

CHAPTER 5

Dry, cool weather moved in over the Shenandoah Mountains from the west, pushing a refreshing breeze down its flanks through the Eastern foothills into the pale-green foliage of early spring. The wind was so strong that it picked up loose bits of dust, pollen, threads of grass, and the smoke from countless abandoned campfires, creating a thick, powdery fog.

Col. Rittenhouse sneezed once, then two more times in rapid succession as he struggled with the laden air.

Sam had pulled down the wall tent and was busy binding the poles together; he had already folded and wrapped the canvas. Rittenhouse's two large travel chests had been dragged off to the side along with his metal bed frame and mattress. As he did often when doing rote work like this, Sam hummed a song and went about his tasks with enthusiasm.

Rittenhouse stared at his servant as if transfixed, but in fact, he was thinking of things that had nothing to do with Sam. The lethal gravitational forces of battle were being exerted, and he felt like one of those pieces of grass blowing by his face, completely at the mercy of forces beyond his control.

"Sam," the Colonel said.

The servant stopped binding two small poles and looked up.

"Yes, Colonel?"

"Could you come here for a moment?"

"Yes, Colonel."

Sam ambled over and stood in front of Rittenhouse. He looked at Sam's face. Its color was profoundly black, with deep fissures crisscrossing his forehead and running down his cheeks. Sam's nose was very broad and flat, and his gray hair and beard merged into a single bushy sphere encircling his face.

"How old are you, Sam?" he said. "I realize I don't even know how old you are?"

"Um, I don't rightly know, Colonel," he said cautiously. This was not the kind of conversation that he normally had with Rittenhouse, and he was always on guard for sudden changes in mood and behavior from white people. It was a lesson every black man had learned, though in fact, Rittenhouse had proved he was a kindly enough man.

"I'm guessin' I's about fifty," he said. "What do you think, Colonel? Lookin' at me, do you figure I's about fifty? I just got no idea, and that's the God's truth. I bet yer guess is about as good as mine, maybe better."

Rittenhouse laughed. "Well, fifty seems like a good round number."

He kept staring at Sam in a wistful manner until Sam grew nervous.

"Colonel?"

"Yes, Sam?"

"You called me over here, and I reckon you was goin' to tell me somethin'," he said. "Was you?"

"Oh, yes, of course," Rittenhouse said, reaching into his pocket and pulling out an envelope. "Sam, inside this envelope is the address that I need you to send those two trunks over there to."

"Colonel?"

"You know, in case something happens to me today and I don't come back. From the battlefield."

"You cain't be talkin like that, Colonel," Sam said, shaking his head back and forth sternly. "Just bad luck to be talkin' about not comin' back. I'm just going to be forgettin' we even talked like this."

"Sam, I need you to promise to ship those trunks back to my wife."

"Yes, Colonel," Sam said taking the envelope and quickly stashing it in his back pocket.

"And Sam, there's $22 in this envelope, and that's for you," he said, extending another one. "In case I don't come back. That's yours to keep. I also talked to Major Slattery and told him what a great manservant you are, and he said he'd try to find you another officer if something happened to me."

Sam refused to make eye contact with Rittenhouse and showed his displeasure in the subject by moving his feet and peering off into the distance as if he were looking for a long-lost friend.

Sam finally turned away, shaking his head, and slowly took up the work of dismantling the tent. He knew the wagon would come soon, and it wouldn't wait for a servant who hadn't packed his master's belongings fast enough.

"Col. Rittenhouse?" a voice that seemed out of breath called from nearby.

Rittenhouse turned to see Lt. Rhys rushing up to him; the exodus from camp was in full swing now and horses and mules could be heard expressing their displeasure. Above all other sounds were the threats and cajoling from noncommissioned officers trying to get their charges in marching order.

"Col. Rittenhouse, can I have a word with you? Capt. Lynch wanted me to report something to you."

"Lieutenant, surely you know we're on the move, son. Are you stowed away and ready?"

"Yes, I did that earlier, sir. But I need to tell you that it happened again last night."

"What in the heavens are you talking about, Lt. Rhys?"

"There was another one last night, sir."

"Another *what?!*" Rittenhouse said.

"We lost another soldier last night. In the 239th. This one was from Company B, sir."

Rittenhouse stared at the young man for at least twenty seconds, before the junior officer spoke up.

"Colonel?"

"Another one?" Rittenhouse said slowly.

"Yes, sir, that makes three."

"How did he die?"

"He was cut up while he slept, sir."

"Didn't his tent companion notice anything, for God's sake?"

"He was out relieving himself, sir. He was mighty upset because when he got back to his tent in the middle of the night, he went back to sleep. But when he woke up, well, his friend was dead."

Rittenhouse mulled his options. The entire corps was going into action this day, and while they expected to be in reserve, they could just as easily be pulled into a full-on battle that would leave hundreds—perhaps thousands—dead and wounded. It would be folly to distract his commanders with this single death. They simply had too much on their minds this morning to focus on anything but making war.

"Lt. Rhys, we'll try to make sense of this at the end of the day, but as you know, we have Bobby Lee's army to worry about right now. You need to get your mount and meet me over at the brigade HQ right away. Right away."

"Yes, sir," Rhys said, turning and running back toward the temporary regimental corral.

Titus had just reached a small crest and could see before him the long lines of men and horses moving toward battle. The infantry always went first, followed by hundreds of supply wagons. But they all went in the same direction. It reminded Titus of what happens after a heavy spring rain, with small creeks and tributaries rushing together to combine into a single raging river.

A fine dust had risen from the dirt road that led south as the thousands of thin-soled shoes pulverized it. The rains earlier in the week had evaporated, and the powdered and rutted roads nearly shook with the tons of flesh crawling across it. At times like this, Titus could not imagine how the Army of the Potomac could lose a battle; its soldiers were well fed, well armed and well prepared for battle. Even now their blue uniforms reflected brightly in the sun, a massed force ready to smash into the butternut-clad forces of the Secessionists.

And yet, there were signs that all was not well.

Titus noticed that some soldiers already had left the line, dropping to the side of the road feigning a sore foot or some other malady. He felt angry at these miscreants but he trundled ahead with the thousand of other soldiers, ready to do his darndest to keep the Union together, as painful and dirty a job as it was.

There were so many men clustered around the makeshift Union Third Division headquarters of Gen. Paxton that Lt. Rhys felt claustrophobic. He kept to the outer ring of junior officers and administrators. Periodically he rolled up on the toes of his boots to keep an eye on the broad-brimmed hat of Capt. Lynch.

Rhys had never heard the sounds of battle before and from the west he could make out the unmistakable thump of artillery. Both North and South used the same weapons—even many of the same bugle calls—so Rhys could not tell what the nature of the engagement was. Still, he knew that Major Gen. Joseph Hooker had amassed his Union Army of the Potomac here and was intending to break through Lee's outer defense of Richmond.

Looking south from his vantage point, Rhys could see thousands of Union troops magnificently arrayed along an open patch of land more than a mile long. All of the infantry had unsheathed their bayonets, and they glinted in the clean spring air. He could not imagine how any Rebel army could hold up against this mass of powerful men and machines.

Out of the corner of his eye, he saw Lynch's distinctive hat rush by.

"Capt. Lynch, sir," he yelled.

Without turning, Lynch said, "Come quickly. We have a message for Col. Rittenhouse. It appears the left flank is in the air and needs closing."

Lynch found his horse, a tall chestnut-colored saddle horse he called Slim, and mounted it in one fluid motion.

"Rhys!" he yelled, "Where the blazes are you?"

"Coming right behind you, sir," Rhys said trying to find his horse, a small jet-black mare named Nancy. "I'll follow."

He tried to catch up to Lynch but it was nearly impossible as he dodged equipment, wagons full of ammunition, artillery limbers, and caissons flying in the opposite direction, wayward mules that had broken free, and the countless band of supporting personnel who were either ferrying something to the front or actively avoiding the front.

Since Titus was slightly taller than Buster, and men were placed in order of height in companies, there were three soldiers between them in Company I. Still, Titus could easily see the back of his friend's head pivoting nervously from side to side as they waited in a clearing.

They had dumped their knapsacks in a pile under several magnificent white oaks and the soldiers were aligned in two long lines facing south.

Together with the 223rd and the 240th regiments, the 239th made up the Second Brigade of the First Corps.

Titus could hear the artillery from at least a mile to his right. And while there was some anxiety among the waiting troops, it had also been explained that First Corps was in reserve, and it was unlikely to see action.

The NCOs tried to keep their companies quiet and attentive but as the morning wore on, a gregarious nature overtook the troops as the relief of not going into battle sank in. At one point Buster dropped out of line and came back and slipped in front of Titus; the other soldiers simply readjusted in line to make space.

"What do you make of the day so far?" Buster said. "We goin' to get into it today or not?"

"Hell, I don't know. Seems they're keepin' us away from them hollerin' Secessionists, which is OK by me. Cain't say I'm eager to go eatin' any lead."

"I just don't like all this waitin'," Buster said. "Makes my belly sour. It gives me gas."

"Everything give you gas," Titus said, "including just plain air."

"Well, this here waitin' gives me worse gas," he said. "Ol' Schmidt up there in line just told me he'd as well shoot me full of lead instead of them Rebs just to stop that smell."

"So that's why you sashay back here—to contaminate me now?"

"No, I'm all gassed out, I reckon," Buster said. "I just needed a change of scenery."

There was a sudden stiffening in the ranks that rippled from west to east, as if someone had pulled a rope taught.

"What's goin' on?" Buster asked.

Ahead they could see their company commander, Capt. Fetzer, yelling something as he walked down the line toward them.

"Get ready men," he yelled, "we're going in! Get ready men!"

After Fetzer turned and walked back up the line, the drum call to order was heard and all three regiments stiffened like a giant writhing, nervous snake.

"My belly is achin' again," Buster said.

"So help me, you better keep your bowels in order," Titus said. "I ain't goin' to be assaulted by you and Johnny Reb at the same time, by God."

The three regiments double-quicked in a long line, first west through a clearing, then south past a small, forlorn abandoned farmhouse, finally filtering out eastward so that the troops faced a recently plowed field, its corduroyed rows parallel to them.

About fifty yards to their rear stood the edge of a tangled, second-growth forest; to their front, three-quarters of a mile away across the plowed field, was the start of another patch of forest. The eight hundred men of the 239th were stationed at the end of a long line, with the 223rd to their right and the 240th farthest right.

Titus looked out over the furrowed field at the line of trees facing them across the way. He squinted to sharpen his eyesight, but he could still not see any trace of the enemy. He glanced off to his far right, past the 223rd and 240th, to see how they were connected to other regiments in battle, but the curve of the field, combined with a slight rise in elevation in that direction, made it impossible for him to see anything of note.

Much farther to the right, past the 240th, he could hear the volleys of rifle fire and the urgent, rhythmic booming of field artillery.

"You reckon there's Rebs over there?" Buster said jutting his chin toward the line of trees in the distance across the plowed field.

"Hell if I know," Titus said. "Cain't figure out why they'd put us into line unless they've got a hole to plug."

"Shut yer traps," yelled Sgt. Wheeler as he paced heavily behind the two rows of soldiers facing the empty field. "I swear I'll run this Enfield and its bayonet up the ass of the next soldier that keeps on yapping."

After Wheeler moved on, Buster muttered, "I'll run my Enfield up his ass if he don't quit yellin'. He's givin' me a case of the nerves."

"Buster, you better not get me in trouble for slippin' out of line," said Pvt. Christopher Wells who stood to Buster's left. "Why don't you go back where yer supposed to be? That Wheeler fellar is a hard man, and he'll have us both shackled and whipped."

"Don't worry about Wheeler, worry about them Rebs across the way," Buster said.

"I'd like to be worryin' about them, but I don't see a damned one of them Rebs," Wells said. "Titus, you think they got us out here for nothin', just to keep us busy and all?"

"I don't know nothin'," Titus said. "All's I know is that we're the far left wing of this army. Ain't nobody to our left, so it's just us out here. Don't reckon I like bein' the far left wing of any army."

"Damn, you're right," Buster said looking around. "We're the end of the line out here. Let's just hope them butternuts just kind of forget about us."

"You can tell Gen. Paxton that we're in position and have seen nothing of the enemy," Col. Rittenhouse said, turning to Capt. Lynch. "Are you sure this is all that he directed us to do?"

"His orders were for you to move the brigade to the left of the 13th Michigan and hold down the left flank. There were no orders for you to advance."

"But what if the 13th Michigan moves out? What are we to do then?"

"I was given no additional orders," Lynch said.

Capt. Lynch, Lt. Rhys, and at least ten other officers were clustered around a small folding table and chair that Col. Rittenhouse sat in. It was situated under a dogwood tree about fifty yards behind the middle of the 223rd Pennsylvania Volunteers. Behind the group of officers were two horse handlers keeping tabs on the officers' mounts as they grazed on a patch of scruffy grass.

On the small folding table flapped a map that had one corner held down by a glass flask half full of amber-colored whiskey.

Rhys was confused, as were most of the officers. The orders the colonel had been given were not very specific, and he could understand how Rittenhouse might be perplexed. Meanwhile, the sounds of battle coming from the west were growing in intensity creating a palpable tension in the group of officers.

Lynch suddenly turned to Rhys and said, "Lieutenant, please transmit the following message to Gen. Paxton's staff: First, what are the orders for Col. Rittenhouse if the 13th Michigan moves forward? Second, what is the brigade to do if engaged by the enemy across this field? Do you understand the message, Lt. Rhys?"

"Yes, sir, I do." At that Rhys grabbed Nancy from one of the handlers and took off racing in the direction of Gen. Paxton's position. He had not expected to take on the responsibility of a messenger. Now he was racing across the rear sections of regiments engaged in battle with a message that more than two thousand soldiers depended on.

And just as quickly he lost his way.

Earlier he had simply followed Capt. Lynch and paid scant attention to landmarks and geographic details. He pulled up near a group of soldiers sitting lazily under a tree smoking pipes and chatting.

"Men, can you please direct me to Gen. Paxton's headquarters? I have an important message," he said, trying to calm his mare. "It's all right there, Nancy," he said gently to the horse.

"We're just quartermasters in the 13th Michigan," one soldier said without removing the pipe from his clenched teeth. "We don't know nothin' about Gen. Paxton's whereabouts."

Rhys kicked his heels into Nancy and took off toward the southwest keeping a lookout for a mounted officer who could direct him. Meanwhile he heard the pounding of artillery nearby and worried that he would not be able to deliver his message before Rittenhouse's brigade came into trouble.

"DAMN IF I DON'T SEE SOME COMMOTION OVER that way," Pvt. Wells said staring across the field to their front. "I can make out somethin' goin' on over there."

Titus squinted and could see the unmistakable movement of men and horses as they emerged from the line of trees.

"Looks like they got some Napoleons they're unlimberin'," Wells said.

Titus indeed could see a battery of artillery being arrayed toward them across the furrowed field, and he felt a jolt of electricity as he pondered that fact. He had never been shot at before, either by a two-ounce Minié ball or a twelve-pound cannon ball, and he was unsettled by the prospect.

He heard a high-pitched whine next to him—it sounded like a cat in heat—and he turned to see Buster's face twisted into a kind of sneer.

"Eeehow," Buster uttered between pursed lips.

"What are you doin'?" Titus asked.

"Eeehow," Buster repeated.

"What's wrong with you?" Titus asked. "Stop that noise; yer givin' me the chills."

"Are they aimin' those pieces at us?" Buster said.

"Looks that way," Wells said. "I'm told that's how they fight wars these days. They point and shoot."

"Eeehow," Buster said again, taking a step backward out of line.

"Where do you think you're goin'?" Titus asked.

Buster said nothing but had now taken several steps out of line.

"Get back in line here," Titus said. "Don't be a damned fool. Get back here."

He hesitated, looked at Titus, and then took another tentative step away from the line.

Titus stepped back and grabbed Buster by the front of his field jacket, pulling him up into line next to him.

"So help me, you better keep yerself right here next to me, or yer goin' to be in a hell of a lot of trouble," Titus said. "Stop your damn silliness."

"WE WANT THEM TO KEEP THE FAR RIGHT flank of the enemy *occupied* so the enemy doesn't roll up our left flank, do you understand?" Gen. Paxton said, grabbing Rhys's arm for emphasis. "Rittenhouse's brigade should occupy their right flank to keep them from doing that. Send out pickets to engage them, but you are not being supported, so you should not advance *en masse*. Do you understand?"

"Yes, sir," Rhys said. "But what if the 13th Michigan advances or retreats, sir?"

"The brigade should remain in contact with the 13th at all times, for God's sake," Gen. Paxton said. "There should be no doubt about that."

"Of course not, sir," Rhys said. "Thank you, sir."

Rhys paid more attention to the course back to Col. Rittenhouse, dodging cavalry, supply trains and, ominously, ambulance wagons carrying the wounded back to field hospitals. The sounds of battle were much louder now, and while he could not actually see the engagements, he could feel the thump of artillery and saw an errant Rebel artillery round hit the tops of a copse of trees a hundred yards to his left. And for an instant he thought he could hear the whiz of a lead ball rush past his face.

Nancy was also harder to control. She fidgeted from the commotion, and he found himself keeping up a continuous stream of reassuring messages to her.

"It's OK, girl, everything is going to be fine," he told her. "Everything is going to be fine."

"COMPANY I, STEP OUT," SGT. WHEELER YELLED. "WE'RE going into a skirmish line. Fix yer bayonets, men."

"I don't like this," Buster said as the company took several steps forward. "We don't need to be way out there by ourselves."

"Shut up," Titus said.

Capt. Fetzer walked directly behind the middle of Company I and gave the order to move forward. As the men moved out, Sgt. Wheeler spread them so that there was ten yards between each man; behind them, the gap they left in the line was quickly plugged as other companies re-sorted.

Titus tried to keep an eye on his squirmy partner, but it was difficult to do that and walk forward slowly without tripping over the uneven ground.

Ahead of the skirmish line, several huge puffs of gray smoke emerged, followed almost simultaneously by the thundering explosion of artillery. Titus hesitated slightly as he tried to determine where the balls were headed. He thought he saw two of them arch over the skirmish line and heard them crash in the tree line behind the nervous rows of the 239th.

"Halt!" Capt. Fetzer yelled, and his order was repeated down the line.

Titus could now see the Rebel artillery battery—consisting of three Napoleons—being reloaded. Near the artillery unit, but mingled into the tree line, appeared at least a company or two of Rebel infantry.

He did not like being exposed this far in front of the rest of the regiment, especially with an active artillery battery in front of them. Yet he also knew that a sparsely manned skirmish line was unlikely to be targeted by artillery. Titus was more worried about whether the Rebels in the tree line would be sending their own skirmish line out soon.

The next salvo of Rebel artillery sounded and the shells arched overhead and hit the tops of the trees behind, this time much closer to the full regiment to their rear.

It was while Titus was turning his head back to face the front that he caught sight of Buster skulking ten yards behind the skirmish line. He was not running to the rear; in fact, Buster was facing forward, but every few seconds or so he took a little step backward, farther away from the skirmish line and closer to the regimental formation.

Titus thought of running back to grab his friend and pulling him to the front, but he also worried that his movement to the rear might confuse others about his intentions.

And just as he mulled this option, he caught sight of Sgt. Wheeler running after Buster. He came up on the recalcitrant soldier, yelling something unintelligible but with enormous vigor, and commenced to swing the barrel of his rifle hard into Buster's backside.

Apparently persuaded, Buster speedily took his place back into line.

Titus would have laughed out loud if his throat was not so dry from the exhaustion of the day.

RHYS DELIVERED THE ORDER TO RITTENHOUSE AND REPEATED it three times; each time he repeated the order, the colonel took a small sip of whiskey.

"They want us to engage but not advance?" Rittenhouse said, almost to himself.

Rhys was careful to answer Rittenhouse's questions with as little subjectivity as possible, but he was also aware that the actual order itself was ambiguous, and he was self-conscious about having to defend it. And very briefly he felt a sudden thrill at being the center of attention. All the officers in the group weighed his words as if they were religious truths that needed to be studied, albeit with haste.

"So they simply want us to hold the Rebels' right flank in place so that they don't roll down onto the 13th Michigan? Is that it?" Rittenhouse asked.

"It seems that way, sir," Rhys said, looking furtively at Capt. Lynch for advice.

"OK, thank you, Lieutenant," Lynch said.

Rhys nodded, and then stepped away from the group of officers as they started to discuss their next steps. He reached for his canteen and greedily drank its contents until it was nearly empty.

He strode back to the makeshift corral and patted Nancy on her sweaty neck. As he did so, he found that his hand was shaking.

———————————

THE FIRING STOPPED AS QUICKLY AS IT STARTED. The Rebel battery limbered up and disappeared into the tree line. Titus looked to his left and right and saw the other members of Company I looking around.

"Is that it?" he heard Wells yell.

"I reckon," Buster yelled back. "We scared them all the way back to Richmond, we did!"

CHAPTER 6

The wildly flickering candle made it more difficult to read the list, so Lt. Rhys closed one of the front flaps to the small, two-man wall tent. The cold weather had whisked through the area and was supplanted by a warm and powerful breeze from the south that had blown all day and into the early evening.

"Damn it, Rhys, it's getting warm enough in here without you making it worse. Why do you have to close the tent, for God's sake?"

"Hang on there," Rhys told his tentmate, Lt. Joseph Spangler. "I just need to study these names one more time."

"You ain't still thinkin' about those poor fellars back there that died a few days ago, are ya?"

"Yes I am, Joe," Rhys said. "I seem like the only person in this whole damned army who's worried about those dead soldiers and who killed them."

"You know how many men the Union lost down here in the last couple of days? Thousands, I reckon. And yer just worryin' about three soldiers who died before the battle even started? Somethin's kind of funny about that, Rhys. You best be careful how Capt. Lynch takes to your mullin's."

Rhys frowned at Spangler and shifted closer to the candle, which was now more docile. "I told you, Joe," he said, "there's somebody out there in a Union uniform killing our boys. And I aim to get him before he does it again. Hell, it could be *you* next. Did that ever occur to you?"

"No one's gonna sneak up on ol' Joe Spangler and stick a knife in him, you best believe that."

"Well, if you're so damned smug about your abilities, then why don't you help me out?"

Spangler, rail-thin and tall, reached out his long arm across to Rhys, who sat on his bed sideways facing his tentmate. "Give me that damn list."

Rhys held the paper out and Spangler grabbed it, bringing it close to his face. The paper listed three men, their rank, their company, how they died, and where they were found. Each entry finished the same: "Mark made with blood found on forehead of deceased in a cross or X shape."

Spangler studied the list, wiping a drop of perspiration off his forehead as it gathered in the heat of the tent.

"They all were found with that damn mark on their heads?" he asked.

"Yep, all of them. Very peculiar and vexing," Rhys said.

"Well, that is somethin' strange, to be sure," Spangler said. "And you say it couldn't have been one of those Rebs sneakin' up in the dark and dispatchin' our boys?"

"It's unlikely," Rhys said. "I already told you that the last one was killed in his tent when his buddy went out to pee. Wasn't gone more than 10 minutes. It had to be someone in the regiment, is what I'm thinking. And someone whose tent was close by."

"I know you told me all this stuff before, but I'm just havin' a hard time thinkin' that in the middle of all this organized killin' going on, some blue coat is killin' his fellow soldiers," Spangler said. "And damn it, Rhys, I got to open that flap or I'm goin' to melt."

Spangler tossed the piece of paper to Rhys and stood up, stooping to make sure his head avoided the apex of the tent, and threw open the closed flap. He stepped outside into the gathering darkness that was illuminated by hundreds of camp fires and permeated with the pungent smell of smoldering wood.

Rhys looked at the piece of paper.

1. *Pvt. Seymour Hesh, Company H, throat slit at latrine in daylight, mark on forehead.*
2. *Pvt. Joseph Meir of Company C, impaled on bayonet, on picket at night, mark on forehead.*
3. *Pvt. Cuddy of Company B, stabbed and throat slit in his tent at night, mark on forehead.*

Rhys slowly reread the list. Then put it down on his bed and stared idly at the candle flame that now jumped wildly in the warm breeze creating moving shadows on the tent walls.

"Joe, what do you reckon I should do about these fellars?" Rhys asked. "Should I remind Capt. Lynch about them?"

"If I were you I'd forget about them soldiers and get back to soldierin'. I don't think you'll see another dead Union soldier at the hands of that killer, whoever he was. This whipped army is on the move back north and you'll have more men run over and killed by runaway horses and wagons in one day than killed by this renegade. I wouldn't bother Lynch with this craziness."

Rhys exhaled a long, morose sigh. "I believe, for the first time, Joe, that I will abide by your advice. I think this was just one of those strange moments in this war that are not explainable and not worth worrying about."

THE SLOW, STEADY, MONOTONOUS AMBLE MESMERIZED TITUS. THE first mile or so of a hard march was always difficult as his body got used to the straps of his stuffed knapsack, the bouncing of the canteen on his left hip, the Enfield as it dug into his right shoulder, and the countless irritations from his thin-soled shoes.

But after a while, with the rhythmic slapping of thousands of shoes hitting dirt simultaneously and the contrapuntal clanging of odd pots and pans hung from knapsacks, Titus would fall into a reverie of sorts, staring at the back of the man to his front, each step an exact replica of the one before, the entire march blending into a walking dream.

During these marches he would often let his mind wander to his family's fifty-acre farm near Shade Gap in Pennsylvania. The oldest of five children, he was the only male child and bore the brunt of the farm's hard work. His father, Jacob, was a humorless man who demanded much of his oldest child. When it came time for Titus to be granted a portion of the family's acreage to start his own farm, his father had balked.

"There ain't enough to give away," Jacob had told him one evening after dinner. His mother and sisters sat silent and petrified in the jittery candlelight. The confrontation had been brewing for months.

"I reckon you could pare off about five acres next to Sutter's property," Titus had responded. "Ol' man Sutter's got at least a hundred acres and he'd be glad to let me buy some of it one day."

"Son, I don't got enough land to let you have any of it," his father said. "We barely can get by with what we got."

"Well, if I up and leave, who do you reckon is goin' to help you work this land?" Titus asked, to the gasp of his youngest sister, Marlene.

"You ain't thinkin' of leaving us, are you son?" his father asked sternly.

"I cain't stay here for the rest of my life workin' yer farm like a hired hand," he said. "I want to have my own life and my own land. I don't want to wait around here until yer too old."

"But you cain't just up and leave us," his father said. "We cain't get by without you."

"Well, then give me them five acres and we'll both get what we need," Titus said.

"I cain't do that son, I just told you so," his father said. "Yer goin' to have to wait for yer time to come."

The next morning, after feeding the horses, pigs, and chickens, and before breakfast, Titus wrapped up his meager belongings in a woolen blanket, tied the ends together into a tube and placed it over his shoulder into a blanket roll. He walked downstairs past the kitchen while his mother was fixing breakfast with two of his sisters, and said simply, "Good-bye, Mom."

He remembered his mother dropped an egg onto the flagstone floor, covering her mouth with both hands in alarm. Marlene ran to Titus and threw her arms around his right thigh and started crying.

Titus gently pried his sister's arms from him, saying, "Don't you worry, Marlene, everythin' is goin' to be OK. Don't you worry now."

He never saw his father, who he knew would be cutting down two locust trees near Sutter's land to be split and used for rail fencing.

And Titus had never been back to the farm. He had written three letters to his mother in the two years since. He had taken on work as a laborer for a furniture factory in Shippensburg, and after proving his worth on the job, was eventually promoted to an assistant shift supervisor.

He had even started to court a young woman named Annabelle Miller, the seventeen-year-old daughter of one of the factory's foremen. But everything changed the day Col. Rittenhouse had galloped into town with a small martial band playing patriotic music. The colonel was raising a brigade of Pennsylvania boys from the county, and Titus and his friends found Rittenhouse's speech enthralling. The War Between the States had been going on for less than a year, and it had hardly made a dent in the lives of the folks in Cumberland County.

"They want to just split this grand republic of ours in half! Just 'cause they want to! Can you imagine that? Are you going to stand for that? What if we let them do that and later on they say they want Pennsylvania to be in their new country? What do you say about that? You going to let them take your land or your neighbor's land?!"

Titus got caught up in the yelling and shouting, and soon Rittenhouse had the whole town worked up into war fever. Before Titus knew it he was one of the forty-three men standing in line to register for service in the Union Army. It had happened so fast that Titus, now plodding along in a line of a hundred thousand Union soldiers more than a year later, could hardly believe it.

THE COLUMN MADE A REST STOP JUST NORTH of the small town of Morrisville. Buster stood with Titus and a group of soldiers smoking pipes. The day had started out sunny, with the warm breeze from the south shepherding the retreating Army of the Potomac north toward Washington. As the morning wore on, clouds began to veil the harsh sun providing a measure of relief for the wool-clad soldiers. Still, by the time the column came to a halt, many soldiers had started discarding the heavier items in their packs onto the roadside, littering their path north with the detritus of an army in retreat.

"I got me half a mind to go find a chicken or a duck on that farm way over there," Buster said, pointing his chin toward a small, weather-beaten structure a half mile across a tilled field and a small stream. "Or maybe just some eggs. I need somethin' beside hard tack and that stuff the Union Army calls bacon."

"Leave them poor folks alone," Titus said, spitting onto the dusty soil of the roadway. "This area's been picked clean by both armies so many damn times I reckon those people are about as poor as you can be."

"Besides that," said Pvt. Wells, "you'd be kind of late to the party. I can see foragers already makin' their way to that farm."

And sure enough, a ragtag group of Union soldiers could be seen running toward the house across the stream, trying to get their hands on anything of value before the column started up again.

"I do kind of feel sorry for them people in that house," Wells said, "even though this is Jeff Davis's territory."

"Yer jest don't got a stomach for war," Buster said. "Not that I got a hankerin' fer it so much. But who said it was goin' to be a Sunday stroll? Them people over there are lookin' to break our country apart, and I for one don't care so much about their feelin's. I want to end this damn war quick enough so as I can get back home and do somethin' useful with my time."

The men smoked their pipes quietly, mulling Buster's comment while the warm breeze swept the tobacco smoke away from them and down the road filled with thousands of hastily assembled tripods of bayoneted rifles, butt ends planted on the ground and bayonets meeting and crossing at the top. It was the standard Army method for keeping rifles clean and ready during breaks, but Titus always thought they looked more like miniature Indian teepees.

A single gunshot erupted from somewhere near the farmhouse, and thousands of soldiers on break instantly craned their necks in the direction of the gunfire. There were rules, of course, against foraging, but there were also plenty of soldiers who did not care about the rules.

"Well, that ain't a good sign," Buster said. "Some greedy soldier just got kilt or some Southern citizen just got dispatched to heaven. Either way it's seems kinda like a waste to me."

The drum call to fall in sounded, and up and down the line thousands of soldiers emerged from the shade like a flock of pheasants being flushed from a meadow by dogs.

Titus emptied his ash by banging the pipe on his boot, stashed it away in his tunic pocket, and readied himself for a day of more hard marching.

THE WHITE CANVAS TENTS REFLECTED BRIGHTLY IN THE half-moon, and Lt. Rhys walked slowly down the walkways and past the smoldering campfires. The army had marched nearly thirty miles that day and the foot soldiers were tired and less boisterous than normal. Rhys always felt a tinge of guilt for being able to ride these long distances, but not so guilty that he considered walking with the infantry.

He heard someone calling his name and turned to see Capt. Fetzer standing next to a campfire twenty feet away.

"Hello, Captain," Rhys said.

"What brings you over here in the early hours of the evening?" Fetzer said. "This isn't the usual haunt of the colonel's staff."

"Oh well," Rhys said. "Was just taking a walk."

"I hope you aren't here for the reason I'm thinking of," Fetzer said, scratching his thick black beard.

"I don't think I understand what you mean, Captain."

"I'm sure you do," Fetzer said.

"Believe me, Captain, I have many qualities but mind reading is not one of them," Rhys said.

"Ha," Fetzer said smiling weakly. "Well, have a good evening then, Lieutenant."

"Of course, thank you, Captain," Rhys said self-consciously.

The young lieutenant looked up at the half-moon, its all-encompassing brightness blanketed the Army of the Potomac in a beam of muted blue light that seemed unreal. He walked on through the regiment and then turned and retraced his steps, taking a parallel alleyway back to his tent.

He looked up at one point and noticed a soldier walking down the path toward him, the man's head whipping back in forth in the moonlight. Rhys recognized the soldier and approached him, whispering, "Aren't you Dr. Morse's aide?"

Pvt. Sandler walked up to Rhys, attempting to keep the conversation quiet. The drum roll for "all quiet" had long ago sounded

"Yes, sir. Pvt. Sandler, sir," he said.

"What are you doing out walking around the camp at this hour, if you don't mind me asking?" Rhys said.

"Well, sir, I'm sort of looking for someone," Sandler said.

"Who are you looking for?"

"Umm, well, I suppose I can tell you," he said stepping forward to whisper even lower. "It's the doctor."

"Dr. Morse?" Rhys said.

"Yes sir."

"I don't understand," Rhys said. "Where is Dr. Morse? And why do you need to find him?"

"Well, he, um, just sometimes takes off. At night, sir. Just gets up and leaves his tent. Most times it don't bother me much, but like tonight, one of the patients is pretty sick. I was hoping he could come back and attend to the poor fellar."

Rhys took this in slowly, trying to make sense of Sandler's information.

"Does Dr. Morse do this often?"

"Sometimes."

"Does he always return to his tent later?"

"Mostly."

"Do you know where he goes?"

"Nope."

"Well, good luck in your search," Rhys said yawning suddenly. "If I see the doctor, I'll send him back to you."

"Thank you, sir."

They parted, and Rhys ambled back to his tent, amazed at how easily his eyes had adjusted to the moonlight. He felt he could see as clearly as if it were daylight, and eventually found his tent, flopping down on his bed without taking off his clothes. He fell asleep instantly and dreamed he was standing in an endless field of wheat in late summer, the blonde strands swaying like ocean waves in the breeze.

––––––––––––––––––

BUSTER KEPT READJUSTING THE BLANKET STUFFED BEHIND HIS back against the bark of the small maple tree. He was still burning with indignation about Company I being put on picket duty that night. They had pulled duty less than a week ago and should have had more time between rotations, but such were the numerous insults and stupidities of army life. Buster sometimes had a difficult time getting over these petty degradations and stewed over them for far too long. And tonight was one of those times.

"*Damn sergeant of the guard,*" he steamed. "*He hates Company I. Just darn hates us. Our captain does nothin' when he picks on us. Just ain't right.*"

The only good thing about pulling duty that night was the fact that they were far enough north, near Warrenton, that they were out of harm's way. That meant the pickets, spread in a large semicircle pointing south and southwest, were more comfortable nodding off from time to time.

And while night pickets were forced to double up at one point because of the knife killing of several soldiers, the order had been rescinded since company commanders felt the danger diminished the farther north they traveled and away from Chancellorsville.

Buster kept fidgeting below the tree, listening to the cacophony of late spring insects in the Virginia countryside. The half-moon had arced three-quarters of its path across the cloudless sky, plunging the thin second-growth forest into semidarkness, crossed by long black shadows of tree trunks.

Buster smirked when he heard Pvt. Wells snoring twenty yards to his left.

Well, he thought, *this is as good a time for some sleep as any.*

He dreamed about his neighbor's prized heifer, how it had broken out of its pen, and how he had tracked it down himself, through unfamiliar terrain, past a vast farm of some sort, and into a town that sort of looked like his hometown of Gladstone, Pennsylvania, but also didn't look like his hometown. In his dream, when he finally cornered the heifer in the town's general store, the heifer suddenly turned into Mrs. Barnes, his schoolteacher from long ago. She commenced to scold him about some infraction that he could not comprehend.

When he woke, he was just as pleased to be rid of Mrs. Barnes and he shook his head against the tree trunk to speed the unnerving interchange away.

Readjusting to the waking world, he tried to judge the time; with the moon now almost completely descendent, and with no noticeable glow to the east, Buster guessed it was about 4 a.m. or so.

He was startled by a noise perhaps twenty feet behind him. It was probably a possum or raccoon, he thought.

The noise started up again, and Buster registered a prickle of alarm because he could swear the noise sounded like hesitant footsteps, starting and then stopping. If the sergeant of the guard were checking up on the picket line, he'd often just walk straight out creating enough noise to be heard in advance in order to give exhausted troops the dignity of avoiding being caught asleep.

But these steps behind him seemed intermittent, more like stalking.

Buster could feel his heart thumping in his chest as he reacted to the presence behind him. He reached down to his side and moved them to the five-inch sheathed knife he kept on his belt, letting his fingers rest on the deer-antler handle.

Hell, could just be a big ol' deer, he thought. *Just you calm yerself, Buster, and don't wake the whole damn Union Army.*

Buster turned and peered around the right side of the tree trunk looking back toward camp. The noise had stopped and he could see nothing behind him except a hundred different shades of black. The bark of the maple tree felt rough and almost painful on his cheek as he strained to see. After several minutes of this, his fear receded and he turned back, letting his head rest on the tree again. He took his hand off the knife handle.

Buster closed his eyes and thought again about Mrs. Barnes and the heifer. As a child he had learned that if he wanted to get back to sleep right away after waking from a dream, he just had to *think himself* back into the dream he'd just exited. Sometimes it worked and sometimes it didn't, but it was worth a try tonight.

He bore down with all the energy he would typically use for a bowel movement, and tried to think his way into the darn dream, but that heifer would just not show its ugly face.

The sound of steps behind him started again.

Buster sat bolt upright with his back against the tree, the blanket falling to the ground. Pulling his knife out of his sheath with his right hand, he turned, stood up, and stepped from behind the tree into the inky blackness of the forest.

"Damn it, who are you out there? Don't you go sneakin' up on a man like that. This ain't no game."

The only response came from Wells who was stationed twenty yards away to his left.

"Buster," Wells hissed. "Yer havin' a bad dream. Quit yer yellin.'"

Buster was going to tell Wells to mind his own damn business, but he suddenly grew tired and realized that he might indeed be overreacting. All this marching had put him on edge. He settled himself back down under the maple tree and tried to conjure up an image of Mrs. Barnes, the teacher. Perhaps she could provide the gateway back into sleep that he so desperately wanted.

CHAPTER 7

They didn't find the body right away. With so many men eating and growling their way around camp in the early morning it was hard to tell he was missing.

At roll call his absence was noted, and his company's sergeant tried to figure out whether he was in sick call or had deserted. The regiment had a number of desertions and it was hard to tell who might skedaddle. Still, the sergeant didn't think his missing soldier was one who would run away.

It was only after they had figured out that the last time anyone had seen him was on night picket that they went out and found him.

LT. RHYS WAS ASHEN FACED AS HE FOLLOWED Capt. Fetzer through the smoky camp fires and clots of men. Behind Rhys walked a taciturn Dr. Morse. As they made their way soldiers grew quiet and watched the officers as if they were a trio of Grim Reapers themselves.

Word had spread rapidly about the latest body and the soldiers were now visibly distressed. The other deaths near Chancellorsville could no longer be tossed off as the work of a Rebel soldier sneaking into camp.

After pushing through the scrub pine and saplings the officers came upon two Union soldiers standing idly smoking pipes. Without speaking one of the soldiers took the meerschaum pipe out of his mouth and pointed its stained white stem to a spot about twenty feet away.

Flies had already found the body and Rhys noticed two large black ants were crawling on the man's face; one emerged from the dead man's nostril.

Rhys quickly looked up at Fetzer, in a mocking you-thought-this-was-over-look, but the captain avoided his glance and instead looked down pityingly on the private, his throat slit from ear to ear, the thick blood now coagulated on his tunic in gobs that looked to him like black oatmeal.

Dr. Morse kneeled down and gently grabbed the dead man's chin and moved it side to side. "That's funny," Morse said, almost to himself.

"What's that you say?" Fetzer said.

"Oh, well, this poor fellow's campaign hat is still on, which, given the struggle that probably occurred, seems odd. You can see he's lying here on the ground, but his head is propped up on this little log and his hat is on, all proper. Like he was posed, perhaps."

"Doctor, what about his forehead?" Rhys asked.

"I was just thinkin' of that," Morse said smiling slightly.

Rhys was fond of Dr. Morse and his idiosyncrasies, but he thought that at times the good doctor's reactions were just plain strange.

Morse gently lifted the dead man's cap and put it down next to the body. The soldier's face was unnaturally white from the loss of blood, and the skin contrasted sharply with the man's thick black hair, which fell down halfway to his eyebrows.

Morse tried to brush back the man's locks, but they appeared glued to his forehead.

"Mmmm," Morse said absently as he reached into his pocket and pulled out a thin pen-knife and unfolded the steel blade. Delicately, he pried the strands of hair that appeared stuck to the dead man's skin.

With most of the hair pried from the man's forehead, Morse gathered the stiff strands with his knife blade and lifted them up and pressed the hair back onto the top of the man's head.

Rhys, Fetzer, Morse, and the two guards that had inched over to the inspection, all bent forward to look at the exposed man's forehead.

After a few moments, Morse said, almost to himself, "Well, that's different."

"I reckon," said Rhys.

On the dead man's forehead was a shallow series of lines cut with a sharp blade; the horizontal cut was two inches long, the vertical cut was three inches.

"These cuts were made after this soldier died," Morse said. "The fellar had pretty much bled out by the time our killer made his mark and then carefully posed him in full uniform."

"Hell," said Fetzer. "I reckon this is just a damned mess."

THE SUN HAD RISEN OVER THE TREE LINE to the east bathing the camp in light and warmth that was not welcome. The long march of the previous day had made the men, the horses, and the mules ornery and lethargic.

Sam had set up a small table and chair in the shade of Col. Rittenhouse's wall tent, along with several other chairs. Sam could tell that the colonel was agitated about something because he and his guests spoke in somber, hushed tones. Sam steered clear of the men by taking his time washing the breakfast cooking items.

"This is just preposterous," Rittenhouse said to Capt. Lynch. "We have a Rebel assassin in our midst? And we haven't caught the bastard yet?"

"Well, according to Lt. Rhys here, and our surgeon, Dr. Morse, it might not be so clear that our killer is a Rebel sympathizer," Lynch said. "Isn't that so, Lieutenant?"

"Um, yes, Capt. Lynch, there are some circumstances that seem unusual, and, well, it's not clear that our men are being killed to support the Secessionist cause," Rhys said, squirming a little on his small folding chair.

"Capt. Lynch, what the hell is this man talking about?" Rittenhouse said, dropping his arms to his side in exasperation and ignoring the junior officer.

"Colonel, he's trying to explain that we might have a killer in our midst, but the killer may not be motivated by sympathy for Secessionist ideas," Lynch said. "Isn't that correct, Dr. Morse?"

"Indeed, that may be the case," Morse said.

"Dr. Morse, do you think you could elaborate a little more for Col. Rittenhouse?" Lynch said, prodding the doctor.

"Well, I'll try, I suppose," he said. "Given what we've seen with the bodies, and the marks made on the bodies, and especially this last body, it's likely that the killer is, well, just a killer and not necessarily a Rebel sympathizer."

"What marks?" Rittenhouse said. "What in the hell are you talking about? Is this related to the incidents we had back near the Rapidan River when we had Rebels sneaking into lines and killing one or two of our men?"

"In retrospect," Morse said, absently twisting the hair at the tip of his dark-brown beard, "we may have misjudged those killings. It appears that there have been a total of four murders of men in the regiment at the hands of this killer. After he kills them he puts a mark on their foreheads; it looks like a cross or a perhaps a 'plus' sign used in mathematics. Hard to tell, actually, but the mark was on the forehead of each of these murdered men."

Rittenhouse shook his head back and forth as if he was trying to get away from a nettlesome insect.

"Have you men been drinking too much busthead?" the colonel said.

Lynch shrugged, more out of frustration than in answer to the colonel. "I know this is an unusual set of circumstances," he said, "but this is our best evaluation of the killings. We owe it to the men of the 239th to protect them from this man, I think you'd agree."

"Listen," Rittenhouse said. "I'm not willing to grant you that our killer is *not*, in fact, a Secessionist, but for the sake of your theory, if he's not killing to aid the Southern Cause, why in God's name do you think he's killing our men?"

Dr. Morse turned to Rhys, and the lieutenant cleared his throat. "Well, we think the killer might enjoy the act of killing."

Rittenhouse's eyes betrayed a flash of incredulity followed instantly with anger. "This man likes killing his own fellow soldiers instead of killing Rebels?! Dr. Morse, surely this cannot be your theory? There is a war underway with thousands of men killing each other, but this regiment has a man who takes more pleasure in killing his own comrades?"

Morse smiled briefly, if unexpectedly. "Yes, that is true. Our killer is unbalanced. Very unusual, I would say. And very good at what he does, unfortunately."

An awkward silence fell over the four men as Rittenhouse stared, his mind processing the strange and confusing information. After what seemed like several minutes, Rittenhouse spoke.

"Find the killer," he said looking directly at Capt. Lynch. "Do whatever it takes, but find that bastard so that we can hang him before he takes any more men from this regiment."

"Should we call in the provost marshal?" Lynch asked.

"Those idiots?" Rittenhouse said. "I will not have Col. Charleton and his gang of pitiful thugs involved with our brigade. I want Lt. Rhys here and the good doctor to find our demented soldier. You must be trying to test me, Lynch, by mentioning the provost. You know the general hates them."

"Just thought that I'd ask," he said gamely.

"No," Rittenhouse said, "we'll not trouble any outsiders. Ha! The provost marshal, for sure."

CHAPTER 8

The ten companies in the 239th were identified, like all infantry companies, using the letters of the alphabet starting with Company A. Each company was led by a captain, who was in turn supported by up to three lieutenants and as many as thirteen noncommissioned officers if the company was at full strength. Later in the war, the 239th, like most hard-fighting regiments, would have its officer corps completely replaced due to the twin scourges of battle and illness.

But at this point, most of the officers had been in charge of their companies from enlistment, and in many cases elections were held to choose their own commanders, a practice that would not last.

The ten company commanders were sitting on the grass in front of Lynch, Rhys, and Morse. Lynch had called the meeting with the officers in a small clearing away from camp. The day had been warm and muggy as summer began to settle in over the Virginia countryside.

"Men, we're hoping to talk to you in confidence about these unfortunate killings that have been following us recently," he said. "I'm sure you know what I'm talking about, because there are rumors taking hold among the troops."

As Lynch spoke, Rhys looked at the faces of the officers sprawled in the grass. Some smoked pipes, others fiddled with beards or mustaches, but most just stared in what Rhys recognized as the "army stare"—the half-attentive, half-bored visage of men assembled for the thousandth time in their brief military careers to hear someone direct them, inform them, train them, or harangue them. In 90 percent of these episodes, the information imparted was meaningless or redundant, so all soldiers—including, but especially, infantry officers—learned to adopt a quasi-attentive demeanor while their true wishes were to be elsewhere.

Still, because of the strangeness of the subject, Rhys noticed more attention than could be expected. The latest death had clearly spooked some of the soldiers in the 239th, including the officers and noncommissioned officers.

"There are many theories about these killings," Lynch said. "Some are quite fanciful, others are more realistic. But whatever the truth, we must prevent further deaths by being diligent around camp. These are our orders moving forward, and these must stay in place until you are directed to change the procedures."

Lynch then listed a host of changes include doubling up on picket duty and guard duty so that there were two men together at all times. Latrine visits must be at least two at a time, the same for wood gathering, and any other duty taking men away from camp. At night there would be new patrol duties of two soldiers together walking through camp.

After listing the numerous changes to camp protocol, Lynch turned to Rhys and Morse. "Col. Rittenhouse has also appointed Lt. Rhys here and our regimental surgeon Dr. Morse to investigate the killings to see if we can flush out the intruder and hang the bastard at our earliest convenience. Meanwhile, the colonel is asking you to cooperate with these two officers so that we can rid ourselves of this scourge. Is that clear?"

Not a single officer nodded approval or even changed demeanor. Rhys noticed that they simply stared blankly or fidgeted sullenly.

"Go ahead, Lt. Rhys," Lynch said.

"Thank you, Captain," he said, stepping forward. "One of the obvious theories we have is that our killer is a Confederate spy and assassin who has infiltrated our unit and is doing his nefarious work when he has another soldier alone. That is why the new rules that Capt. Lynch just listed will hopefully prevent further killings. But we'd also like to ferret out the intruder and bring him to justice. And we'd like you to help us identify any men in your companies who have expressed any allegiances with the South that you think we should know about."

"Hey there, Lieutenant," said a red-haired burly officer sitting near the front, "I got me a sister that lives in Atlanta. Am I one of yer suspects?"

The group erupted in chuckles.

"Damn right, Baker, you're on my list fer sure," someone yelled.

"Once again," Rhys said, trying to regain their attention, "we just need your help to identify anyone who you think might be a Confederate spy. Just let me know and we'll follow it up."

"How yer goin' to follow it up?" asked another officer in the very back sitting in the shade of a small tree.

"We'll question him about his allegiance, and if nothing else, we'll at least scare him into stopping his murdering ways."

The group fell silent as they fidgeted more aggressively, another group behavior that communicated increasing boredom.

"Are there any more of them theories you talked about, Captain?" the redhead asked Lynch, "besides that Rebel assassin theory? 'Cause we heard other ideas about them killin's."

Lynch turned to Morse, who during the meeting squinted distractedly into the assembled group as if he were observing an experiment.

"What else do you think might be going on here?" Lynch said. "Dr. Morse, please share with the officers what you have suggested as an alternate theory."

Morse frowned, sucked in his cheeks in thought, and then said, "Well, another theory we have before us is that our killer, is, well, a man who likes killing."

Rhys could see the group of officers frown, almost in unison, as they thought about Morse's comment.

"Come again, would you, Doctor?" someone asked. "I didn't quite get what you said."

"I said that our killer could just be a deranged man who enjoys killing people," Morse said matter-of-factly.

"Is there any chance," the same officer said, "that we can capture him, and then slip him through Rebel lines so that he can do his work on their men?"

Laughter again broke out, this time with more nervousness.

Lynch jumped in quickly to keep control. "And as part of this investigation, Lt. Rhys and Dr. Morse would like you to forward to them the names of any men in your companies that you think might be of a deranged and dangerous demeanor."

"I seen someone like that just two weeks ago," another officer said after a brief pause. "It was in Washington. Name was Abraham Lincoln. He's from Illinois and is crazy and as dangerous as a hoot owl."

After that explosion of laughter, Lynch quieted the group down by raising his hand and reminding them that they would each be interviewed by Lt. Rhys. They'd be asked to account for their entire company over the past week, including any unexplained absences at night by their men and non-commissioned officers. That ended the meeting. The officers trundled back to their units, anxious to get back to the real work of an army, which is to wage war.

BUSTER STOOD IN FRONT OF THE SUTLER'S TENT and stared at the numerous items for sale arrayed across the oak-plank table.

"I don't see no cards," Nate said. "He's got no cards."

The sutler emerged from the tent like a flushed pigeon, cooing with excitement.

"What do you have on your mind today, boys?" he said, adjusting his wire-frame glasses. "I got newspapers from Baltimore and Philadelphia, tobacco, razors, anything you want, really."

Titus watched Buster with amusement. He could never predict what his tentmate was going to do one moment to the next, but all day he'd been acting in a peculiar way, even by Buster's standards.

"You got any of them playin' cards?" Buster asked. "I got to play me some poker, and I need some of them cards."

"Well, indeed I do have some playing cards," the sutler said, grinning widely. "They're slightly used, but you'll find them sufficient for your purposes, I'm sure." He entered his tent and re-emerged a few moments later with a deck of cards.

The deck had an elaborate blue design on top and was bound together with brown twine.

"How used up are they?" Buster said.

"Oh, not much at all."

"Can I see them?" Buster said holding out his hand.

"Not that I don't trust you, young man, but my policy is to exchange money for products at the same time. It's a rule that has worked well for me."

"Well, how do I know you got all the cards in that deck?" Buster said. "What if I take it back to my tent and I find out there's but fifty-one cards?"

The sutler teased apart the string knot and slowly counted the cards, snapping each one for histrionic emphasis. He looked up at Buster periodically without missing a count in an exaggerated show of confidence and honesty.

At the end he said, almost wearily, "There you have it; fifty-two cards for your gambling pleasure, young man."

"And how much are them cards goin' to put me back?" Buster asked, squinting into the afternoon sun that glowed orange over the sutler's tent.

"It'll be the same price you'll find for a deck of fine cards sold everywhere out here—two dollars."

"Two dollars!" Buster said, dancing in a circle and looking at Nate and Titus to demonstrate shared umbrage. "Are you sutlers workin' for Jeff Davis or Abe Lincoln's army? Yer crazy if you think I'm goin' to pay one dollar for that bunch of paper."

The sutler just smiled. "Well, you're welcome to think about it, boys. If you change your mind just come on back, and we'll transact."

"Now wait a minute," Buster said. "How about a dollar for them old cards? I got me a dollar right here," he said slapping a bill onto the tabletop.

The sutler stared at it for far too long, Titus thought.

"That won't do it," the sutler said. "Not anywhere near what these cards are worth."

"Hey, wait a minute," Buster said, suddenly remembering something. "Hey, I got me an idea." He reached into his partially open tunic and pulled out a pint bottle of amber liquid.

"What if I toss this here bottle of busthead into the mix, and knowin' how you sutlers work, you'll just water this stuff down and sell it for double the price you paid fer it."

"I take great offense to that charge; that's not how I run my business," he said, adjusting his spectacles again. "Perhaps you're thinking of someone else."

"Here," Buster said pulling the cork out of the glass container. "Take yerself a swig of that and tell me what you think."

He reached out and took the bottle gently in his long, bony fingers. "Now you boys wouldn't poison a hardworking sutler here just to get your playing cards, would you?"

Even Titus laughed at this exchange. Titus was now fully engaged in Buster's grand scheme to trade whiskey for cards.

The sutler took a generous swallow, closed his eyes, left them closed for several seconds, then returned the bottle. Opening his eyes, he said, "That indeed is whiskey, and a good batch, too. I'll take the bottle and the dollar, and we have ourselves a deal."

"The whole thing?!" Buster cried. "Yer a slippery one fer sure. And a good day to you, sir." Buster slipped the bottle into his tunic, grabbed the one dollar bill, turned and walked away so abruptly that Nate and Titus were still standing at the sutler's table when Buster stopped and turned back.

"Damn you," he said taking the few steps back to the table. Reaching into his tunic again he pulled out the bottle and banged it onto the table, throwing the dollar bill down as well. Holding out his hand he said, "Now I want them cards."

"This is indeed a deal, young man," the sutler said putting the deck into Buster's hand while simultaneously grabbing the bottle with his other hand. "And a good day to you fine soldiers."

Titus and Nate had a difficult time keeping up with Buster as he beelined it back to his tent, past the tents of the 223rd, the commissary, and finally their regiment.

"Hey, damnit, Buster, slow down there," Titus said. "You can play cards any time. Me and Nate here don't feel like double-quickin' for a card game."

"I got to get away from that sutler," Buster said looking over his shoulder.

"Well you got his cards and he's got yer whiskey, so what are you rushin' for?"

Buster stopped, looked furtively behind him, and caught his breath.

"It ain't what it seems," Buster said, a smile spreading across his face, his crooked teeth showing brightly in the sun.

"I don't get it," Nate said. "You gave him much too much whiskey for them stupid cards. I cain't figure you out sometimes, Buster."

Buster reached inside his tunic and pulled out what looked like a half-full pint of whiskey.

"I thought you gave him the whiskey," Nate said. "Seen it with my own eyes. Didn't he Titus?"

Titus nodded.

"Well I give that crook a taste, as they say, of his own medicine," Buster said, grinning. "I switched them bottles on him when I turned away."

"What was in the other bottle?" Titus said.

"If you boil the bark off an oak tree long enough, it renders down to that brownish color that sort of looks like busthead. That's what I give him."

Nate laughed so hard he started to tear up, and Titus just shook his head, smiling but not saying a word.

When they got back to their tent, Buster retold his story to a wider group, embellishing the details and creating great whoops of laughter, while Titus looked on with a grudging admiration for his spirited tentmate. Typically, Titus did not countenance robbery of any type, but sutlers, the civilian merchants who followed armies throughout their campaigns, were a universally despised group, so it mitigated his sensibility on the issue.

Later, after he was exhausted from his storytelling, Buster untied the string and stared at his booty. Slowly he counted the cards silently; then he counted the cards again, this time out loud. After a third count he handed the deck to Titus.

"My mind's all jumbled with all this fussin," he said. "Can you count these damn cards?"

And just as he suspected, Titus ended with "…fifty, fifty-one."

"That son of a bitch robbed me!" Buster yelled.

But Titus was laughing so hard he couldn't hear the howls of indignation from Buster, and he barely noticed the deck of cards fall to the ground from his hand, spreading out like brightly colored autumn leaves on the red Virginia soil.

CHAPTER 9

Lt. Rhys sat in a small wooden folding chair with his closed writing box on his lap, a pencil in his hand, and a blank piece of paper staring up at him.

Dr. Morse sat across from him, casually scanning the Virginia countryside. The rolling countryside south of Warrenton pulsed with life as deciduous trees and underbrush exploded in a late spring riot of green.

"I can't possibly see why I've been chosen to help find this devilish creature who's preying on these troops," Morse said. "I'm a physician, for God's sake. I had twenty-three men at sick call today, and I have one very sick young lad who will likely not make it through one more night. I don't really have time to ferret out this killer. Besides, why doesn't Rittenhouse push this further up the command ladder and get someone in here who knows what they're doing?"

Rhys had by now become accustomed to the recalcitrance of the doctor, and while Morse outranked the young lieutenant, Rhys had come to the conclusion that the doctor simply complained a lot, but would comply when pressed. And he knew the doctor had a weakness that could be utilized—he had a thirsty intellectual curiosity about solving problems and could not resist a challenge.

"Because he's embarrassed, I suppose," Rhys said.

"What would Rittenhouse be embarrassed about?"

"Well, the Union Army just suffered yet another defeat south of here at Chancellorsville," Rhys said. "I've heard that we had a significant advantage of two-to-one over Bobby Lee's army, and we were still thrashed. With so much attention being paid to the thousands of casualties that we just received, I'm guessing Col. Rittenhouse is afraid he'll be ridiculed if he says he needs help tracking down a Rebel spy who has killed four soldiers."

"This is no Rebel spy, I'm certain of that," Morse said, raising his chin slightly to take in the listless breeze huffing from the southwest. "We have a lunatic who is doing all of this damage."

"Well then, Doctor, why don't you help me find him?"

Rhys wrote down the number one on the paper, ignoring the doctor's entreaties. And truth be told, he was just as confused and ill prepared for this task as the doctor was. But he refused to disappoint his superiors and would drag the doctor with him whether he liked it or not.

"Our murderer has only killed men in the 239th Pennsylvania Volunteers; he has not apparently killed any soldiers in the brigade's other regiments nearby, the 223rd and the 240th. I've asked over there and neither regiment has reported deaths like these here. So, let's just assume the killer is in the 239th then."

"Why would we assume that?" Morse said, rising to the bait. "Wouldn't it make more sense for the killer to be a member of another regiment? He wouldn't be recognized and perhaps would feel less guilt for dispatching men not from his own regiment?"

"But surely, if your premise is correct, Doctor, guilt shouldn't be a part of his thinking, would it?" Rhys said. "You just said he was a madman and, in that case, remorse has little to do with his actions."

"Hmmm," Morse said. "A point well taken."

"But for the sake of argument," Rhys said, "if the killer was from, let's say, the 223rd, our intruder would have to traverse perhaps two hundred tents or more to have killed Pvt. Cuddy," Rhys said. "He was the poor fellow, remember, whose tentmate simply went to relieve himself, and in that period of time he was stabbed and slashed? That particular tent was in the center of the camp and it just seems unlikely he would be able to sneak over and return unnoticed. No, I think we have to assume our killer is here, in the 239th."

The doctor did not reply.

Rhys wrote the number two down.

"Our killer is an enlisted man, he's not an officer, since our officers are all mostly accounted for," Rhys said.

"In that meeting with the company commanders," the doctor said, squinting for emphasis, "did it not occur to you that one of the soldiers sitting smugly on that grassy hill might be our killer?"

"Yes it did," Rhys said, "but as a group they do not seem like the type to wantonly slice up their charges. I know I have many interviews to go with those company commanders, but my instinct is that we're not looking at company commanders as the killer."

"I just don't agree with your conclusion about officers," Morse said.

"But will you grant me this one small exception so that we can move on?"

"Well, not if the killer is indeed an officer, then we're wasting our time completely," Morse said.

"I will put a little star next to number two," Rhys said. "We can revisit this question later."

"Hmmph," Morse said.

"Now, number three," the lieutenant said. "Our suspect, if that's what we're calling him, is very handy with a knife and in fact, besides our regimental butcher, must have the sharpest knives around. He has nearly decapitated two of his victims. So we should look for men who have possession of large knives and perhaps are constantly sharpening them."

"In public?" Morse said.

"Excuse me?" Rhys said.

"Why would our suspect sharpen his knives in public?" the doctor said. "That might lead to suspicion. He may do it at night or off somewhere on guard duty."

"That is an excellent point," Rhys said. "But you will grant me that he has an extraordinarily sharp knife?"

"That is granted," he said.

"Well, then, number four—our killer is driven to mark his victims. He always marks their forehead with a cross or an X," Rhys said.

"Yes, isn't that peculiar?" Morse said, suddenly showing genuine intrigue. "I find that so odd. What could that mark mean? Is it the crucifix? Does it have some religious significance? A very interesting thing."

"Number five," Rhys said quickly, feeling as if he had finally tapped into the doctor's interest level, "and I think this may be our best lead yet, our killer is absent from his tent for long periods of time when he's doing his nefarious work. His tentmate will have noticed these absences and we will have an opportunity to discover this fact as we interview more subjects."

"Ah, but does he even have a tentmate?" Morse said.

"What do you mean? They all have tentmates. You know the army method of giving each infantryman half of a tent. They choose their tentmates and button the two halves together into a single two-man tent."

"But you are not very observant then, Lt. Rhys," the doctor said. "There are men who either have lost their tentmates to sickness, death, desertion, or God knows what reason, and they live in half tents. Surely you've seen the handful of lean-to's these soldiers employ as protection from the elements?"

"Damn, you are a clever one," Rhys said, genuinely pleased with Morse's observation. "It's true; there are always some men who tent alone. Of course. And those soldiers never have to be observed by another tentmate. Damn, that is fine thinking, Dr. Morse."

Pleased that he had accomplished his singular goal of engaging the doctor in their investigation, Rhys sat back in his chair and exhaled. The two sat surrounded by the assorted domestic sounds of camp life—laughter from a group of soldiers sharing a joke, the thumping of two riders racing by, the lone bark of a dog.

"Isn't that odd?" Morse suddenly said, as if he were finishing an internal argument.

"I beg your pardon?" Rhys said.

"What?" Morse said confused.

"You just said, 'Isn't it odd,'" Rhys said. "Or I thought that's what you said. Perhaps I misunderstood."

"Oh that," Morse said. "I was just ruminating."

"About the investigation?" Rhys said hopefully.

"Well, yes, I suppose," Morse said. "Isn't it odd that all of the men in this camp—in one way or another—are being trained to murder men wearing another uniform? I mean, we are preparing to murder other soldiers with rifles, bullets, swords, and artillery."

"Don't you think the word 'murder' is a little strong in this instance?" Rhys said. "I would think we're defending the Union. Killing Rebels is just a means to preserve the Union. I would not call that 'murdering.' And I'm not sure I understand the connection with our investigation."

"Ah, young Lt. Rhys," Morse said, smiling, "but just think about it. This is a camp full of murderers—granted, the murdering is being sanctioned by our government—but we are men being trained to murder a group of other men. And yet there is a murderer in our midst who is not murdering the right people; he's breaking the rules of murdering, as it were. Isn't that the oddest thing? War is so perplexing, wouldn't you say? Actions and behaviors we wouldn't tolerate in civilian life are encouraged and tolerated here. And yet, even in this topsy-turvy moral environment, there are perversities we won't tolerate—such as murdering the wrong murderers."

"If you'll permit me," Rhys said standing up, "I'll decline participation in this philosophical discussion about war. Each day here is a challenge, and I consider it a victory just to complete my tasks, much less take on the moral justification of the war to preserve the Union."

"Ha," Morse said smiling and waving his right hand in the air. "Pay no attention to my ramblings. I'm a doctor, not a moralist. Go find your murderer and we'll all sleep a little better."

Five soldiers sat on the edges of a rubberized gum cloth and were silently focused on each other. In the center of the cloth was a deck of cards and a pile of coins. Behind the card players stood a group of a half-dozen onlookers arrayed in a half-circle.

Poker playing had recently taken hold in the camp, as had a strange new game called baseball. But Buster was not athletic enough to play that game well, and the rules seemed too difficult for him to comprehend. Poker, although new to him, was much more interesting and he had taken to it quickly, earning admirers, detractors, and a fair amount of currency.

"Well, I guess I call you," one of the soldiers said, putting down a coin.

Three of the soldiers put down a matching coin and a fourth threw down his cards saying, "I'm out, fellars."

The first soldier put down his hand showing a pair of jacks.

"Hee, hee," Buster said smiling as he put down a pair of queens, a pair of clubs, and a single spade.

84

"Damn," the third soldier said putting down a pair of jacks.

The fourth soldier just threw down his cards without showing them. "I'm gettin' tired of you takin' all my money, Buster. Go find some another fool to play with."

Buster scraped the coins together into a pile and then meticulously scooped them into a small leather sack with a drawstring at the top.

"How's about tomorrow, boys?" Buster said. "See if you can get some of this money back."

"Go rob someone else," one of the soldiers said as they left.

Titus watched the scene with a group of bystanders, and after the group dispersed, he sidled over to his tentmate.

"Buster, you ought to be mindful of the fact that you're takin' hard-earned money from these folks," he said. "Fer you it's just a fun game, but them guys don't have much money to start with, and you might be makin' some of them pretty mad." "Oh, don't you worry about them," Buster said, humming to himself as he folded the gum cloth. "They just love playin' the game. They don't take none of this personally."

Lt. Rhys had interviewed half of the company commanders, and it went pretty much as he expected. Dr. Morse refused to participate in the interviews, so Rhys was left to himself to glean what he could from the infantry officers.

One officer, Capt. Slayton from Company B, could barely control his disdain for the entire interview. Rhys wondered if the captain even believed that men had been murdered in camp.

"Nope," was the answer that Slayton gave to nearly every question. "Have you noticed if any of your men demonstrate strong allegiance to the Southern Cause?"

"Nope."

"Have any of your men acted peculiar to their fellow soldiers in a manner that might cause others to fear him?"

"Nope."

"Have any of your soldiers shown an obsession with sharpening knives?"

"Nope."

"Is there any man under your company that you think we should talk to about these deaths?"

"Nope."

And Rhys's final question was the only one Slayton could not answer himself: "Who in your company tents by themselves?"

Sitting in a chair outside his wall tent Slayton turned his weathered face and yelled, "Lt. Parker, please come here. Lt. Parker!"

"Yes, sir," came the reply from nearby.

Lt. Parker arrived soon afterward and stood in front of the two men in chairs.

"Ask your question again," Slayton said.

"Lieutenant, are there any men in your company who tent alone? If so, could I have their names please?"

Lt. Parker pursed his lips in thought.

"Well, there's Cpl. Haines, and I think the only other one is Pvt. Schmidt. He's the one with gas."

"Gas?" Rhys said.

"Yeah," Parker said, "Schmidt had two other tentmates but they couldn't abide by the man's gas. He sometimes eats that sauerkraut them Germans like. No one can stand to be in a closed tent with him."

"Sound like a killer to you?" Slayton said, looking at Parker and smirking.

CHAPTER 10

In the beginning Morse suspected that men were malingering when they answered sick call. He could tell they simply wanted to get out of the relentless parade drills and other repetitive duties that soldiers trained for. Others simply were homesick, or so it seemed.

But over time Morse's opinion about sick call became more nuanced. Indeed, there were always some malingerers who showed up, but increasingly many soldiers were visibly ill with an assortment of maladies from respiratory distress to digestive problems. He was not prepared for the volume, the severity, or the chronic nature of the illnesses.

The most common complaint the men had was diarrhea caused by dysentery, and Morse did not know how to prevent it, much less treat it. He had initially given mild doses of quinine and a shot of whiskey, but then it had the unfortunate effect of creating long lines of sick men that he suspected were interested in the whiskey.

So he switched to issuing a common medicine called blue mass. That seemed to help only some sufferers. So he administered turpentine, which he had read was a useful medicine for treating diarrhea. In some severe cases, in which men were withering away, he administered laudanum.

Nothing seemed to work. In fact, he suspected that the turpentine was harmful. At least the laudanum calmed the men's bowels, so that was one treatment he could use. But again, he had limited supplies of this opiate, so he reserved it for the sickest of the sick.

If the soldiers stayed sick, he could always ship them to hospitals in Washington or Virginia. But increasingly they simply died in his care, moaning through the night and then suddenly perishing.

The utter volume of sick men, combined with his inability to help them, began to wear him down. In the week that the brigade had withdrawn to Warrenton, his field hospital had been overrun with sick soldiers. Privately he began to doubt his abilities as a physician. He had taken to dosing himself nightly with several drops of laudanum mixed with a healthy dram of whiskey.

His aide, Pvt. Sandler, seemed immune to the sad spectacle and could be heard reciting lengthy verses of scripture to some of sickest patients. Morse wondered how Sandler coped with only the salve of religion; he did not drink alcohol and declined Morse's offer of laudanum.

Then again, the regiment was full of religious groups and assorted teetotalers warning of the dangers of alcohol, so he was not surprised at Sandler's behavior. In fact, he was secretly envious of people who could rely on the succor of an Almighty God at times like this. It appeared to be a sensible and less expensive approach than relying on whiskey and opium.

"I GOT A STRANGE ONE FOR YOU," SAID Capt. Farley, of C Company.

Lt. Rhys had nearly completed his interviews of the company commanders, and it was clear that no one believed there was a killer in their midst. The officers' reactions to his interview varied from barely disguised boredom to outright hostility.

"You do?" Rhys said.

"Yep, we got a strange man in our company that you should talk to 'cause he pretty much scares daylights out of us," Farley said.

Rhys searched the ruddy, clean-shaven face of the officer sitting before him for even the slightest inflection of sarcasm; he was growing tired of the mocking from the company commanders.

"That's what yer askin' for, ain't it?" Farley said.

"Well, yes," he said. "One of my questions was whether your company housed anyone that you considered a threat to your fellow soldiers or was a Southern sympathizer, anything like that."

"Then I got someone fer yer list Lieutenant."

"You do?"

"Ain't that what I just said?'

"Yes, you did," Rhys said. "So who is he, and why do you think we should interview him?" Rhys had reverted to using "we" when talking about the investigation, since it suggested that a team was busy at work on it. But of course just he and the good doctor were the only ones flailing about on this task.

"He's off in his head, that's why," Farley said.

"Do you think this man is capable of killing people?" Rhys said.

"Hell," Farley said laughing, "ain't that what we're all doin' in this damn army? We're here to kill men. And those butternuts on the other side are here to kill us. We're all supposed to be killers."

"I mean is this fellow capable of killing his *own* men?" Rhys said as he felt the creeping derision from Farley.

"Like I said, he's an odd fellar that kinda spooks the other soldiers, includin' the company sergeants, and I was told that's the kind of man yer lookin' fer."

"What's this man's name?"

"Ruder. Pvt. Wilf Ruder."

"And by any chance does this Pvt. Ruder sleep in a half-tent by himself?"

"Hell yes, he does," Farley said.

THE BATTALION CAMPED TWO MILES SOUTH OF WARRENTON for eight days and the smell of ammonia grew proportionately to their stay. The weather seemed to stall over Virginia building up heat and concentrating the odor of urine around the camp.

While soldiers were directed to use the open-air latrine fifty yards from camp, they often simply walked a dozen feet into the brush on the outskirts of the camp to urinate; after thousands of these trips the odor of accumulated ammonia permeated the area, wafting through in blankets of pungency that caused men to snort and cough to clear their throats.

Rhys had convinced Dr. Morse to join him in a walk through camp that evening to get him out of his infirmary. Lately he noticed the doctor was more withdrawn and even morose as he tended to the sick and malingering soldiers. Rhys had nearly given up trying to keep the doctor participating in their investigation.

Rhys, on the other hand, was determined to do as he was told and to do it well. It made no difference to his sense of duty whether his task was to manage a firewood detail or to find a killer. Both were tasks that required his utmost attention, albeit the second task was more vexing in its nature.

The daylight was long now as the earth tilted toward the summer solstice and the two officers walked silently through the edge of camp; Morse lost in self-reflection and Rhys at a loss in how to engage his companion.

The sharp creosote smell of smoldering campfires tended to mask the odor of concentrated human urine.

"It must be their diet," Morse said suddenly.

"Pardon me?" Rhys said.

"What?" Morse said.

"You said something."

"I did? I thought I was just thinking. Isn't that odd that I just said it."

"Still, what did you mean about a diet?" Rhys persisted.

"Oh, the diet. Yes, well, I've been thinking that there must be something wrong with their diet since a great number of men come to me with stomach ailments. Of course some men do seem to have an illness unrelated to their stomach, but many do have stomach problems. Very peculiar."

"Which part of their diet is causing them problems?" Rhys asked, pleased to have engaged the doctor in any conversation, even though the lieutenant had no idea what Morse was talking about.

"Mmm, that's a good question. I'm wondering if it's not something *in* their diet as much as something that's *missing* from their diet," Morse said. "I mean, you and I eat different foods than they do. Yesterday I had a potato, for instance, and I don't think these men have seen a potato in a while."

They continued to walk through the early evening shadows while some soldiers greeted the doctor as they cooked their meals in small groups.

"Hey, Doc, how yer doin'?"

"Doc, my stomach is better now."

"Doc, you got any more of that whiskey?"

Morse appeared to brighten somewhat as soldiers called to him, so Rhys decided to jump in while he could.

"Dr. Morse, I've completed my interviews with the company commanders about suspects they suggest we interview," he said. "I have a list of seventeen men, including those men who sleep alone."

"What men?" Morse said.

"The men to interview."

"What are you talking about, Lieutenant?"

"We were directed by Col. Rittenhouse to investigate the murders of several soldiers, don't you remember?" Rhys said. "Surely you remember that?"

"Oh that," Morse said, raising his right arm and brushing the air as if he were chasing away a horsefly. "I don't think I can be of much good there. I'm a doctor, for God's sake."

"But Dr. Morse, we were *ordered* by Rittenhouse, remember? Should I contact him and tell him that you refuse to participate?" Rhys was suddenly angry with Dr. Morse's obstinacy, angry at the company commanders for being disdainful of him, angry at the army for putting him in this situation, and increasingly angry that no one seemed to care that a killer was in their midst.

Morse stopped walking and squinted hard at his young companion. "You are a petulant one, do you know that, Rhys?"

The lieutenant held his ground and stared back at the bearded physician. Laughter could be heard nearby as a group of soldiers repeated a joke.

After several seconds Morse sighed in a slow, exaggerated manner. He seemed almost forlorn, Rhys thought.

"You realize the war hasn't even really started yet for us, don't you?" Morse said.

"I suppose that's true."

"I'm burying a man almost every other day now from sickness and not a single one has been on the end of an angry Rebel Minié ball."

"Dr. Morse, are you going to help me investigate these murders?"

"Yes, yes, yes, of course I will," Morse said.

"Well, of the seventeen names, five of them sleep alone. I thought we'd concentrate on them to start. What do you think?"

"Yes, that will do," Morse said turning around and heading back to the infirmary. "I need my nightly dram of whiskey."

NEARLY TWENTY MINUTES HAD PASSED SINCE THE TWO men had gone off into the forest scraping past tree branches, dodging spider webs, and tripping over the gnarled roots of luxurious deciduous trees in full fledge. Finally Pvt. Blute complained.

"I ain't goin' no farther," he said suddenly and pulled up next to a towering pine tree. "There ain't a damn thing out here and I shoulda followed my better judgment instead of followin' you."

Buster, sweat saturating his open tunic and cascading down his temples, stopped ten steps ahead, planted the butt of his rifle onto the floor of the forest and caught his breath. "I'm tellin' you, Nate, there's a farm nearby; I can smell it," he said. "You come all this way already, you'd be missin' out on the larder that we're gonna get. You best stick by my side."

"I cannot fathom why I fall fer yer crazy ideas, Buster," Nate said. A huge salty drop of perspiration gathered at the tip of his nose. "This foragin' is just not fer me. I'm headin' back in. Only problem is that I don't know which way is back to camp."

"Then you better come with me, because if you head back by yerself you'll end up in Richmond all by yer lonesome self," he said. "I'm goin' just a bit longer and then I'll turn 'round. So come on."

"I swear, Buster, you are the devil in disguise," Blute said. He stood up and shuffled forward, his rifle balanced on his right shoulder in a decidedly unmilitary fashion so that his right hand fit snugly around the barrel.

Ten minutes later they broke into a clearing and stared at a small forlorn farmhouse and barn a quarter mile away in the afternoon haze.

"I told you, Nate," Buster said. "See?"

"All right, I see a farmhouse but I came fer the victuals."

"Don't you worry, there's somethin' good to eat over there, but let's be prepared just in case there's trouble nearby," Buster said, reaching into the leather cartridge case on his hip and pulling out a paper-wrapped ball and powder charge. He ripped the paper wrapping with his front teeth and blew the shredded paper into the air, poured the charge down the barrel, and then pushed the Minié ball in as well. The thickness of the lead bullet kept it from falling all the way to the bottom. Buster teased the ramrod out of its place under the rifle barrel, flipped the rod, and put the flared end down the barrel, ramming the ball all the way to the bottom. He replaced the rod in its small sheath under the barrel in one swift push downward with the tip of his right index finger. Lifting the rifle butt off the ground, he cradled the barrel in the crook of his left elbow, pulled back the hammer to its half-cocked position with his right hand, reached into his cartridge box again, pushed aside the bristles holding the percussion caps, grabbed one, and put it on the small metal nipple under the half-cocked hammer. Holding the hammer firmly with his right thumb, he pulled the trigger and gently released the hammer so that it rested tightly against the percussion cap.

By loading the rifle this way and keeping the hammer down, Buster could walk a fair distance without dislodging the cap. He could easily cock the weapon when needed and fire it, assuming he had several seconds to spare.

Blute had mirrored the procedure but was slower and more circumspect. "Better not be any trouble out there, Buster. I ain't lookin' to get myself kilt for a damn rooster, that's fer sure."

"Just quit yer worryin'," Buster said, sliding along the tree line toward the farm house. "I smell food over there."

It took the two men twenty minutes as they remained inside the tree line, skirting the open field to the north, looking for signs of activity. The field they were walking around had been roughly tilled, but there were weeds and grass growing in the furrows and Buster figured that something had happened to prevent the seeding.

When they were within a hundred yards of the house, Buster stopped several yards inside the tree line, knelt next to a small scrub-pine tree, and stared at the buildings.

"What do ya see?" Nate whispered.

"Nothin' yet," Buster replied in a barely audible tone. "Just lookin.'"

The farmhouse was a tiny one-story building with a small covered entranceway held aloft by two rough-hewn four-by-four posts.

As was the custom in the South with hot summers and cold winters, the farmhouse had been built in the lee of a giant oak tree that plunged the structure into a deep purple shade during the hottest part of the summer, but during the winter, when the leaves were missing, the house was warmed by the sunlight.

The house's siding had been bleached by the sun to a deep gray color. Four meager windows, two downstairs on either side of the door and two upstairs, made the house appear perfectly square and symmetrical.

But there was an overgrown quality to the yard, with weeds and grass growing right up the side of the house. A dirt path led to the front door, and Buster judged the path had been used regularly or it, too, would have been completely overgrown.

Buster was mostly interested in the single-story barn that was about fifty feet away from the house at the rear. It had never been painted either and had an almost iridescent shimmer of gray in the harsh sun. He looked closely for signs of movement or even the cackle of a hen or neighing of a horse; anything to suggest there was something of value in the barn.

After ten minutes of watching, Nate whispered, "What the hell are we waitin' fer?"

Buster stood up and continued to circle around the farmhouse inside the edge of the forest. The two soldiers found themselves staring at the back of the house with the barn door facing them from their left.

And then Buster heard it.

Buck, buck.

He turned and looked at Nate, smiling broadly.

"C'mon," he said, pausing briefly at the edge of the trees. He took off running to the back of the barn with Blute in tow. He waited a few minutes longer and then inched around to the barn side door and looked in. There was a scattered pile of old hay, the faint smell of horse manure and in the far corner was a stall with three chickens, clucking to themselves and furiously pecking at the ground.

"Remember," Buster whispered, "keep yer rifle out front sideways and help me push them back into a corner so we can grab them, OK?"

Blute nodded, and the two men stepped slowly into the cooling shadows of the barn and turned their rifles horizontal to the ground in front of their chests to make them seem wider than they were.

The three hens immediately noticed the men and one of them made a kind of screech; the other two jumped upward in alarm.

"Hey there, girls," Buster said to them warmly, "how you all doin' today? Don't worry about nothin', we're just here to say hello."

After a minute of painstaking advancement, with Nate jumping sideways at one point to keep a hen from escaping, the men had the three hens cornered in the back of the stall. The chickens voiced their displeasure by chattering and flapping their wings, and Buster kept glancing at the barn door to see if anyone had heard the commotion.

"Remember, you grab their legs and point them backward and put them under yer armpit, they'll just kind of lay there. You hold them chicken legs tight and soon enough they'll jest quiet themselves down," Buster said. "I'm goin' to go in first to get two of them and you just keep them penned. I got some string and I'll hobble they's legs."

"Hell, my mouth is already waterin'," Blute said.

Buster rested his rifle against the pen divider and then lunged at the hens, grabbing one, then another by their legs and quickly putting them under each arm facing backward. The two captured hens yelled and squawked as Blute chased the remaining free one, almost crushing it with his stomach as he fell on it.

In short order Buster hobbled the two hens' feet together with a short length of string and held them upside down with their feet tied together. He hobbled the third hen and gave it to Blute to carry back.

Buster held the two hens facing backward under each armpit and gave his rifle to Blute to carry. Cautiously, he moved to the entrance of the small barn and peered outside, squinting a little in the blinding sunlight.

"We're goin' back the same way we come, just follow me Nate," Buster said as he strode quickly outside and headed to the forest.

He jumped in alarm when he heard a voice from behind say, "Where you goin' with our hens?"

Buster and Blute turned to see a woman with two small children at her side staring at the soldiers. The woman appeared to be in her mid-twenties, with long, dark brown hair tied back with a piece of faded red ribbon. She wore a patterned dress that hung on her thin frame, but the exact details of the fabric pattern had long ago faded. Her face was tanned and freckled, but her eyes were dark brown dots of anger focused upon the two soldiers.

"Um, we's takin' them back to camp, ma'am," Buster said. "We're mighty hungry these days."

"What do you reckon we're gonna be eatin' after you take our last animals?" she said. "Them eggs is all's we got."

Buster had a difficult time looking at the woman because her eyes seemed to pierce him, so he looked away and focused on the little blond-haired child who clung to her right leg. The boy's hair ran down to his shoulders and he wore a pair of thin overalls with a rag of a shirt. He was barefoot and appeared to be about four years old, Buster thought. The child seemed more curious than scared, and kept shifting a little by grabbing his mother's leg tighter.

On the woman's left side was a very small girl with long, blonde hair that was tied back with a piece of string. The girl was only about two years old, Buster figured, but she had huge, round blue eyes that shone back at him in alarm. She too hugged her mother's leg tightly, even though the woman had her arms around both children, squeezing them to her thighs.

"So ya'll think that these two chillens can eat hay and bugs after you take them hens? Look at them and you tell me what I'm supposed to feed them?"

For the first time in the brief interchange Buster noticed a tinge of desperation flicker across her face, but it was soon replaced with that burning, accusatory glare that unnerved him and forced him to break off eye contact yet again.

"Ma'am, it weren't us that started this here rebellion," Blute said. "You should be askin' your kinfolk about who done started this thing. We're just tryin' to get by, that's all."

"Well, I didn't start this rebellion either," she said. "Every soldier—gray or blue—that comes near this godforsaken farm steals me blind. I'm just a poor woman with two chillens and three hens, and after you leave I reckon we're gonna just starve to death so as you boys can have a meal."

"Well, I'm sure yer husband is sendin' money home to ya to buy food," Blute said. "I sure as heck know what side he's fightin' on."

"He ain't fightin' on any side; he's kilt," she said, the bones on her cheeks now plainly clear as she clenched her teeth.

Buster's two hens started clucking, as if some signal passed from the woman to the animals. He raised his eyes and looked at the field beyond the farmhouse, feeling a strangeness that he could not articulate.

"Yer just sayin' that to make us feel bad fer yer condition," Blute said, "but I got me a brother is kilt, too at the hands of yer boys. And he got a wife and one kid himself."

There was a pause as the two soldiers stared at the woman and her two children.

Buster slowly bent over, dropped one of the hobbled hens on the ground and then unsheathed his knife. The steel flickered radiantly in the sunlight.

"What the hell are you doin' Buster?" Blute said. "Hey wait one damn minute..."

But it was too late; the string came off easily and the two hens took off toward the barn about as fast as hens could scoot.

Buster took several steps and grabbed Blute's left hand that held the third hen, while Blute tried desperately to keep it away from his partner.

"Let go for damn's sake," Buster said.

"I swear you are a fiend," he said as Buster cut the string and forced Blute's fingers apart to release the last hen.

The woman said nothing as Buster took his rifle back from Blute and started walking toward the tree line with Blute behind him cussing all the way.

Right before he entered the cover of the forest Buster turned and looked back over his shoulder.

She stood exactly where she had during their interchange and her children still clung to her legs. He thought he saw a tear slide down her dusty cheek, but it might have just been the sun's glare, he couldn't tell.

CHAPTER 11

The candles and lanterns created strange, elongated shadows in the huge wall tent. Several large moths the size of a child's hand relentlessly plunged toward a whale-oil lantern, each attack announced with a ping as the glass cover was hit.

The body odors from the crowd of officers, combined with the heavy gray cigar smoke made Rittenhouse consider stepping outside. But of course he could not; something serious had occurred and the ranking officers of First Corps were clustered around Gen. Paxton waiting to hear the news.

Rittenhouse pressed his chin against the shoulder of an officer in front of him and squinted in concentration. He heard the general speaking loudly, but to no one in particular.

"He's on the move, men; he's on the move north," Paxton said. "He's taking that army of his and circling up into Maryland to swoop down on Washington from the west and north."

"I thought Lee was just outside Richmond?" someone said.

"No, he's gone, and taken his army with him," the general said.

"He's headed to Washington?" someone else asked.

"That's what we've been told. We're breaking camp first thing tomorrow and will take up a blocking position with part of Second Corps to shield Washington. This is very serious, men. Lee's on the move."

There was a brief chattering among the officers as they processed the news. Rittenhouse, too, made some perfunctory remarks to a colonel standing near him, but was filled with a secret admiration for Gen. Robert E. Lee. The Southern general acted decisively and with speed, something the Union Army could not bring itself to do.

How are we ever going to put down this rebellion if our generals continue to be whipsawed by indecision and incompetence? he thought. *Damn that Robert E. Lee.*

He tossed and turned several times before sitting up on his elbow.

"Smitty," he whispered. "Smitty. Get up. I need to piss."

They had just been issued yet another regulation calling for all soldiers to urinate at least fifty feet away from camp. The smell had started to bother the troops and he'd heard a rumor that Doc Morse thought it was the vapors from the urine that was making so many soldiers sick.

But even crazier yet was the second part of the new regulation: if a soldier needed to pee at night he had to be accompanied by someone. The senior staff was convinced that there was a Rebel assassin in their midst and was waiting at night in the woods to kill wayward Union soldiers, or at least that was the rumor.

Dick Perry did not believe there was an assassin, or an Indian or anyone else lurking in the woods to kill him. He was more worried about raising the ire of Sgt. Lemley if he was caught breaking the rules. In point of fact Perry would prefer to meet an assassin in the woods alone than be dressed down by Lemley in front of the entire company.

"Smitty, wake up, I got to pee."

His tentmate turned away from Perry saying, "Go piss on yerself. I ain't gettin' up."

Perry furiously weighed his options as his bladder began to throb.

Hell, he thought, *I'm just going to pee right near camp and the hell with them stupid new rules.*

He crawled out of the tent on his knees and stood; even though clouds blocked out the moon he could easily make out hundreds of pale canvas tents strewn over the surrounding fields. Here and there the embers from a neglected camp fire glowed like fat, inert fireflies.

Perry arched his back and stretched his arms straight up as if reaching for a passing cloud. He carefully tiptoed past a half-dozen tents until he came to the edge of camp. He took several timorous steps into the forest, pushing aside some low hanging branches and was fumbling with the buttons on his britches when he noticed a light flickering ahead of him deeper into the trees.

He stared and wondered who was walking around in the woods in the early morning hours with a lantern or candle. Forgetting momentarily his need to urinate, Perry took several steps deeper into the tree line to see who might be there.

After a half-dozen steps, he still had trouble seeing the source of the light that flickered twenty or thirty feet ahead. The light seemed to be stationary, but it was impossible to make out anything else.

That's kinda odd, he thought. *This situation is not to my likin'. I reckon I should get myself out of here.*

Perry backtracked slowly without urinating until he was back in the camp again. Even standing at the edge of the forest he could still make out the flickering light from inside the tree line.

Maybe I'll just pick another spot to do my business, Perry thought. *I'm sure that light in there ain't nothin'. All them damn new rules has got me spooked.*

He walked farther along the treeline and then took five short steps into the brush, unbuttoned his fly, and peed. Looking into the trees, he was happy that he could no longer see the flickering light.

As Perry made his way back through the maze of tents, he noticed two of the night guards sauntering his way.

He walked up to them and whispered, "Hey, fellars. You want to see somethin' kinda peculiar?"

"What are ya talkin' about?" one of the guards whispered back.

"C'mon," Perry said. "Follow me."

He led them to the edge of the forest and pointed to the flickering light.

"You all see that in there?" Perry whispered.

"I cain't see nothin'," the first guard, Pvt. Schiller said.

But the second guard, Cpl. Sullivan, replied quickly, "Yup, I see somethin' back there."

"Ain't that kind of odd?" Perry said.

"I guess so," Sullivan whispered. "Who's in there this time of night?"

"That's what I was thinkin'," Perry said. "You reckon we should maybe see who's in there?"

"It ain't none of our business," Schiller whispered. "That light there ain't hurtin' no one. Let it be."

"No, we're on guard duty, and that's what we's supposed to be doin'," Sullivan said. "C'mon."

He led the way into the brush, pushing forward with the tip of his rifle. Behind him in single file was Perry, followed reluctantly by Schiller.

The light became brighter and as the men drew closer to the source; the intervening leaves and branches accentuated the flickering effect. After twenty seconds of progress the three soldiers came upon the source of the light.

On the floor of the forest sat a small, white, half-melted candle. The leaves and dead branches appeared to have been cleared from around the candle leaving a clean space of about three feet in diameter.

But a foot behind the candle, stuck into the ground, was a hand-made cross of some sort. The vertical stick was about two feet tall and a half-inch in diameter; the horizontal stick was a foot long and was tied perpendicular to the first stick with string.

The three soldiers stared at the setting.

"What do you reckon is goin' on?" Perry asked.

Neither of the two guards spoke.

"What do you reckon?" Perry asked again.

"I got no idea," Schiller said. "But I'm gonna get out of here. We can report it to the sergeant of the guard and he can figure the damn thing out."

All three soldiers turned in unison and made their way back to camp, but halfway there Cpl. Sullivan stopped and said, "we cain't let that candle stay lit; if it starts a fire we're gonna be in big trouble. It'll burn down the whole damn forest and cause a helluva row. You wait here and I'll go put it out."

Schiller said, "Hell no, I ain't waitin'," and kept walking toward camp. Perry stopped briefly but then decided to follow Schiller out to the edge of camp. The two men stood there in silence waiting for Sullivan to return.

Nearby, a sleeping soldier coughed in a tent.

From inside the forest, Perry could hear twigs snapping and branches being pushed aside. This was followed by silence.

After several minutes Perry turned to Schiller and whispered: "You reckon he's OK in there?"

"I don't know why he ain't here yet," Schiller said.

"You reckon we should go get him?" Perry said.

"I ain't goin' in there," he said.

"But what if he's in trouble?" Perry said.

"He ain't in no trouble," Schiller said.

"How do you know?" Perry said.

The guard didn't answer.

After several minutes Perry said, "Wait here, I'm gettin' a candle." He re-traced his steps to his tent, crawled inside, pulled a half-used candle from his belongings along with a knife, and returned to the guard. He lit the candle, held it with his left hand and kept the knife in his right hand. Reluctantly, Schiller followed with his rifle pointing forward and the two went back into the forest, trying to retrace their steps.

But the light source had disappeared and they were forced to stumble around looking for the make-shift cross.

"Hey, Sully," the second guard said in a loud whisper. "Sully? You out there?"

There was no response, just the agitation of hundreds of insects as they adjusted to the two intruders.

After several minutes of searching, Perry stumbled upon the cross and snuffed-out candle. There was no sign of Sullivan.

"Damnit, Sully," Schiller said louder now. "Where the devil are you?"

Nothing.

After another ten minutes of searching the two men returned to the camp, half expecting to find Sullivan there.

"Maybe Sully went to report somethin' to the sergeant of the guard," Schiller said. "I'm goin' to check that out."

Perry went back to his tent and looked up just in time to see the clouds part briefly to let a shaft of blue-white moon glow rake the camp. The tents shone luminous and then went dark as the moon slid again behind the clouds.

Well, that's sure an odd turn of events, he told himself as he crawled back inside the tent.

CHAPTER 12

Lt. Rhys stood looking at the makeshift cross and scratched his chin absently. "This is what you came upon last night?" he said to the two soldiers standing next to him.

"Yes sir, that's what we seen," Schiller said. "Only the first time the candle was burnin', ain't that right, Perry?"

"Yep," Perry said. "The candle was burnin' down, and we just looked at it and then left. But as we said, Sully went back to snuff out the candle. And that was it. We never seen him again. We waited but he just didn't come out."

"And you went back in to look for him?" Rhys asked.

"Yep," Perry said. "And Sully was gone. But the candle was out."

Rhys looked at the two soldiers, at Company C Commander Capt. Farley, who stood behind them, and then again at the strange area on the forest floor.

"Capt. Farley, do you think that Pvt. Sullivan deserted? Was he the sort to want to skedaddle?"

"I can't say he was, I can't say he wasn't," Farley said. "Men are skedaddling all the time."

"Have you searched the area for him?" Rhys asked.

"We've done a quick search and no one's found him, though I know you're aware that we're breaking camp today and there's a lot of activity," Farley said. "In fact, we got to get back to the company or it'll take us damn near a week to catch up to the regiment."

Rhys looked at the small wooden cross and candle, bent down and peered carefully at the forest floor.

Kneeling, he slowly picked up the candle stub and held it close to his eyes looking for any sign of ownership or origin; but it was a standard US Union Army-issue candle. He tossed it onto the ground, then pulled the cross out of the ground and held it in front of his face, looking at the string that bound the cross-members together. Again, it was the standard brownish twine a soldier could buy from any sutler. He stood up holding the cross.

Peering closely at the forest floor he kicked the dead leaves aside and walked in a semicircle; he stopped at one point and leaned over.

"Hey," he said. "Captain, does this look like blood to you?"

Farley and the other two soldiers hurried over and looked down at a brown leaf that Rhys was pointing to using the wooden cross as if it were a toy sword.

Streaked across the leaf it was a dark brownish line of mostly dried fluid a half-inch wide. Rhys picked up the leaf and handed it to Farley, who held it up in the murky light of the forest with his left hand.

"Mmm," he said, touching the swath with the forefinger of his right hand. Something sticky came off on his finger and he squeezed it between his thumb and forefinger. "It just might be blood, lieutenant," Farley said returning the leaf to Rhys.

"Watch where you're stepping men," Rhys said looking down at the forest floor again. The men spread out, looking carefully at the brush and leaves on the forest floor.

"Hey," Farley said, "look at this." The group peered at the large green leaf of a maple sapling that was only twelve inches off the ground. It was smeared with a brownish-reddish streak.

Rhys looked in the direction the two blood-streaked leaves seem to lead. He thought he could make out something in the distance and he walked straight toward it. As he got closer to the pile of leaves he saw a human hand exposed, palm upward as if in supplication.

When they uncovered Sully from the shallow pile of leaves and brush they found that his neck had been nearly severed, with black dried blood covering his tunic. Sullivan's campaign hat was down over his eyes as if shielding him from the sunlight streaming unevenly through the forest canopy.

Rhys gently pulled the cap off Sully's face. On his forehead a cross had been cut into his forehead, the coagulated blood stuck to the cap's bill so tightly that he had to pry it away.

"Damn!" Perry said stepping backward. "I told him not go back in there!"

Rhys stood up and tossed the cap down next to the body.

"This is a fine turn of events," he said. "Just fine."

THE WAGON RIDE HAD JUST STARTED, AND DR. Morse was already irritated at the day in front of him, bouncing along a deeply corrugated, dusty road in an endless train of wagons, cavalry, artillery caissons, and limbers. A serpentine row of blue-colored foot soldiers led the army north, the thousands of boots pounding the soil so thoroughly that a reddish dust rose up and engulfed the horde as if it were a thin fog.

Morse's back was already sore from the incessant jolting, and his driver, a young black man named Billy, was humming a song that Morse knew would be repeated all day.

Morse did not like all of the moving about, though he knew it was absolutely necessary for a field army to be in constant motion. Still, he was increasingly partial to the certainty and stability of staying put and hated having to pack up the hospital supplies, his own belongings, and caring for the transportation of his patients. He was able to ship two very sick soldiers to one of the large hospitals in Washington, but he was still responsible for six men who were in various stages of illness.

And one of them, a noncommissioned officer in the quartermaster's corps, had a mysterious illness he had never seen before that he guessed from his readings was erysipelas. The sergeant's skin had turned bright red on his arms and thighs and was accompanied by pustules. He also had a fever and was in constant pain, so Morse had given him blue mass and, increasingly, laudanum diluted in whiskey.

Morse was intrigued with some folk remedies that Dr. Calloway, the 223rd's surgeon had shared with him, including teas made of Virginia snake-root, but he had yet to try them.

He sat, feeling morose and distracted, in the front of the wagon as it bounced along the road to Centreville. He was not really doing the fulfilling work he had anticipated—saving the lives of grateful soldiers wounded in battle. All doctors secretly felt the deep satisfaction of a thankful patient, and Morse thought it would be much the same in the army.

Instead, all his waking hours were spent tending to men with intestinal difficulties or more serious illnesses that he could not diagnose nor salve sufficiently.

And to make matters worse, he was being hounded by a lieutenant to help solve a series of apparent murders that had taken place within the regiment.

I'm a physician for God's sake, Morse stewed, *not a policeman. I'm here to help the infirm and save the lives of men punctured by pieces of Rebel metal, not ferret out killers. This army has lost its collective mind.*

Awakened from his sour reverie by the driver's humming, Morse said, "Billy, can you please hum another song?! My God, man, I'll never make it to Centreville before going stark raving mad!"

He knew there was a hole in the sole of his left shoe, and a thin strip of cowhide he slipped into the shoe was supposed to save him from another blister. But now after an hour into what was likely to be a long hard march, Titus's left foot was aching and he could not stand it any longer.

Falling quickly out of line, Titus dropped his rifle as he sat down and pulled off his knapsack. It tumbled a few feet down a gentle slope, clanging as his frying pan jostled against his tin cup.

The ragging started even before Titus had his shoe off.

"Hey there Titus, don't forget to say hello to my parents when you git home in a couple of days."

"Titus, most of them skedaddlers wait a little longer before they make the ol' I-got-me-a-sore-foot-trick."

"Hey Titus, them Rebel cavalrymen are hot on our trail. You best be mindful of that on yer way home."

He ignored them all as he readjusted the cowhide in his shoe.

Hell, if they give us a decent pair of shoes I wouldn't have to keep putting stuff in there to save my damn foot, Titus thought. *And I ain't no skedaddler either. I'd already be in Shippensburg if I wanted to do that.*

As he laced up his shoe, Titus heard branches breaking behind him in the edge of the forest and turned to see two men on horseback picking their way toward him. His heart skipped a beat when he recognized who they were and quickly stood up and reached for his pack.

"What do ya think yer doin' there, soldier?" one of the riders said. Titus looked up to see the closer of the two men was riding a coal-black horse with a single white streak between its large, wet, black eyes.

"I ain't doin' nothing 'cept fixing my shoe," Titus said, hurriedly pulling on his knapsack.

"Don't you go gettin' any ideas there," the second rider said, pulling up behind Titus. "You just get yerself back in line there."

Titus bent down and picked up his rifle, then looked up at the hulking presence of two huge horses and their riders towering over him. Like most soldiers he dreaded coming into contact with provost marshals, men charged with chasing down deserters and bringing them to justice. While Titus had no direct knowledge of bad behavior by marshals, he had heard enough stories of their capricious, sometimes violent acts that he avoided them at all cost.

"I told you I was fixin' my shoe," Titus said. "Cain't a man fix his own shoe? I ain't got no horse to ride."

"That's 'cause you ain't worthy enough to have a horse," laughed the first rider.

"I reckon that's true," Titus said as he turned back to the torrent of blue-coated soldiers plodding north on the dusty road. He had the choice of just squeezing back in line and catching up later with his company, or to double-quick ahead to get back with his unit. He chose to catch up and was sweating profusely when he was able to slip in to his original slot.

But the teasing didn't stop.

"Hell, Titus, I thought you'd be in Maryland by now," someone said, "but I see them marshals changed yer mind."

But he didn't pay much attention since he was already daydreaming about the foreman's daughter back in Shippensburg.

CHAPTER 13

"**W**hy you askin' me all them questions?" said Pvt. Ruder. "I don't see you askin' anyone else questions."

Rhys sat on a small, wooden folding chair to the side of his wall tent and in front of him stood a small, very thin black-haired private from Company B. His name had been volunteered to Rhys by his company commander as someone who both slept alone in a half, lean-to tent and also who was considered "menacing."

Rhys decided he'd focus on the soldiers who slept alone as the most likely suspects, but he did not know if this approach was reasonable, nor did he even know how to conduct an interview.

The most common response from his fellow junior officers when he complained about his new assignment was a perfunctory shrug of the shoulders. In fact, his mission to investigate an apparent series of murders was no more or less bizarre than any order given a junior officer.

"You are most certainly not the only soldier in the 239th I'm talking to, Pvt. Ruder," Rhys said. "Please sit down. Rest assured there are many more men I will speak to."

"Well, I don't like it much," Ruder said, scratching the tip of his nose feverishly.

"Tell me," Rhys said quickly. "Have you always tented alone?"

"Alone since when?" he private said.

"Since the brigade broke from winter quarters," Rhys said.

"I reckon I have since we broke camp up in Fairfax Station," Ruder said.

"Any particular reason you don't want to share a tent with one of your fellow soldiers?"

"Since when is it anyone's business how I choose to sleep? I thought they jest wanted me to kill Rebels and not worry about findin' someone to tent with."

Rhys smiled. "So you prefer to sleep alone?"

"I reckon."

"What's so bothersome about sleeping in the same tent with another soldier?"

"Does Capt. Farley know I'm being bothered by these here questions?"

"Yes," Rhys said, "your company commander knows we're talking."

"And he agreed to let you ask me them questions?"

"Why are these questions so bothersome to you?"

"'Cause they're stupid questions, that's why."

"Do these questions make you angry?"

"Damn right they do."

"Why?"

"'Cause I don't like people botherin' me. It's bad enough that I got to be in this army and spend my days marchin' 'round in circles. Now I got to explain my sleepin' habits."

"Do folks bother you here?"

"They's always botherin' me. I know they talk about me. I can hear them say things."

"What kind of things do they say about you?"

"Why don't you ask them?"

Rhys smiled. "But go ahead, what do they say about you?"

"They say I'm 'a strange fellar.' One of them started callin' me a 'crazy duck,' and now some of them make quackin' sounds when I'm nearby."

"Soldiers are always doing foolish things in camp, especially when they haven't seen any real fighting," Rhys said. "They're just bored and restless."

"Well, I don't much like it."

"Have you been in any arguments with soldiers?"

"Why would I want to do that?"

"I'm just asking. Perhaps you were angry at someone for saying something."

"I'm sure as hell angry at them but ain't nothin' I can do. I just mind my own business and hope I can get out after my time is up."

"Tell me, did you know any of these soldiers?" Rhys said, reading off the names of the five men who were killed over the previous several weeks.

"Those names are of them dead boys."

"Yes. Did you know any of them?"

"You think I'm the fellar that kilt them?"

"No, I didn't say that."

"I reckon you think I did, that's why yer feedin' me them questions."

"My job is to find out what happened to these men," Rhys said. "Why do you think these men were killed?"

"Why don't yer go and ask them?"

"Well, it's a little late for that," Rhys said.

"I'll tell you why those boys are dead," he said. "'Cause they was unlucky, that's why."

"You think someone here in the regiment is a Confederate spy and is doing the killing?"

"I heard that them boys got their necks cut and some mark scratched on their heads."

"Yes, that's mostly true. Does that sound like a Rebel assassin to you?"

"No sir, it don't. Sounds like a crazy man."

"Really, what makes you say that?"

"'Cause whoever is doin' the killin' seems to enjoy it, that's why."

"How do you know the killer enjoys it?"

"You ever slit a pig's throat?"

"No. Can't say I have," Rhys said slowly.

"For a split second, after you do the slicin', the pig knows he's gonna die and he tries to squeal, but he's helpless. And jest fer an instant, the butcher feels powerful, like he's the hand of God doin' his work."

"The hand of God?" Rhys said sitting forward and looking at the fidgeting soldier. "Why the hand of God?"

"Well, that's how my Pa tells it, anyway," Ruder said. "That's what we think of when we're slaughterin' them animals. It's God's work. But you seem like one of them city folk and I bet you don't do no slaughterin.'"

"No, I don't slaughter animals," Rhys said.

"It's funny, but now we're slaughterin' men in the thousands in this damned war and I don't reckon it's God's work."

"None of this seems to be God's work," Rhys said nodding. "Not a single thing."

RHYS HAD BEEN LOOKING FOR THE YOUNG SOLDIER for quite a while, but no one seemed to know whether he was on guard duty, sick call, foraging for wood, or deserted. Such was the disorganization inherent in such a large army that at times a man could get lost, and then reappear suddenly. When armies were on the move it was even more confusing, as soldiers dropped out of line with sore feet or for any number of reasons and then would be lost for days until they caught up with their unit.

Because so many soldiers had deserted, daily muster cards were the only available source of information about who was present for roll call. And the assumption was that a missing soldier was a deserter unless there were extenuating circumstances that a fellow soldier might impart to the officer managing roll call. Many soldiers reported as deserters were often not deserters at all but had been temporarily left behind, complicating the record keeping further.

Still, as Rhys sought out Pvt. Loren Seibert of Company C he was aware that he might not even be in camp. His name had been forwarded to Rhys as someone who should be interviewed, since he slept alone in a lean-to and was deemed suspicious for reasons that were not explained by sergeant who delivered the note from the company commander.

"Hey there, soldier," Rhys said to a tall, gangly corporal who sat at a campfire whittling a small oak branch. "I'm looking for a private in Company C named Seibert. Loren Seibert." The sitting soldier was so tall that his knees, when splayed outward, suggested the giant wingspan of a blue heron.

"Why you want that fellar for?" the solider asked.

"I just need to talk to him, that's all," Rhys said.

"You checked with the sergeant of the guard?"

"Yes I have," Rhys said. "No one knows where he is. You figure he might have skedaddled?"

"Heck if I know," the soldier said, concentrating on a small carving detail.

"I can't even find his tent," Rhys said. "Do you know where his tent is?"

The soldier stopped whittling and looked up, his face dark from soot and sun and stared at Rhys for several seconds.

"No, cain't say I know where he sleeps," the soldier said. "Fact is he don't really set down each night like the rest of us. He bunks by hisself. We don't have much to do with him, and he don't have much to do with us."

"Yes, I understand he sleeps by himself," Rhys said, looking around the camp.

"Hey, wait! Are you that officer that's tryin' to figure out who been killin' boys at night around here?"

"Yes, I'm that officer."

"Is that why yer tryin' to find Seibert?"

"I've been talking to a lot of soldiers," Rhys said. "I might even want to talk to you."

"Me?" the soldier said, frowning. "Why me?"

"You may have some information that I need. Like I said, I'm talking to a lot of men so you shouldn't draw any conclusions about who I'm talking to," Rhys said.

"I don't know nothin'," the soldier said.

Rhys sighed. "So you don't know where Seibert is?"

"No, I don't know where 'the owl' is," he said, returning to his whittling with fervor.

"What do you mean by that?" Rhys said.

"Huh?" he said.

"I thought you said something about an owl."

"Oh, that's just the name we give him," the soldier said.

"Seibert, you mean?"

"Yep, Seibert 'the owl.' He hates when we call him that," the soldier chuckled. "He got them big eyes and barely makes a sound. And he makes a hummin' sound to hisself."

"Well, if you see him walking around could tell him Lt. Rhys is looking for him?"

"Well, just look for a card came, you might find 'the owl' there," the soldier said.

"Cards, as in gambling, like poker?" Rhys said.

"Yep, 'the owl' is always playin' cards, and winnin' a lot, too. Might explain why he ain't too well liked."

"Well, again, if you see him could you let Seibert know I'd like to talk to him?"

"Sure," the soldier said unconvincingly.

———————

BUSTER WALKED UP AND DOWN FOR AT LEAST a half hour. The new camp had the clean odor of freshly cut wood and newly trampled grass. More important, it was not yet drenched with the smell of horse manure, human urine, and the cast-off garbage of thousands of men on the march. And for now, anyway, the camp had an additional smell for Buster: the unmistakable fragrance of money.

The paymaster had just finished his visit to the regiment, and soldiers were flush with greenbacks. Somewhere, Buster knew, someone was playing cards, and he wanted in.

He really did not know many soldiers outside of Company I, but he found that when it came to poker, anyone with money was welcome. And providence was partial to him that afternoon because he finally heard voices from a crowd and turned to see men standing around looking downward. It was either a fistfight, or a card game.

He sidled up to the conclave and inched his way to the front. Four men were sitting around a small crate that that had been fashioned into a card table. The players were sitting on grass and the bent stalks gave off a pleasant aroma.

Buster watched the game for a few minutes, and when a hand ended he said, "Is there room for another player, boys?"

The four men playing and the half dozen watching all looked at Buster. One of the players said, "Where you from, soldier?"

"Company I," Buster said. "Just got my pay and am lookin' for a card game."

"We'll be glad to take some money off yer hands there, soldier," one of the players said. "Sit on down here."

A soldier stood up and said "I'm done. Them is my cards so hand them over. I shoulda charged you fellars for usin' my cards. Maybe I coulda made some money."

"You cain't take them cards," one of the seated soldiers said.

"Don't worry none, boys," Buster said. "Got me a deck I just bought from a sutler."

"Well get yer butt down here and let's get playin', so we can take all yer money from ya!" Even Buster laughed at that comment.

"Hold yer horses, there," he said. "I'm comin.'"

It was not that Titus was beholden to Buster, or had been asked by Buster's parents to look after their son. In fact, Titus did not know Buster's family or any of his kin. But in the forced camaraderie of soldiering, men often developed strong relationships that were suited to the peculiar demands of war but would not stand up to ordinariness of civilian life.

Titus felt an almost paternal obligation to try and protect Buster from his sudden enthusiasms and predilection for mischief. Perhaps Buster reminded Titus of his hellion of a sister named Maureen, or maybe Buster said and did things that Titus wished he could do. But whatever the cause, Titus tried to keep an eye on his young charge. Of course it was no easy task, given Buster's impulsive nature.

So when he overheard two soldiers walking by discussing a big poker game that Buster was in the middle of, he took off in search of his tentmate.

It took him fifteen minutes to find the game, which was not hard, given the small crowd of about twenty that had gathered. He pulled up to the rear of the onlookers, who were absorbed in the drama taking place at their feet.

"Damn, that's sure a lot of money," someone said.

Titus gently, but purposefully, inched and shoved his way to somewhere near the front. Sticking his head out around the shoulder of another bystander he finally got a glimpse of the players.

Four men were arrayed around the crate and one of them was indeed Buster, who rocked back and forth on his haunches completely absorbed in his hand. Clockwise to Buster's right was a huge man with a black bushy beard; his insignia showed he was a corporal in the quartermaster's unit. Sitting directly across from Buster was a dark-haired infantryman of medium build, high cheekbones, and very large, dark eyes; the third player was directly underneath Titus and he could only make out an unruly mop of sandy hair.

Titus instantly noticed the pile of money on the small crate; by the standards of an ordinary infantryman, it was a huge amount of money and Titus instantly felt a rush of anxiety. His instinct told him this was too much money for soldiers to be fighting over and could raise emotions to a higher than normal pitch.

Still, Titus marveled at Buster's attitude, which he knew all too well: cocky, confident, and unbowed. As he watched Buster rock back and forth gently, he could only smile.

Titus heard the dark-haired soldier across from Buster humming to himself while he stared at the pile of money, his cards face down on the small box top. The man toyed with a small black porcelain-coated crucifix that hung on a thin chain around his neck, flipping it over, then back again repeatedly.

"I reckon that song yer hummin' there is kinda gettin' on my nerves," the sandy-haired card player said. "I asked you to quit that damn sound a while ago."

"Yeah," Buster said. "Quit it, would ya? I'm tryin' to concentrate."

Without acknowledging either of the two men, the dark haired man said, "I call yer."

There was a pause as the three other players weighed their chances. The crowd murmured in anticipation of the climax to this duel.

The sandy-haired man put down his cards first; a pair of twos and a pair of tens. Buster put down his cards next. There was a brief burst of cheer as he showed three sixes. The quartermaster threw down a pair of aces disgustedly.

The group of men now waited for the dark-haired player to show his cards, but he had cupped his right hand over them on the box top. He suddenly let his gaze lift up, and he stared harshly at Buster as if it were a private conversation between the two. Everyone waited for the player to show his hand but he continued to stare at Buster, his sharp features even more pronounced now as his faced tautened, his large dark eyes focused on Buster.

"C'mon, Seibert," someone said gingerly from the crowd. "Let's see 'em."

Titus prided himself on his general awareness and focus during times of stress, but even he was caught off guard by what happened next.

As if lifted by an explosive charge of tremendous force, the dark-haired player catapulted across the small crate sending the cards and greenbacks flying into the air. The man landed on top of Buster forcing him onto his back. The bystanders scattered in the standard method employed by soldiers when a fight broke out: they stepped back far enough not to be caught in the melee but still close enough to perversely witness the gruesome violence that could erupt.

Seibert sat on Buster's chest while Buster shimmied underneath trying to push the man off. A couple of bystanders yelled out, "Hey," and "Careful there," as Seibert drew a long thin-bladed knife out of his belt and shoved the tip of it on the left side of Buster's neck. The man used his left hand to shove Buster's chin upward so that his neck was exposed.

Buster had stopped wrestling to get away as he felt the knife point on his neck.

"Hey Seibert," someone said from behind Titus. "Just you calm down there. Ain't worth gettin' hanged fer. Just let that fellar be."

Titus notice that the tip of the knife had pricked Buster's neck and a small red bead had formed on his white, stubbly neck.

The entire mass of men froze awkwardly in a pose that Titus had often seen in one of those tintypes floating around camp.

Pushing aside the man in front of him Titus jumped at Buster's attacker, grabbing the man's knife hand with his right hand and whipping his left arm around the attacker's neck yanking him up and away from Buster. Instantly other men jumped in pressing the attacker to the ground and removing the knife.

Titus noticed that the moment he pulled the man off Buster, the attacker went limp and did not resist his disarming. In the end the man just sat up and stared at Buster with a gaze that made Titus shudder.

CHAPTER 14

He carried the half-empty bottle of Old Crow in the crook of his left arm and his notebook in his right hand, walking as fast as he could so as not to draw attention to the sloshing bottle of bourbon he had purchased.

In the dim light of early evening he thought he was safe from the mischievous eyes of thirsty soldiers who were known to employ almost any trick or sleight to pry a bottle of bourbon or whiskey away from anyone, even a junior officer.

He found the doctor sitting in front of the medical tent staring absently into the sprawling camp. The creosote smell of a smoldering fire nearby masked the otherwise fetid camp odors.

"Dr. Morse, how are we this fine evening?" Rhys asked.

"Oh, hello there, Lieutenant," Morse said, hardly pivoting his head in Rhys's direction. "It's indeed a fine evening. The air is cool, the insects are few, and I haven't lost a soldier in three days."

"Ah yes, the rate of illness, I gather, is still fairly high," Rhys said sitting next to Morse. "It must be a burden to care for all of them."

"A burden for me, no; for them, very much so," Morse said looking away again into the camp.

Rhys was hoping to re-engage him with their investigation this evening even if it meant buying a half-filled bottle of Old Crow to entice the doctor.

"You're not here to talk about this killer you're stalking, are you?" Morse said, still looking away. "I don't think I can accommodate you this evening on that score. I have enough death lurking inside that tent behind me and don't feel I can motivate myself to help you find your killer out there."

"Oh, well, I was just hoping to get your impressions of some soldiers I've been interviewing," Rhys said quickly before the doctor's attention floated completely away into the smoke. "And I brought you a gift as a token."

"A gift, you say?" Morse said turning. "No one brings me gifts."

"It's a bottle of Old Crow. I'm told it's a very tasty bourbon whiskey from our rebellious cousins."

"Mmm," Morse said, eyeing the bottle. "I bet that it's far tastier than the medicinal whiskey they provision us with here." He leaned over and picked up the bottle, looked at the black label in the dim light, pulled the cork out and smelled the concoction.

"Well, let me grab two glasses, then, to test this fine nectar," he said standing. "I assume you'll join me?"

"Yes, of course," Rhys said, though he was not a drinker of any ability or interest.

The doctor returned with two small glasses and poured sizable portions in each.

"You know," he said, "I'm not incapable of discerning your motive for proffering this gift. But at the same time I'm not so stubborn that I can turn down bourbon like this. Does Capt. Lynch know what a scoundrel you have become?"

"Ha, you give me too much credit," Rhys said.

"Do I?" Morse said.

"Well, no, I suppose not," Rhys said, chuckling as he took a sip of the tepid brown liquid. "I was hoping you would indulge me on my interviews."

"I grant you an indulgence this evening," Morse said, fluttering his left hand in a mock royal gesture.

"Is it possible to bring out a lantern so that I can read my notes?" Rhys asked.

"Of course, my young man," Morse said motioning at the hospital tent. "Grab any light source that suits your fancy, while I consume my most welcome bribe."

Rhys spent more than forty-five minutes detailing the five interviews he had conducted with soldiers that had been recommended by company commanders. All of the interviewees slept by themselves in half-tents.

Initially Morse was polite and seemed to feign interest, saying things like, "Is that so?" or "That's very interesting." But as time went on and the bourbon had its effect, Morse grew more irritated that he was being forced into this charade to pay attention. Yet he was also unable to avoid engaging the intellectual problem that Rhys was presenting.

"What makes you think any of these men is the killer?" Morse said suddenly.

"Well, I don't know for certain, but they match some of the criteria of our killer: they sleep alone and therefore could move around without waking their neighbor; and they are reported as 'peculiar' in some fashion by their commander."

"Ha! Peculiar! Half this damn army is peculiar!"

"Well, that's probably true, I suppose," Rhys said, still trying to sip his way through the drink Morse had poured. "But what else do we have to go on?"

"You have nothing to go on, except that he has some perverse affinity for slicing throats like a butcher, and he likes to mark his victims," Morse said, his voice rising as he absently batted away a small moth drawn to the lantern.

"Well, what do you think then of Pvt. Ruder?" Rhys said. "He sleeps by himself, is viewed by his peers as strange, and admitted to me that he's slaughtered farm animals in the past by slitting their throat."

"Don't you think that every farmer in this army has slit a throat or two of a barnyard animal in the furtherance of his pastoral duties? Really, Lieutenant."

Rhys sighed heavily, sat back in his small chair and drank the rest of his bourbon in one gulp, wincing as he did so.

"Capt. Lynch reports that Col. Rittenhouse is adamant about not calling in the provost marshal on this case," Rhys said, "but to be honest, I don't know what to do any longer. I'll have to report to him that it's beyond my capability to find this man."

"Oh, don't be so hard on yourself," Morse said pouring his third drink of the evening. "You will find this man, but it will take time, that's all."

"But how will I find him?" Rhys said, his voice rising in exasperation. "I don't know what to *do* to find him."

"Be patient," Morse said. "He will emerge. Keep up your interviews. Keep asking questions. This man is driven by madness and not by reason; he will present himself at some point and you must be prepared to move quickly."

"You think so?" Rhys said. "Truly?"

"Of course I do. Why would I lead you on?"

"To get more bourbon?"

Both men laughed heartily, but Rhys's laugh was the louder and more fervent of the two.

THE NOTION HAD BEEN RATTLING AROUND IN RHYS'S head for several days and he had suppressed it with all his might, sometimes even shaking his head back and forth briskly as if that motion alone would dislodge the thought from his mind.

But the idea simply would not go away, and it hid like a field mouse in the corner of a room waiting for a moment of silence to race out into the open.

Finally, more out of fatigue than any other motive, Rhys simply decided to deal with his problem. He spent several minutes one evening writing out the reasons he needed to test his new and troublesome theory. He drew a line vertically down the center of a piece of paper and wrote the word "Yes" at the top of the left column and the word "No" on the right column. Every fact or event that supported his suspicion he put in the "Yes" column; every contradictory or exonerating fact he put in the right column. After twenty minutes of scratching out the lists by candlelight he put down the paper, stooped, and walked outside the wall tent. He stretched his arms high into the starlit sky, arched his back and rolled forward on his toes and yawned sharply.

"Damn," he said softly. "Damn. Damn."

Going back into the tent he sat down on his bed, picked up the paper and reviewed again that the list on the "Yes" side was very much longer than the list on the "No" side.

"Damn," he said again to himself.

"Damnit yourself, Rhys," said Spangler, his tentmate, rolling over in his bed. "Put out the blasted candle. It's drawing bugs in here and driving me crazy."

"Sorry," Rhys said, blowing the flame out with one long troubled breath.

RHYS FOUND THE MAN HE WAS LOOKING FOR the next evening after nearly an hour of traipsing up and down the informal alley of tents. Even though he was desperately looking for the man, he was determined to make the encounter look accidental.

"Hello there," Rhys said.

"Good evening," Sandler said stopping.

"I was just thinking about you," Rhys said, "and here we are. Isn't that odd?"

Sandler looked at Rhys and smiled slightly. Even Rhys winced at the awkwardness of this exchange.

"You were looking for me?" Sandler said. "Is someone sick?"

"No, no, it's not about that. Actually it wasn't anything important, really," Rhys said starting to walk casually down a freshly trampled grass path. "It was just something you said awhile back."

Sandler walked beside Rhys and looked quizzically at the lieutenant.

"Something I said? What was that?"

"Well, awhile back I ran into you one night in camp, and you said you were looking for Dr. Morse. Do you remember that? It was quite late."

Sandler stopped walking, and Rhys stopped next to him. There was a brief silence as the two men looked at each other in early evening darkness.

"Yes," Sandler said slowly. "I remember that."

"You said that Dr. Morse sometimes leaves his tent at night and you have to look for him."

"Did I say that?" Sandler said.

"I believe that's what you said," Rhys persisted.

"Well, the doctor does sort of walk away," Sandler said. "Sometimes."

"At night or during the day?" Rhys asked.

After a pause, Sandler said, "At night."

"Is he gone for long?"

"I'm not sure what you are suggesting," Sandler said, irritation suddenly evident in his voice.

"I'm not suggesting anything," Rhys said quickly. "I was just trying to clarify what you meant."

"I didn't mean anything."

"But you said you were looking for the doctor and that he wanders at night sometimes."

"Yes, he does wander."

"Why does he wander? Is he looking for someone? Does he have trouble sleeping?"

Again, Sandler said nothing while he seemed to consider the question very carefully.

"He gets confused," Sandler said finally.

"Why does he get confused? I've had many conversations with the doctor and while he might be considered a little eccentric, perhaps, I've not noticed him being confused."

The right side of Sandler's smooth face was illuminated by a lantern nearby and Rhys saw his facial expression move decisively into a frown.

"The doctor is fond of whiskey," Sandler said.

"And that's what makes him wander?"

"That and his other habit," Sandler said.

"What is that?"

"He is fond of laudanum, too."

"Oh, I see," Rhys said. "I did not know that. He takes it each night?"

"Most nights he puts several drops in his whiskey and then falls asleep," Sandler said. "But sometimes he wakes up and walks away."

"Where does he go?"

"I don't know. He just wanders. If I wake up and he's not back, I'll try to find him. Sometimes I'm too tired to search for him."

Silence fell again between the two men.

"Why are you asking about the doctor's night habits?" Sandler said.

"No reason, really, I was just curious," Rhys said.

"You won't tell the doctor that I was talking to you about this, will you?"

"Of course not," Rhys said. "I'm sure with the kind of suffering he sees that the doctor's entitled to seek comfort in this manner."

———————————

"I FIGURED HE WOULD HAVE KILT YOU IF I hadn't jumped him," Titus said, taking a nibble at a piece of hardtack that he had fried in bacon fat. "How in the hell do you get yerself into these situations?"

"It weren't that bad," Buster said. "Yer always makin' it seem worse than it is. He weren't goin' to kill me. He was just showin' how manly he was."

"Well how come you got yerself a nick on the side of yer neck there? You think that fellar Seibert was just playin' around?"

Buster, Titus, Nate Blute, and Pvt. Walter Bucklaw were assembled around the small campfire finishing up their individual cooking. As was the case throughout the regiment, informal groups of soldiers pitched tents near each other and shared the same campfires.

"I heard from someone who was there at that card game that this Seibert fellar accused you of cheatin'," Blute said. "How was you supposed to have cheated him?"

"Hell, I didn't do no cheatin'," Buster said, the flames from the fire bathing the side of his face in a yellow wash. "He was just sore 'cause he lost, that's all."

"How much did you win in that game?" Bucklaw said. "I heard it was a load of greenbacks."

"I ain't gonna tell ya how much 'cause I don't want folks talkin' about it," Buster said, poking the fire with a short stick. "Next thing I know, I'll have it stole from me."

"You think one of us is gonna take it from you?" Bucklaw said.

"No, not you fellars, them others that might hear you talk about it," Buster said.

"Well, you wouldn't have any of that money if yer pal here hadn't jumped in to save you," Blute said. "I ain't heard you thankin' him at all."

"He don't need to thank me," Titus said, chewing the hardtack slowly. "I know'd he'd do the same fer me."

"A course I would," Buster said. "We're pals and we stick together. Especially in this here den of thieves."

"But I got some advice fer yer," Titus said, inspecting his hardtack closely in the firelight to look for weevils. "Stay away from that Seibert fellar. He was mighty bothered by you takin' his money and gave you the eye."

"I ain't afraid of him," Buster said.

"You should be," Titus said.

"I ain't," Buster repeated.

"You ain't listenin'," Titus said. "Stay clear of him."

"He better stay clear of me, is all," Buster said.

Capt. Fetzer marched Companies H and I over a mile through the underbrush and along the river to relieve two companies of soldiers guarding a river crossing.

With Confederate cavalry spotted nearby, the area had been reconnoitered, and a river ford was found. It was deemed a vulnerability to the thousands of Union troops and supplies camped upriver. Fetzer was in charge of the detail, and he and Company H commander, Capt. Franklin, spread their men out in the open, shallow rocky riverbank as a visual impediment to any Rebel scouts that might try this route.

Fetzer did not believe there was going to be any action to his front this day, since the commander they relieved had reported the area was quiet.

Titus took off his furrowed, worn boots and stained socks, resting his rifle on a large granite boulder. Rolling up his pants legs he stepped gingerly into the fast moving stream, careful not to stumble on the cannonball-size stones underfoot. The water was clear and cold, and he stared down at his bone-white feet through six inches of water. He flexed his toes back and forth repeatedly, and smiled at the simple pleasure it gave him.

He bent down and scooped up a handful of sparkling water, and tossed it over the back of his neck. He bent down again and repeated the motion several times until the collar of his tunic was soaked with icy water.

"Hell, Titus," Buster said standing next to him in the water. "What in God's name are we doin' out here on such a beautiful day with guns ready to kill any damn Rebel we see? Don't seem right. Days like this—sun shinin', cool breeze, and cold, peaceful water—well, it makes me consider skeddadlin'. Just plum droppin' my rifle and headin' home, away from all this craziness."

Titus gave Buster an exaggerated frown, shaking his head. He had long learned that sometimes it was just best not to answer Buster and let him talk himself quiet. Once Buster got any verbal encouragement whatsoever, he might keep going for quite a while.

The water rippled by swiftly as the two companies of soldiers took the light duty in stride and made the most of the day.

Titus was the first to see it and he nudged Buster with his elbow.

The two men stared up river.

"Do you reckon he knows we're right here?" Titus said.

Blute, who was standing in the water behind Titus, looked upstream and saw a Union soldier rowing slowly toward them, his back exposed as he methodically swept the oars through the water. The rower was moving at a rapid pace, given the combination of current and rowing strokes.

Titus knew it was unusual to see a single enlisted Union soldier in that kind of conveyance, and he wondered if the rower knew he was approaching a large group of other Union soldiers. The rower seemed nonchalant and unaware of his surroundings, lending the event a strangeness that was not lost on Titus.

As the rowboat approached the only sound was that of the crystalline water rushing in small violent torrents through the shallow ford. Nearly every soldier on the bank watched the scene with amusement.

It took Titus only a few moments to figure out what was playing out in front of him, and when it became clear he quickly turned to see what Capt. Fetzer was doing. Much would depend on how the captain would react.

He could see Fetzer pointing to the rower and talking to and one of his lieutenants.

"Hey there, soldier," someone yelled from the shore. "How ya doin'?" The salutation was more a gentle warning from a fellow foot soldier than it was a true greeting.

The rower turned and seemed startled to see so many soldiers right next to him on the shore. He appeared to be a young man, perhaps in his early twenties. He was not wearing his cap, and his field jacket was unbuttoned showing his white tunic underneath.

The rower bounced quickly over the rough ford and was now moving away when Fetzer yelled out, "Soldier, what are you doing out there? What unit are you in?"

The rower grimaced and shrugged his shoulders as if he couldn't hear what Fetzer was saying.

Fetzer and two sergeants were now running toward the water's edge, commanding the rower to approach them.

But the rower, now ten yards away and moving quickly downstream, simply shrugged.

"Halt, damn you," yelled Fetzer.

Fetzer turned to the soldiers on the bank behind him and yelled, "Shoot that deserter! Someone shoot that bastard before he gets away."

Titus, like every enlisted man in the group, was not going to shoot the man floating away. Feeling both sorry and envious for the man in the boat, they were not going to interfere with the current pulling the man away from them. The deserter faced so many other obstacles in his long journey home that this event did not warrant an aggressive response, at least from his fellow enlistees.

"Shoot, damn you!" Fetzer screamed at his charges.

Several men made halfhearted efforts to raise their weapons, slowly stumbling about with their footing.

A sergeant standing next to Fetzer raised his pre-loaded Enfield, half-cocked the hammer and reached into his leather case for a firing cap. He snapped one onto the nipple and pulled the hammer back all the way until it clicked loudly, the mechanical sounds harsh in the pastoral setting. The sergeant took several steps into the water, leveling his rifle at the rower who was not more twenty yards past them.

The rower, his chest now facing them as he moved downstream, seemed unaware that someone was pointing a weapon at him and he continued his steady pull on the oars, lost in thought.

The sergeant's rifle discharged in a rush of blue smoke and a split second later the front of the rower's tunic fluttered as the man fell onto his back, his face pointing skyward and his head resting over the bow. One of the oars fell out of the man's hand and floated free.

Then, as if he were a puppet on a string, the rower sat bolt upright and stared in the direction of the shooter. He stayed that way for ten seconds or so, and just as suddenly he slumped to his side letting the other oar hit the water and float gently away.

They found the body in the rowboat a quarter mile downstream lodged against a large willow tree that had fallen into the river, its long spindled branches catching every bit of detritus the river offered, including deserters in rowboats.

While the men of Companies I and H knew the consequences of desertion, and had seen their share of apprehended soldiers being led back into camp in chains, it was not common at this point in the war to see men put to death.

"Why would they shoot a poor fellar like that?" Buster said to no one as they marched back to camp later in the day.

"I'd like to take a shot at that sergeant who did the killin'," someone else said.

"He better look out for himself next time we're in the line of battle," someone else said. "That man might find himself with a ball in the back of his skull."

"It just ain't right," Buster said. "He weren't hurtin' no one."

The long line of soldiers made their way back to camp after an hour of trampling through the late afternoon light, tired and played out from the drama. As was the practice at the time, the soldiers discharged their weapons, which had been loaded while on picket duty, shooting at trees that some pretended were "that damn murderin' sergeant."

Titus was quieter than normal around the campfire that night. He turned in early and was fast asleep before the moon rose over the warm Virginia countryside.

CHAPTER 15

For the first time since he had started the investigation, Rhys felt uneasy in the presence of another soldier. There was something about the man sitting across from him that disturbed Rhys and made him feel threatened, but he could not figure out what it was.

The soldier being questioned never motioned in a threatening manner, raised his voice, or even scowled. What was it about this man that was so unsettling?

"There was a report recently about an incident involving you and a card game," Rhys said looking down at a piece of paper in his lap. "I believe there was some problem at the end of the game, and you attacked a man. Is that correct?"

Pvt. Seibert stared at Rhys for a few moments before saying, "Might have been."

"Did you attack someone?" Rhys asked.

"If they say so, then I did," Seibert said flatly.

"But what do you say?" Rhys said.

"I guess so," he replied.

"You guess you attacked this man?"

"I guess so."

"The report says that you pulled a knife out and put it against the man's throat," Rhys said. "Is that correct?"

"Guess so."

"It says you were not put on report because you accused the other man of cheating, and there was no way to determine the truth of your charge, so they let it go. But I was told that some of the men in your company are frightened of you. It appears that you sleep alone in a lean-to and don't have any friends in the company."

"Why do I need friends?"

"You don't need friends, it's just that you don't seem to like being around people. And the fact that some men think you're menacing is kind of unusual," Rhys said. "I've been told me that some men in your company won't even serve guard duty with you. Why do you think men are bothered by you?"

"Ask them."

"But I'm asking you," Rhys said, trying to engage the man seated across from him.

Seibert shrugged. "Don't know."

Rhys noticed Seibert, a painfully thin black-haired man in his midtwenties, was bored and unaffected by anything Rhys said to him. He tried another approach.

"Do you know why I'm interviewing you?" Rhys said.

Seibert shook his head.

"I've been charged with investigating a series of killings that have plagued our regiment," he said. "I use the word 'killings' because it may be the work of Rebel assassin in our midst. But to be honest, I think these are murders, not assassinations."

Seibert suddenly pursed his lip tightly and stared harshly at Rhys.

"Why do you say that?" Seibert said, eyes narrowing.

"Why do I say 'murders'"?

"Yeah."

"Because I think the man doing the killing is someone who is not fighting to preserve the Confederacy," Rhys said with sudden conviction. "I think the killer is just a plain murderer. He likes to kill people. And he's got plenty of people around him here to kill. Simple as that."

"So that's what you reckon?"

"Yes. And I plan to find him and bring him to justice," Rhys said. "Either that or a Rebel ball will bring him down. Either way he'll be stopped from killing our men."

"Good luck, then," Seibert said.

Rhys had nothing more to say and the two men sat across from each other in silence for a minute before Rhys sent the man on his way, glad to be rid of him.

SAM WAS PROUD OF HIS ABILITY TO FIND food for Col. Rittenhouse and while other servants were scrambling to please their masters, Sam had tracked down and paid handsomely for a live chicken. He had decapitated it, gutted it, plucked it and singed the remaining hairs off the carcass and now it was nearly done roasting on the spit, the drops of oil from it hissing as they hit the coals below.

But Rittenhouse had just returned from a meeting and was agitated. He told Sam that they were breaking camp before dawn and were in for a long march.

Rittenhouse was so distracted that he forgot he had invited guests for a meal that evening, and when Sam reminded him respectfully, he sighed and said, "Yes, of course. I suppose there's time for that."

To Sam, there were always sudden changes of plans in this army. To date, there had been no real battles for Rittenhouse's regiment, only skirmishes that had been inconsequential. All of the servants were pleased, of course, since it was well known that in units that had seen heavy fighting, the officer corps was often decimated. And that meant that servants were suddenly marooned without masters. It took time to find another sponsor, and it was a worrisome time for a black man at the periphery of the machinery of war.

And here in Virginia, if by chance Rittenhouse's regiment was overrun or the supply train captured with Sam in one of the wagons, there were rumors that Rebels were executing former slaves on the spot.

Sam had set out dinner on the folding table for Dr. Morse, Capt. Lynch, and Lt. Rhys, who had shown up and were busy sipping whiskey. Sam made sure he heaped the plates with collard greens and carrots that he was able procure, and he was not immune to accolades they threw his way about his cooking. It was his way to ensure he could find a sponsor should anything untoward happen to Rittenhouse.

"Is it true that Lee is into Maryland already?" Lynch asked Rittenhouse as the men sucked on their chicken bones and wiped their hands on the sides of their pants.

"Yes, it seems that way," Rittenhouse said. "The entire First Corps is moving in a blocking motion to protect the capital. There has been much debate about whether we should press against Richmond while he's heading north, but wiser heads have prevailed, and we'll concentrate on protecting Washington."

"What if Lee is not heading to Washington at all?" Dr. Morse said.

"Well, Doctor, what else would he be doing?" Rittenhouse said.

"Perhaps he's just heading into the heartland of the North, collecting provisions and making a statement to our European friends that the South is a force to be reckoned with."

"Mmm," Capt. Lynch said. "With no disrespect, Doctor, that sounds like you're suggesting Lee's on a political mission, not a military one."

"Yes, perhaps I am," Morse said, "but I'm a simple physician and know nothing of these larger affairs. It was just a comment."

"Your opinions are always welcome here, Doctor," Rittenhouse said. "No one is certain what that scoundrel Lee is doing, but we know we're on the march tomorrow. For this brigade it could be an eventful time. I'd be lying to you if I said I wasn't vexed by the possibility of confronting this Rebel army head on."

"I guarantee that the brigade will do you proud," Capt. Lynch said, raising his glass, "and the state of Pennsylvania."

"Here, here," the group concurred, and downed their drinks.

Lt. Rhys grimaced as he sloshed down the whiskey. He wondered if he was ever going to get used to the amber-colored liquid that others seemed to relish.

"Hey there, Lt. Rhys," Rittenhouse said suddenly, "I understand we have had no new incidents from this Rebel assassin in our midst. I was hoping you and Dr. Morse there were going to ferret this man out for us so we could all watch him twist and turn on the gallows. Have you two chased this bastard away from us once and for all?"

"Well, we don't quite know if we've chased him away," Rhys said. "There have been no more deaths primarily, we think, because of our diligence in removing the conditions that the killer prefers to work under. We have doubled up on pickets and have regular patrols in camp all night long."

"Ah, then you think we've licked this scourge?" Rittenhouse said.

"Well, in a roundabout way, perhaps we have," Rhys said. "I'm praying we will not see another killing simply because we have made it impossible for him to do so without identifying himself."

"But I want that bastard hung!" Rittenhouse said. "And I was hoping we could do it before being dragged into battle or having that damned provost marshal get involved."

"The lieutenant is trying his darndest," Capt. Lynch jumped in. "He and the doctor have done an excellent job investigating, and I think they might even have a suspect. Isn't that correct, Lieutenant?"

Rhys was thankful for Lynch jumping in but was caught off guard by the mention of a suspect, and he furiously tried to remember what he had said to Lynch that he might be referring to.

"We do have a suspect?" Morse said.

"Yes, you know, that farmer you were telling me about," Lynch said. "I thought you said he looked like a possibility."

"Oh him," Morse said. "Hardly a real candidate for killing people, in my opinion. Farm animals, perhaps, but not people."

Before Rhys could reply, he heard the clanking of swords and the group turned to see two men of captain's rank walking briskly toward them in the murky light of early evening.

"Col. Rittenhouse?" one of the officers said.

"Yes, that's me," the Colonel said.

"We have new orders for you from Gen. Hooker," he said handing him a folded piece of paper. "The Second Brigade has been ordered to break camp immediately and proceed to Maryland."

"Immediately?" Rittenhouse said. "The men are just bedding down."

"Immediately," the captain said. "With the utmost haste."

"But the men haven't drawn rations," Rittenhouse said.

The two captains shrugged in unison and walked away into the darkness, the sound of their clanging swords lingering behind them.

As he stumbled through the darkness, trying to fall into the rhythm of thousands of feet pounding the dirt road at the same time, Titus thought about how obedient the company had been when ordered to break camp in the middle of the night.

The men barely complained and did exactly as they were told, rolling up their gum cloths, unbuttoning tents, and packing away their belongings into knapsacks.

He marveled at how little resistance he and the other soldiers gave to enormously disruptive orders, like marching through the night at a moment's notice. Yet, when it came to small, inconsequential orders, like firewood details, or picket duty on a cold rainy night, he and others would complain until they were red in the face and daydream about deserting.

As he finally fell into a marching rhythm that suited him, Titus began to daydream again about squiring the manager's daughter around the little town of Shippensburg. If nothing else, it took his mind away from the numbing monotony of walking in the darkness for hours on end, following the man in front of him with as much fealty as if he were his personal guidepost for salvation.

Titus looked eastward and noticed the smudge of a sunrise.

Where the hell are we goin' in such a hurry? he wondered.

HE HAD BEEN WALKING THROUGH THE UNDERBRUSH FOR at least five minutes, pushing farther into the treeline, looking for a good spot to ease his bowels away from the thousands of other men doing the same. Buster passed men bent over emptying their waste onto the rich forest floor, and they would nod or ignore him completely as he went around them looking for his own spot.

The sun had been up for only an hour and the long dark shadows sliced through the forest, giving off a kaleidoscopic effect as he walked. Buster finally found the trunk of a collapsed oak tree and he quickly went to work, dropping his britches and sitting on the horizontal tree trunk. He pushed his rear out over the other side and he commenced the serious business at hand, grunting loudly as he did so.

He preferred to find his own spot for defecating away from others, since Titus had accused him of making too much noise in the past at the open latrines around camp.

"Yer sound like some ol' barnyard dog gruntin' away," Titus had teased in front of others in the company. "Cain't you jest do yer business without all that damned racket?"

It was not Buster's style to be bothered by anything anyone said about him, but somehow this particular jibe had elicited a lot of teasing. Buster decided he'd just as well avoid further attention to his toilet habits by finding a place where he could grunt as loud as he wanted and for as long as he wanted.

Go mind yer own business about a soldier's habits, Buster thought. *It's a man's right to empty hisself without bother from anyone else.*

After he had finished, and hearing the bugle call to fall in, Buster used some old newspaper strips to clean himself and then headed back to the road, where they had stacked their rifles in pyramids of threes and fours. All around him other soldiers made their own way through the forest to gather on the road.

Buster had walked about thirty steps or so, his head down and lost in thought, when he looked up, startled. Seibert was standing ten feet in front of him.

His card-game nemesis was looking at him with the same, intense, cold—almost rapt—stare that he had employed when he attacked him at the end of the card game. Buster felt a rush of electricity that seemed to emanate from his stomach and radiate outward to his fingers and the very tip of his nose.

Buster hoped his visitor would either say something or move. All around him he could hear men working their way back to the road, but none seemed to be close enough to disrupt this private menacing scene.

After what seemed like too long, Buster said, "You're welcome to stay here, fellar, but I ain't gonna be accused of skeddadlin' while I wait fer you to get out of my way."

Buster took several steps to his right to take a wide berth around the other soldier but Seibert moved to his left an equal number of steps and stopped when Buster did, blocking his way yet again.

"What the hell is got into you?" Buster said. "Are you still sore about the damn card game? If you cain't stand losin', you shouldn't be playin'. Now git out my way before we get ourselves in a tussle."

Buster made a move again to his right but stopped immediately when Seibert reach into his tunic and pulled out a knife. It was about six inches long and slightly curved, with what looked like a white bone handle.

"Just you wait one second there," Buster said. "I reckon you are takin' this thing to the wrong conclusion." The longer he delayed getting back to the road to fall in, the more isolated the two men became as the other soldiers left the forest.

How strange, Buster thought. *There are about ten thousand troops fifty yards from me right now, but I'm about as alone as a man could be. I reckon this meetin' here is not gonna end just right.*

CHAPTER 16

Titus never thought Buster would desert, though he knew his tentmate had blustered about doing so many times. After the deserter was shot in the rowboat, Buster had been particularly vociferous in decrying the army, the war, officers of any rank, and now, especially, noncommissioned officers.

Still, as Titus set up his tent as a one-person lean-to, he was surprised and sad at the same time.

"You reckon he just plum took off fer home?" Blute said.

"Seems that way," Titus said, staking the rope and pulling it taut. "Never figured he'd do it, but I keep gettin' surprised about things that happen in this here army."

"Maybe he come down sick?" Blute said.

"Maybe," Titus said, wearily.

The march had gone on nearly all day, and the men were exhausted and hungry. Rations for five days were being handed out, and Titus, Blute and the others from the regiment made their way over to the long line.

Titus tried not to think about his friend's absence, and the hunger in his stomach made that possible, concentrating his mind on the hardtack, bacon, and coffee he was going to be offered.

Later, sitting around the campfire, Blute and others tried to engage Titus but he was too worried to talk. He simply poked the fire with a stick, rearranging the charcoal remains of the fire idly, as if they were important levers to a complicated piece of machinery.

THE RAILCARS WERE LINED UP FOR AS FAR as the eye could see, and Lt. Rhys wondered how a locomotive could pull a brigade, including horses and wagons at the same time.

"Captain," he said, "do you think we can all get onto these cars?"

"It does look like it'll be crowded, that's for sure," Lynch said. "But we're not going far, so that's some consolation. And if we can't do it in one ride, they'll send back another train."

Movements like this take so much time, Rhys thought, as he tried to calm his horse. When massed together like this, the infantry seemed to turn to molasses, with painfully slow progress to achieve any goal, whether it was to board railcars or simply drill for a commanding officer.

"Have they found Lee yet?" Rhys asked.

"Well," Lynch said, "it looks like his damned Army of Northern Virginia is probably in Western Maryland. They took Winchester, and there was a hell of fight at Brandy Station, we hear. All on horseback. A real cavalry fight."

"Did we prevail?" Rhys asked.

"Damn right we did," he said. "That blowhard Jeb Stuart had his comeuppance at the hands of Maj. Gen. Pleasanton, a brilliant cavalryman."

Rhys was well aware of Lynch's propensity to exaggerate, and he never challenged his claims of Union dominance in battles. He typically received a more sober assessment of battle outcomes in small groups with other junior officers. Still, he would sometimes prod Lynch with queries about battles just to let him extol the prowess of Union forces, if for no other reason than to allow his mentor to puff out his chest a little and buoy his demeanor.

"And we're heading to Maryland then?" Rhys asked. "Is that the plan for the brigade?"

"Yes, that's what Hooker has us doing," Lynch said, "and I dare say, young Rhys, that we will finally see action against this Rebel horde. If they're coming north, then we'll meet them with resolve—and with a whole lot of lead, that's for sure."

"Well, I cannot wait," Rhys said, again trying to steady his mare as the locomotive let loose several screaming whistles. "Steady, there Nancy. Steady, girl. That train won't hurt you."

THE SWEAT WAS POURING DOWN TITUS'S BACK AND pooling at the base of his spine, soaking his tunic. The loading of the railcars had started smoothly enough, but the process soon devolved as officers began to speed up the effort, yelling at everyone and agitating junior officers, who agitated noncommissioned officers, until there was no else to agitate except the infantry.

The men settling into the railcars were a mixture of companies, and Titus was lucky to grab a spot near the open sliding door and against the wall. He jammed his knapsack between his legs and kept his rifle vertical in front him with the butt on the floor wedged between his left knee and the pack, and the tip of the rifle barrel leaning back against the railcar.

The heat rose inside as soldiers readjusted themselves, found friends to sprawl next to, and generally waited for the train to get moving to push some air into the freight car.

"Hey, there you are." Titus looked up to see Buster grinning down at him.

"I been lookin' for my ol' pal," Buster said.

"Well, you found him," Titus said slowly. While he was more than a little relieved to see his wayward tentmate, his nature did not allow him to show too much emotion.

Buster shoehorned his way into a small area at Titus's feet, causing a brief and spirited rebellion by several soldiers who had already taken up space there.

"Give the fellar some room," Titus said. "He just returned from the dead, he did."

Buster wore a thin sheen of perspiration on his forehead, and he unbuttoned his field jacket to cool off.

"You ain't gonna believe what happened," he said to Titus.

As the train lurched forward Buster grew animated in his storytelling.

"What the hell did he want?" Titus asked after listening for a while.

"He never said a damn thing," Buster said. "Couldn't get a word out of him. But he wouldn't let me pass, neither. I tried to scoot around him, but the damned fool would block me each time. And jest when I figured I'd just run fer it, damn if he don't pull a knife out."

"Yer kiddin' me," Titus said. "That damn knife of his that he pulled on you at the card game?"

"Yep," Buster said. "That crazy fool was goin' to cut me up!"

"All because of that card game?" Titus said. "That don't seem right. A man don't act like that unless he's bothered by more than a card game. You must've done somethin' to really burrow under his skin. You sure you didn't do no cheatin' in that game?"

"Titus, I'm tellin' you I don't n'even know *how* to cheat at that game. And I ain't never seen this fellar before that game. I got no idea why he got it out fer me."

"How in the hell did you get out of this mess then?" Titus asked, grateful now for the swirling air from the moving train.

"I could hear the brigade startin' to move out and there we was, starin' at each other. I'll be honest with you—I was thinkin' this was my last day on this earth, that the Lord done seen that it was my time to depart."

Buster stopped and took a long draw of water from his canteen. Titus could tell from his friend's jittery smile that he was genuinely agitated by this experience. Given his friend's typical cockiness and self-assurance, Titus figured his tentmate had been through a harrowing experience.

"I was lookin' around me for somethin' to use as a club or weapon against this here madman, when damn if I don't hear someone from the side of me say, 'What the hell you boys doin' here?' I just about jumped out of my britches.

"There's a marshal on horseback makin' his way toward us, lookin' like he thinks we're stragglers," Buster said. "I look back at Seibert and wouldn't you know that the knife is all gone, and he's lookin' all normal and all. He says, 'We was just makin' our way back.'

"I cain't believe my eyes. One minute he's all fit to cut my throat, next he's just out takin' a Sunday stroll."

"What'd you do next?" Titus said.

"Well, I just started talkin' to the marshal, tellin' him what a nice horse he got, stuff like that, and followin' him out to the road. And when I git out I find my Enfield and knapsack on the side of the road, and the regiment is long gone. But guess what?"

"What?"

"That damn marshal won't let me go!"

"What the hell did he want?" Titus said, now taking a swig from his own canteen.

"He wanted my name and unit, and kept questionin' me, like he was gonna throw me in prison for skeddadlin'."

"Did he do the same for Seibert?"

"No! That crafty bastard just took off; grabbed his stuff and disappeared into the soldiers goin' by. But don't worry, I give that marshal Seibert's name instead of my name. Hee hee. And when he finally let me loose, well, the damn army had just about gone by, so I hitched a ride on a quartermasters' wagon."

"What took you so long to catch up to us?" Titus said.

"Well, them quartermasters eat pretty good," Buster said chuckling. "And I stayed with them last night to enjoy some of their fine victuals."

"Did you find Sgt. Crowley yet? At muster he put you down as desertin'," Titus said. "You better get that fixed up."

"I seen him already," Buster said. "He didn't believe it was me."

The two men jolted along in silence as the train pushed through the Virginia countryside, heading to Maryland.

After several minutes, Titus said, "I told you to stay away from that fellar."

"Titus, I *was* stayin' away from him! He found *me*."

"I don't think this Seibert is right in the head," Titus said.

The two men fell silent again. The car rocked gently back and forth and was full of the conversations and laughter from the other soldiers crammed into the railcar.

"Hey, Titus," Buster finally said. "You reckon this Seibert fellar might be connected to all them knife killin's in the regiment?"

Titus looked at his tentmate and then peered over his head and out the other open railcar door opposite him. The countryside streamed by in a smear of green while Titus considered his friend's question.

"Could be," Titus said finally, letting the rhythmic rocking in the train lull him to close his eyes briefly. "Just you stay clear of him."

THEY GOT OFF THE TRAIN NEAR LEESBURG, RESTED for several hours and then marched toward the Potomac River.

They stopped marching at two a.m., dropped their knapsacks, and slept on the open ground. At seven a.m. they were marching again through a thin, misty drizzle that turned the roads to mud and made the march both more miserable and more physically exhausting. They pushed on through the night until they stopped just short of Edward's Ferry at four a.m.

Titus did not mind marching at night since he was not distracted by the scenery. He could just plod on, following the knapsack of the man in front of him and daydreaming. When the brigade dropped its packs at four a.m. he fell down and went to sleep almost immediately.

He dreamed about his mother and one of his sisters, who were fussing over an article of clothing they were sewing. In the dream, Titus was not sure what the piece of clothing was or who it was being made for, but he stood in the small living room of their farmhouse and tried to communicate with them. In the dream, he could not speak and was struck dumb as he watched them fuss over the item. The more Titus tried to speak, the more frustrating it became that he could not speak. It seemed as if his mouth was glued shut and his tongue paralyzed.

The effort to speak became so frustrating and bewildering that Titus woke to the sounds of his own groaning. In the darkness he could make out the hundreds of shapes on the ground spread out as far as he could see. The sun had only started to hint at sunrise in the east and Titus closed his eyes to try to find sleep again. The rich, pungent smell of the river nearby reminded him how thirsty he was, and he reached for his canteen, taking a long swig.

He settled back down next to his knapsack and fell to sleep immediately, praying that they would delay reveille so that he could rest.

MORSE MAINTAINED A LIST OF NAMES THAT HE rarely read in its entirety, but in the middle of the night on the banks of the Potomac he suddenly couldn't resist looking at it.

He opened the notebook and read over the names, one by one, with the date, location and cause of death listed in a column to the right of the name.

Morse had trouble remembering the faces of many of the dead, and that fact bothered him greatly.

Why can't I remember the face of this Cpl. Silvani? he thought as he adjusted the candle light that flickered in the warm June breeze. *He died just two weeks ago. Was he the one who had an enormous abscess on his stomach? Damn, I can't remember anything anymore. We haven't seen real battle yet, and men are dying all around me.*

Morse closed the notebook and put it snugly onto his lap, as if maintaining physical contact with the written word would help him remember some of the names and faces of the men who came to die in his care.

He pulled out his small pocket watch and tilted it to the cone of light from the candle. It was 2:46 a.m. and while he was feeling the effects of the whiskey and laudanum concoction he drank every night, in recent weeks he'd had to increase the number of tincture drops in his whiskey to achieve the desired effect: to sleep and not be reminded of his sick charges. Unfortunately, the increased dosage also had the contradictory effect of inducing a kind of waking dreaminess that he found pleasant—but irksome, because he wished to sleep, not walk around in a gauzy state of mild euphoria. His aide, Sandler, had taken to hiding the laudanum recently, and Morse was not unaware that he was perhaps acting a little more self-absorbed and distracted than was the norm.

He snapped the watch shut and dropped it back into his vest pocket. Standing up, he was suddenly consumed with a delight in the freshness of the air, the smell of the river, and the warm breeze that rippled the trees and ushered the campfire smoke away.

With a near-full moon radiating through a thin layer of clouds, Morse found himself drawn toward the languorous Potomac River. He sauntered past the snoring mounds of exhausted soldiers who were cuddled like hundreds of kittens. He passed two guards and raised his hand in a kind of hello-what-a-fine-night-it-is-but-don't-bother-me wave. They returned the wave.

After a meandering walk of nearly a hundred yards, Morse found himself at the pontoon bridge that would allow the brigade to move into Maryland and chase down Bobby Lee and his band of insurrectionists.

Immersed now in that dreamy feeling produced by his nightly concoction, Morse was enthralled by the sight of the river as it jostled the pontoons holding the bridge afloat. The river seemed to slither like a thick, black snake with its scales sparkling jewel-like in the moonlight.

Instead of walking back to camp, Morse walked parallel to the riverbank, moving west and into the countryside past a line of pickets, who also nodded to him. He reveled in the bucolic beauty and quiet of his surroundings. He felt giddy and absorbed in the world around him. He listened to the insects, smiling to himself in the knowledge that each chirp and buzz was a private communication between creatures determined to survive in this beautiful but dangerous universe.

"Hey, Doc," he heard someone say. He turned to see a soldier standing twenty feet behind him.

"Hello," Morse said, chagrined that his private reverie was being interrupted.

The doctor turned away from his visitor and looked back at the river, trying to recapture the pleasing mood.

"It's a dark night in a dark world," the soldier said.

"Yes, I suppose," Morse said, only partly turning his head toward his visitor to invoke the notion that he did not wish to converse.

"There are many dark secrets we all carry with us, and the night is as good a place to let those secrets come out, away from all those pryin' eyes," the soldier said.

Although his central nervous system was smothered with the laudanum and whiskey, Morse was able to detect something sinister in the tone and content of his visitor's conversation. And there was a fleeting sense of familiarity, as if he knew who this person was.

On the other hand, his confusion was so profound that he wondered, in fact, whether he was imagining this conversation. Was he dreaming? He had awakened before from confused, garbled situations only to find that he had been dreaming.

He turned to face the man, who stood in the lee of a large willow tree. Morse struggled to concentrate on the man's features, but the lack of light and his dulled senses made it difficult for him to see.

"What's your name, soldier?" Morse asked. "I don't believe I know you."

"You know me," the man said.

"I do? Well, repeat your name to me then. I'm at a loss."

"I'm the one you're looking for," he said.

"You are?" Morse said. "I didn't know I was looking for anyone. I'm afraid you're confusing me, son." The doctor was starting to battle his oily and sluggish consciousness in an attempt to stay focused on this man, whose voice and self-assured tenor was oddly disturbing.

"I think you know what I mean," the man said firmly. "You and that lieutenant are seeking me out."

From his stomach came a sudden swirl, as if a sparrow was flitting about.

"I think you are mistaken, young man," Morse said slowly, careful not to move closer or farther from the man. "I'm not looking for anyone."

"You shouldn't lie like that," the man said, a note of sternness in his voice. "I believe that's a sin, and sins must be expunged."

Morse struggled with a creeping sense of dread and quickly looked past the soldier into the darkness behind him, gauging how far back the pickets were. A silence fell on the two men and Morse, with his physician's penchant for decisiveness, decided to act.

"Are you that cold-blooded fellow that is killing our soldiers?" Morse said.

"Those are harsh words to describe what I am," he said. "It's the Lord's mission I'm on. To thin out the herd of the weak of mind and heart."

"What makes you think they are weak of mind and heart?" Morse said.

"I can tell when I get near to them," the man said. "I can feel it. The weak ones need to be removed in order to make the whole stronger yet."

"What is it about the ones you choose that tells you they are weak?" Morse said.

"It's the smell, I think," the man said. "I can smell their putrification."

"Don't you think the army should figure out who's strong enough to remain and who must be sent away or discharged?" Morse said. "Why do you think you have the responsibility to do it yourself?"

"Only a few are chosen to do this work," the man said. "It's not my choice. It's the Lord's choice. He has given me this gift."

"Well, the army doesn't quite see it as a gift; they see it as a crime that's interfering with their ability to wage war against the Secessionists. Surely you must have a sense that what you're doing is hurting their effort, not to mention the men you're killing. Are you a Secessionist then?"

"I already told you. I have been sent to remove the weak and decrepit," he said. "I'm no Secessionist."

The men looked at each other in darkness, separated by twenty feet of blackness and menace.

Finally Morse spoke. "What are you doing here tonight, talking to me like this?"

"I came to smell you up close," the man said, taking a small step toward Morse. "I was trying to figure out whether you have the smell of death about you."

CHAPTER 17

Rhys mounted his horse and asked an enlisted man to direct him to the Second Brigade headquarters. Capt. Lynch had told him to report there at seven a.m. for a briefing.

"Lt. Rhys," someone called loudly from nearby. He pulled back on Nancy's reins. Turning, he saw Sandler waving his hand. "Lt. Rhys, wait up, please."

"Lieutenant," Sandler said, "I can't find the doctor and we're breaking camp."

"I don't understand," Rhys said. "You can't find Dr. Morse?"

"That's right," he said. "He's just gone."

"I'm sure he's just on one of his late-night walks," Rhys said.

"I don't think so," Sandler said. "He's never gone this long."

"I'm sure he's nearby; maybe getting rations?"

"I've been looking for the last hour and I'm telling you he's gone," Sandler said. "Can't you please just help me look for him? Please? I'm kinda worried about him. He hasn't been himself lately."

"Alright, damnit, but I'll only be able to spare a few minutes. Where's your wagon? Hell, just get up here and we'll get there much faster."

He yanked the private onto Nancy's back and made his way past artillery limbers, ornery mules and thousands of soldiers moving toward to the river.

At the medical wagon Sandler explained that the doctor had stayed up late, as was his habit, and then apparently just took a walk into the night.

"Was he of sound mind?" Rhys asked.

"Well, he likes his tincture, as I told you before, Lieutenant. I've been trying to hide it lately, but I reckon he might have his own stash."

"Have you asked whether he was seen by anyone last night?" Rhys said.

"I asked some of the fellars on picket and they said they might've seen him along the river bank late at night. But I'm just one man; I can't search the whole river by myself. I'll be here till August if I do that."

"What direction did they say they saw him walking?" Rhys said as he looked at his pocket watch. "Damnit, I'm going to be late. This is absurd, an army on the march to save our capital, and I'm off chasing a drunken doctor who's lost in the woods!"

Rhys tied Nancy to a small sapling and dragged Sandler with him toward the river. The infantry was now crossing the pontoon bridge in a long thin line, the regiments crowded together at the entrance of the bridge in what looked like a massive field of blue bobbing caps and rifle barrels.

Sandler and Rhys walked west along the bank of the river about forty feet apart, looking for any sign of their missing quarry. Periodically, more to vent his frustration than out of any hope that it would prove helpful, Rhys yelled out, "Dr. Morse! Dr. Morse, are you there?!"

After nearly ten minutes of looking Rhys stopped and yelled to Sandler, "I think our good doctor isn't here and we'll just have to report him missing."

Rhys took several steps closer to river and noticed a large boulder about fifty feet ahead, jutting above the scrub pine and underbrush. He walked toward it and stopped when he saw the shape of a soldier curled in a ball at the base of the gray obelisk.

He recognized Morse's boots protruding from the ball of a man, and he rushed over with dread, knowing what he was going to find.

Grabbing the shoulder of his blue wool coat he violently threw the doctor over onto his back so that he could see his face and neck.

Morse lay there inert, his arms flopping aimlessly in the dirt.

The doctor opened his eyes and closed them again in the glare of day, covering them with the back of his left hand.

"My God, you're alive," Rhys said. "Sandler! Over here, Sandler. The doctor's here."

Morse sat up and looked around, bleary-eyed and confused.

"Are you all right, Doctor?" Rhys asked.

"Yes, of course I am," he said. "Why wouldn't I be?"

"You disappeared last night," Rhys said. "Sandler here couldn't find you and half the brigade is already across the river. You really shouldn't be leaving camp like that, Dr. Morse."

Rhys and Sandler helped Morse to his feet and led him back toward camp.

"Are you sure you're all right, Doctor?" Sandler said as Morse shuffled his way slowly back to their wagon.

"Yes, of course I am," Morse said.

After several steps Morse stopped, rubbed his eyes, yawned violently and said to Rhys, "I believe I had one of the strangest dreams I've ever had before, Lieutenant. A dark, troubling dream."

"Well, I'm sorry about that, Doctor," Rhys said. "I must be running ahead to attend a briefing."

"Thanks for helping me, Lieutenant," Sandler said as Rhys ran to get Nancy, holding his sword scabbard hard against his thigh so that he wouldn't trip.

Buster slid in directly behind Titus, forcing the soldiers in line to re-sort and to curse Buster in the process.

"Yer goin' to get me in trouble, Buster," a soldier said.

"Oh quit yer complainin'," Buster said.

"Hey, Titus," Buster said. "Can you believe all these folks? They're just lovin' us. Sure beats what we come across in Virginia, that's fer sure."

Titus was shocked at the outpouring from the small town of Poolesville in Maryland. Men, women, and children had come out to wave flags and cheer the thousands of soldiers on. It gave him a thrill, and for the first time since joining the regiment, Titus felt a rush of patriotism.

"It's a far sight better than on the other side of the river," Titus said. "Just wish they'd slow down all this marchin'. It's gettin' tiresome."

The truth was that soldiers were dropping out regularly now, falling behind to catch up later. The marshals were checking stragglers for written passes from doctors or company officers to ensure they weren't deserting.

Titus noted that the general tenor of the march was more festive as they moved through the small towns in Maryland, but also more somber as the brigade's officers and couriers rushed back and forth. And foraging, tacitly allowed in parts of Virginia, was strictly forbidden on Union soil.

That night as the brigade bedded down in fields just north of Frederick, Titus noticed that Buster was in a foul mood.

"If we cain't do no foraging up here, then you'd think they'd give us some better food," Buster said, frying up a small slab of bacon.

"These are our people up here," Blute said. "We cain't be takin' their hogs and cattle. It ain't right."

"But you reckon it's all right to take it from them poor folks in Virginia?" Buster said. "They didn't have nothin' to start with, and we took what was left."

"Hell, Buster, they started this damn thing. I don't feel sorry for them folks at all," Blute said. "They deserve to be treated like that."

"But what happens after we win this thing—and I reckon we're gonna whip Bobby Lee right soon—and them folks we plundered is gonna be part of the same country again. How do you reckon they're gonna feel about us then?"

"I don't rightly care what they think," Blute said.

Titus was glad to see Buster quit talking and focus on eating. When Buster was agitated, he invariably got others worked up as well. Titus was exhausted and just wanted to sleep after dinner, since orders had already come down that they were breaking camp before dawn again.

After several minutes of quiet, Blute said, "I heard that Company B got two of them deserters back. It just ain't right that they give them amnesty jest to get the army back up to full strength."

"It's that big monkey, Abe Lincoln, just messin' everything up," Buster said. "First he says we gotta punish them deserters, then he turns around and says he's gonna give them amnesty. So all them boys who were sittin' home getting fat on home cookin' get to just saunter back into camp like nothin' happened."

"I heard that in Company B, them two amnesty fellars ain't welcome, and they're tryin' to transfer to another company," Blute said. "You reckon we'll get them two fellars? We're down five men at least."

"So help me if they put them deserters with us they might find themselves wakin' up one mornin' with a bayonet up their ass," Buster said, snapping off a piece of hardtack with his canines.

"You two better get some sleep in," Titus said, packing up his gear. "We'll be headin' out early again."

"I swear that they're gonna kill us from marchin' before we even get a chance to fight them Rebels," Blute said. "My legs are so weak right now I cain't even feel my toes."

THE WARM BREEZE THAT HAD MADE THE EARLY evening bearable stopped abruptly around midnight turning the camp into a hot, mosquito-infested caldron. Rhys had stayed up late writing a long letter to his parents, but Spangler had complained so loudly about not being able to sleep from the light and heat the lamp gave off that Rhys finally put out the flame around midnight.

He tried to sleep but his mind was racing with confusion. His investigation into the killings had moved no closer to a conclusion than when he was first given the assignment. It was folly and poor judgment on Rittenhouse's part to appoint Rhys and Morse to try and find the killer. Perhaps it was the colonel's insecurities or his fondness for whiskey, but Rhys now grasped the full absurdity of his task.

And to make matters more complicated, he now had grave doubts about the innocence of Morse, his co-investigator. Rhys had tried to remove the doctor from his private list of suspects based on the facts, but try as he might he could not exclude him. Morse had the sharpest knives in the camp, appeared to walk around alone at night, and was prone to eccentricities that raised eyebrows even among senior officers.

But perhaps his biggest concern was that no one seemed the slightest bit interested in helping him find the killer. The chase to block Lee's army from attacking Washington had drowned out his investigation and every other ancillary activity.

He lay in his bed inside the tent, perspiration forming on his forehead as the heat became unbearable. Spangler had insisted on keeping the front flap closed to keep out the bloodthirsty mosquitoes, but it had only kept the heat concentrated inside.

After tossing back and forth on his thin, straw mattress for several minutes, Rhys finally sat up, pulled his blanket off the bed and went out of the tent. It was especially dark that night due to the heavy cloud cover, and Rhys could barely make out a quartermaster's wagon parked about twenty yards away. Uncertain whether it would rain that evening, he trundled gingerly over to the wagon trying to avoid the pebbles and sticks that hurt his bare soles.

Crawling under the wagon he tried to get comfortable, rolling the blanket into a pillow. After awhile he fell into a fitful sleep, slapping absently at the few mosquitoes that found him there.

He did not know what woke him precisely or how long he had been asleep, but at some point Rhys opened his eyes and found himself staring at the undercarriage of the wagon. He yawned, turned on his side to avoid a root of some type that was digging into his rib cage, and then closed his eyes again, eager to find sleep.

The sound of footsteps caused Rhys to open his eyes. He was facing his tent twenty yards away, its white canvas a dull shape in the darkness. Of course footsteps in an army camp were not out of the ordinary, since there were night guards and soldiers seeking to relieve themselves, but still Rhys was bothered by these particular footsteps. He wondered if that was why he woke.

He sat up slowly on his elbow and tried to scan the darkness around him. *What was it about the footsteps that bothered him?* he thought.

He listened, holding still on his elbow. There, he heard them again off to his left. They were not the plodding, rhythmic steps of a guard on duty or the furtive quick steps of a soldier with a full bladder seeking relief. No, these steps were intermittent; someone nearby was stopping and starting at odd intervals almost as if the person was looking for someone or something.

The wagon allowed Rhys to raise his head just so far, and he had trouble seeing anything clearly. The footsteps started again and stopped just as quickly. He turned his head in the direction of the sound, perhaps fifteen feet away, and realized with dread that the random footsteps he heard were more like that of someone stalking an animal. Or a person.

The hairs on his arms stiffened as he felt a surge of fear course through his tired body.

Someone was trying to find Rhys's tent, and he had just discovered it. He strained to see but could only make the dull light color of his wall tent. The palms of his hands began to dampen with sweat and he found that he could hear his heart pounding in his chest.

My God, it's him, Rhys thought.

His elbow began to hurt as he rested on it, frozen in place as he was under the wagon. And then just when he thought he could not take the searing pain from his elbow he saw the unmistakable outline of a blue shape against the white of his tent. Someone was standing perfectly still in front of his tent, perhaps no more than five feet from the closed flap. Rhys realized in dread that Spangler was alone inside the tent.

Damn, he thought. *That man will kill Spangler thinking it's me. Damn!*

Panicking and short of breath Rhys tried to run though his options: he could stand up and yell, raising a ruckus and scaring away the killer. But he would still not know who the killer was because he would surely take off in chaos. Hell, the killer might simply chase down Rhys and slit his throat once he found out he wasn't in the tent; in the chaos no one would know what was happening or witness the attack.

But still, Rhys had to do something to save Spangler.

Rhys strained to see the blue shape to gauge whether it was moving toward the tent flap, craning his neck forward and tilting his body at an odd angle. To Rhys's surprise and dread, his aching elbow gave way and he fell forward onto his left shoulder.

The noise of his small fall would have been inconsequential in the full light of day but in this little corner of Maryland, in the ghost-like quiet of night, the stumble could be heard clearly. Rhys lay frozen on the ground, leaning on his left side, afraid to move a muscle for fear of giving away his position. Perhaps the killer did not hear him fall after all. Rhys's left ear was planted squarely onto the rough ground under the wagon, but he was still facing his tent. He tried to focus on the shape, but the man had disappeared.

Rhys had a sinking feeling that the killer was inside the tent with Spangler. He was about to crawl out from under the wagon and start yelling when his left ear felt the unmistakable seismic sound of footsteps.

Without raising his head off the ground, he slowly, painstakingly arched his neck backward to look down the length of the undercarriage.

That's when he saw the legs. They were barely visible at the very end of wagon. The legs were very still, waiting. Rhys tried to control his breathing. The killer was so close now that any sound at all would give away his position, even something as small as the shifting of his leg or the scrape of his tunic against the soft grass.

The legs took several tentative steps away from the carriage and stopped. Rhys could barely make out the shape since his head, resting on the ground, was bent backward to the fullest extension of his neck. To see the man, he would be forced to raise his head and shift his body, but he didn't dare.

Then the intruder took several steps back toward the carriage and stopped again. Rhys waited, praying silently for the man to go away, but also hoping that *something* identifiable could be gleaned from the legs. Perhaps the man wore riding boots identifying him as an officer or had some unique feature to his boots, anything that Rhys could use.

And then the worst possible thing happened.

The intruder walked slowly around the carriage and stopped. He was directly behind Rhys's arched back less than five feet away.

More petrifying still was the fact that Rhys did not know what the intruder was doing behind him. He could be leaning over with that damn knife of his ready to slice away Rhys's life. Or he could be staring out into the countryside, or rubbing the sleep from his eyes.

Then the steps commenced again; the man walked away from the carriage and stopped, then repeated this behavior until Rhys assumed he was gone. He slowly stretched his body out of its cramped state, turned his body around and stared in the direction of the intruder, relieved that he had gone.

After what seemed like ten minutes, Rhys crawled slowly out from under the wagon with his rolled-up blanket and stood perfectly still. Behind him he heard steps and saw two guards walking slowly past the far side of his tent, the barrels of their rifles barely discernable in the darkness.

He rushed over to the tent, threw the flap open, and rushed over to the crumpled shape of Spangler on his bed. He grabbed the man's shoulder and roughly turned him over. Spangler yelled in confusion and thrust out his arms to fend off whoever was attacking him.

"It's me, Clive," Rhys said. "Calm down."

"Damnit. Quit tryin' to strangle me then," he said.

"I was just seeing if you were all right, that's all," Rhys said falling back into his bed.

"Goddamn you, Clive," Spangler said, tryin' to calm himself. "Yer turning into a crazy man. You know that?"

Exhausted, Rhys lay back and tried to sleep again. He turned on his side to avoid a piece of stiff straw that poked through the mattress. *Damn*, he thought, as he adjusted again. He reached around to the small of his back to press down the errant shaft of straw. His hand discovered a stick. Quizzically, he pulled out the twig and felt a coldness sweep up from his stomach into his chest and throat. He did not need to light the lantern to see what he held in his hands. Rhys's fingers could easily make out a small wooden cross, perhaps four inches long and three inches across. A piece of string was wrapped tightly to hold the cross members in place.

RITTENHOUSE DID HIS BEST TO PRESENT AN OFFICIAL demeanor of confidence and resolve at briefings, rarely asking a question for clarification unless it was absolutely necessary. He noted some of the other officers in the corps would pepper Gen. Paxton's staff with inquiries that seemed silly, and to his mind, made the questioners appear indecisive and weak.

He was not worried about how and when they'd get into battle; he was more concerned about whether the brigade would hold together in battle. Rittenhouse had been getting an endless stream of reports detailing the exhausted and depleted condition of the regiments. Some companies were down by almost half due to stragglers, the increasing numbers of sick soldiers, and the small—but constant—draining away of deserters. Now that they had crossed over the Potomac he feared that some soldiers would simply go home.

Further compounding his anxiety was the fact that Lee's Army of Northern Virginia was not yet found. Rumors had his army as far north as Harrisburg, but no one knew for sure where he was and that meant that at any moment they could stumble upon his vast army and be forced into battle instantly.

The briefing ended faster than he anticipated, and the group of forty or so officers turned to collect their horses, swords clanking in syncopation to the tension. Rittenhouse walked with Capt. Lynch and Lt. Rhys back to their horses in silence, the smell of cigar smoke strong in the humid air of the last day of June.

"You reckon we'll get a shot at Lee's army this time?" Lynch asked Rittenhouse.

"Hell if I know, Lynch," he said. "That Lee is a wily one. Can't say I want to volunteer the brigade to meet up with him first. Still, whatever God has in his plans for us, we'll do our damndest to make our state and country proud."

When they got to their horses, Rhys suddenly turned to Lynch.

"Sir, can I have a word with you?" he said.

"Now?"

"Yes, if you don't mind."

"We'll follow shortly, Colonel," Lynch said, as Rittenhouse mounted his horse.

The two men stood in the shade of a majestic drooping elm taking a brief respite from the unforgiving sun, which had broken strong that morning.

"What is it that's so pressing?" Lynch asked, looking irritated. He glanced around as most of the other officers were riding off to their commands. "Quickly please. There's much to do."

"It's about that investigation that Col. Rittenhouse ordered me to complete," Rhys said. "I was to work together with Dr. Morse to try to find the man who was killing some of our men."

"Yes, yes," Lynch said. "But the killings have stopped, yes?"

"Well, so far that is true, but I have no doubt that when the opportunity presents itself, the man will continue to kill. I'm certain of it."

"But if we have night guards and procedures that make it impossible for this Secessionist spy to kill, then we've done all we can do," he said. "You've accomplished your task."

Rhys did not wish to debate about whether the man was a Rebel spy or not.

"But I don't feel appropriate for this investigation," Rhys said. "Can we please turn this over to the marshals?"

"But you know that Rittenhouse hates them," Lynch replied raising his voice in frustration.

"Yes, I know, but they are best suited for this kind of work. The doctor and I are not suited to this kind of work. Would you talk to the colonel about it, sir?"

"Today?!"

"No, not today, of course, but soon? I feel like this work is beyond my capabilities."

"Fine, fine, Rhys," Lynch said, turning back to find his horse. "I'll talk to him. Let's stop talking about it now, OK?"

"Thank you so much, sir," Rhys said.

CHAPTER 18

Titus noticed that something was wrong. After four days of a near-continuous, exhausting march through the hot Maryland countryside, there was a sudden change in the demeanor of every officer and noncommissioned officer.

For the first time as a soldier, Titus was suddenly directed to keep his voice down and to avoid any needless chatter that might draw attention. This could only mean one thing—they were in earshot of the enemy.

On the night of June 30, the brigade came to rest next to a small creek just over the border into Pennsylvania. Pickets were set out farther than normal into the surrounding farmland that evening.

Titus, Buster, Blute, and several other members of Company I were allowed to cook their food and boil coffee for only a brief period, and then campfires were doused and men were again prohibited from any loud behavior.

"Hell, I feel like I'm in school, for God's sake," Buster said.

"You never even been to school," Blute said. "So quit soundin' so high-minded."

"Well, I went when I was little," Buster said.

"I don't reckon you would have lasted more'n a week in any schoolhouse," Blute said.

"It still feels like we're in school," Buster said defiantly.

Blute's tentmate, Greg Gillette, had straggled so far back in the forced marches that Blute now slept alone in a half-tent lean-to.

"You think that Greg done skedaddled?" Buster said.

"I don't reckon he would," Blute said. "He just got a bad belly. Lost so much weight that he looks like one of them fence posts we pass all day long."

Silence fell on the group again, and after a few minutes Buster tried to engage Titus, who was more distant than usual in the darkness.

"How far away do you reckon them Rebs is, Titus?" Buster said.

"My guess is that they're right close," Titus said. "We'll likely see them tomorrow."

"How you reckon the 239th'll hold up?" Blute said.

"Well enough, I think," Titus said. "We damn well trained long enough."

There was no bugle or drum roll for the nightly "all quiet," instead guards came through the camp to shut down activity.

The soldiers were not allowed to pitch tents, so camp had the feel of chaos as soldiers spread out everywhere using their knapsacks as pillows. The only redeeming feature to the camp was the weather; a breeze had picked up that evening, feathering the exhausted marchers into a full sleep.

"Hey there, Titus," Buster whispered.

"Huh?"

"You sleepin'?" Buster said.

"Tryin' to."

"I been worryin' a bunch about tomorrow," Buster said, scrunching several inches across the ill-defined demarcation line separating the men's sleeping spaces.

"What are you worrin' about? Just get some rest."

"It's them thoughts I get," Buster said. "They're botherin' me a plenty."

"Whatever them thoughts is, you don't got to worry. Jest get to sleep."

"But I'm worried I jest might try, you know, to straggle."

Titus sighed. "You got nothin' to worry about, damnit, Buster. And I got to get me some sleep, so quit yer yappin'."

To Titus's relief, Buster stopped whispering to him. Titus closed his eyes, listening to the gurgling of the small creek nearby.

"I put my favorite things in yer knapsack," Buster said.

"Huh?" Titus said, struggling at the very edges of sleep to ascertain whether he was dreaming. "What?"

"I put my special things in yer pack," Buster whispered. "They's wrapped in paper and have a string around 'em. I want someone to have them."

"Buster, I swear I'm gonna punch you silly if you don't quit yer—what did you say? What special things?"

"I reckon you would look after my belongin's," Buster said. "Got my lucky deck of cards, my knife—the one you like—and a pile of money from card playin'. You can have it all. Cain't think of anyone else I want to have it."

Titus turned to face Buster in the darkness, the smell of crushed grass, body odor, and wood smoke filling the small space.

"You cain't be talkin' like that, Buster," he said. "I don't want yer stuff, 'cause yer gonna be needin' it yerself. It ain't right to talk like that."

"Well then, jest give it back to me tomorrow at the end of the day," Buster said. "It just makes me feel better thinkin' someone's got my stuff to carry on with."

Titus closed his eyes again.

"I swear, Buster, I don't know who's gonna kill you first, them Rebs or me."

Titus bolted upright, startled by something.

"Damnit, get up," someone hissed, shoving his shoulder. Titus looked around in the darkness and saw that Sgt. Wheeler was quietly waking several soldiers.

"What's goin' on?" Buster said.

"Just shut up and get your rifle," Wheeler said.

"Do we take our kit with us?" Titus asked.

"No, you'll have time to pack up in the morning," Wheeler said softly. "Just come along now. Right now."

Titus, Buster, and several other Company I soldiers groggily followed Wheeler through the maze of soldiers spread out over the ground. At one point Buster tripped over a sleeping man's leg and fell in a pile. The sleeper cursed Buster, but Wheeler kept the men moving forward without bothering to stop.

After fifteen minutes of wending their way through the piles of men, dozing horses, and wagons, Wheeler halted the small group in a clearing.

"Capt. Fetzer found a huge gap in our picket line," Wheeler said. "Don't know how it happened but we're going to fill you fellars into that gap. Now, we're going out together so as not to spook the pickets already out there. You stick with us, and we'll place you one by one."

"Sgt. Wheeler," Buster said, "when do we come back in?"

"We'll pull you in at daybreak, don't worry about that," Wheeler said.

"Just don't forget about us, that's all," Buster said.

Titus nudged Buster hard to shut him up, since the tension in Wheeler's voice was unmistakable.

"Come on," Wheeler growled as he pressed forward through a patch of saplings and shrubs.

After several minutes of walking a voice shot out from in front of them.

"Who's that! Who goes there?"

"Hold your fire, boys. It's Sgt. Wheeler from Company I with some more pickets. Just take it easy."

The small group came upon a single soldier who identified himself as a private from Company C. Wheeler consulted with the soldier about where the other pickets were located to his right.

The soldier was agitated and said he hadn't seen anyone to his right. He warned Wheeler that his sudden appearance had spooked him and that he was briefly tempted to fire at him.

"Damnit soldier, the enemy is out there," Wheeler said pointing away from camp and into the darkness beyond. "Don't you go shootin' your own men behind you."

"Well, don't do no sneakin' around then," the soldier said.

Titus could see that Wheeler was trying to control his temper. After several seconds, Wheeler said in a calmer voice, "Son, we're going to put some men to your right over there. You see in that direction?"

"Yep, I see."

"There's a gap out that way that we're tryin' to fill, do you understand that?" Wheeler said carefully.

"I reckon I do," the soldier said.

"Well, I'm tellin' you that because I don't want you to shoot any of my men," he said. "I'd be mighty angry if you kilt one of my men 'cause you were scared."

"I ain't scared," the soldier said.

"Good," Wheeler said patting the man on his shoulder. "I'm takin' these fellars out this way," he said, pointing to the man's right. "And then I'm going to come back this way and check up on you."

"Sure," the soldier said.

"What your name?" Wheeler asked.

"Pvt. Jelia."

"Well I'll come back through here and call out yer name, Pvt. Jelia, and that's so you won't shoot me, OK?"

Buster chuckled and Titus shoved him again. Fear was palpable in the patches of dark forest and open farmland, and even Titus was feeling nervous.

Wheeler led the way through the brush for about twenty yards and stopped.

"You," he said to one of the group. "You put yer butt here and keep your eyes out in that direction. You got that?"

"Yep," the soldier said.

Wheeler continued on and placed another soldier until Titus and Buster were the only ones left. They kept walking. Titus kept his arms up in front of his face to protect it from the whipping branches Buster generated. Suddenly he heard a commotion ahead and Titus ran into the back of Buster.

"Damnit," Wheeler was saying to someone. "Why didn't you call out when you heard us coming? I just about stepped right on top of you."

Titus found himself staring down at a Union soldier sitting with his back against a tree, his rifle lying across his lap.

"Soldier, I'm talkin' to you," Wheeler said. "What's your name?"

The soldier just stared back. Titus could not see the man and he quickly scanned the area wondering if Wheeler had overshot the area he was trying to fill.

"Seibert," the soldier said.

Titus felt a twinge of alarm and grabbed Buster's arm to hold him back. Titus quickly stepped past Wheeler to look at Seibert. He could barely make him out in the darkness.

"Do you have pickets beyond you over there?" Wheeler said pointing.

"A long ways away," Seibert said.

"How far do you reckon they are?" Wheeler asked.

"Maybe fifty yards," Seibert said. "Maybe more."

"Well, I'm puttin' these two men on the other side of you over in that direction," Wheeler said. "And then I'm comin' back through again. You got that?"

"Yep," Seibert said.

Buster pushed his way around Titus and bent over into Seibert's face.

"You come near me, and I'll shoot you jest like you was a Rebel," Buster said.

"Hey, take it easy there," Wheeler said grabbing Buster by the collar and yanking him up. "The enemy is out there, boy."

"No he ain't," said Buster. "He's right here."

"Goddamnit," Wheeler said in a high-pitched whisper, "can you just fight one war at a time? I swear I'll have you men in chains if you keep this up. It's no wonder Lee can kick our butts whenever he wants."

He pushed Buster away from Seibert. Before Titus followed he leaned over into Seibert's face.

"You leave my friend alone, you hear me?" he said inches from the sitting soldier's face. "You touch him one more time and you'll have me to reckon with."

Titus followed Wheeler for about thirty seconds until he directed Buster to stand guard next to a small pine tree.

"Just stay here until you're called in at daybreak," Wheeler said. "Pick up your kit and find your company if they've already left. You got that?"

"Yep."

"And stay away from that other soldier back there."

"Yep," Buster said sitting down on the warm forest floor.

After another thirty seconds of walking, Wheeler deposited Titus and repeated the orders to remain in place until daylight.

Titus settled into place, and while he felt jittery about the proximity of Seibert and Buster to his left, he also felt a sudden draining of energy that surprised him in its intensity. He briefly closed his eyes, opened them again after a few moments with an enormous expenditure of energy, and then let them slide shut again as if his eyelids were made of granite slabs.

RHYS DECIDED TO GET UP AND WALK SINCE he could not sleep comfortably on the uneven ground. There were no tents allowed during this hurried advance, and he would not have slept in his tent anyway, the memory of the previous night still on his mind.

In the hours that passed since that strange episode, he had been in a daze. At times he even wondered if he had imagined the scene with the stranger lurking outside his tent. But each time doubt crept in, he would simply let his hand fall to his left pants pocket. Inside he had placed the small stick cross he found in his bed. This was the only proof he needed that the killer was real.

It was also clear to Rhys that his stalker had come to see him as a threat. The only reason the killer would seek him out now, he guessed, was because Rhys must have scared him. Was it one of the men he interviewed? Or was it someone else who knew one of the men interviewed? And why did the killer warn him off with his crude handmade cross? Or was it not the killer after all but someone playing a practical joke on him?

God, what does any of this mean? Rhys thought.

But whenever Rhys relived those moments watching the stranger's shape as he stood motionless in the dark outside his tent, there was little doubt the man was the killer. He could not prove it, of course, but there was something—the presence of evil maybe?—that made him shiver at the recollection.

If he thought hard about those interviews, only a couple stood out: Ruder and Seibert. But this was just the product of his instinct, if he could call it that. He had no clues or witnesses. Both of these men could be absolutely innocent, but how was he to know?

And of course there was the problem of Dr. Morse.

As much as he tried to strike the doctor from his list of suspects he could not do so. Disturbingly—and sadly—the doctor was perhaps the single most likely suspect, Rhys knew. A strange, distracted man, the doctor certainly had access to a weapon to slice a man's throat in one quick move. And given his knowledge of anatomy, he would know how to do it quickly and silently.

Furthermore, Morse instilled trust in the troops and would not be seen as a threat if he greeted someone in the dark.

But how could he accuse the doctor of being the killer—he was the savior of so many soldiers! Capt. Lynch might question Rhys's state of mind if he even suggested it.

After mulling his dilemma all day long, Rhys came to a resolution. If the murder investigation was not turned over to the provost marshals as he had requested then Rhys would seek a transfer, pulling what strings he could to get out of the regiment.

What more could I do? he thought.

He wasn't acting irresponsibly or cowardly. And if he didn't leave the unit he might end up with his own throat slit one of these nights. The army simply did not care about an isolated killer in the midst of so much organized killing. The army, Rhys concluded, could take care of itself.

The sliver of a crescent moon produced enough illumination for Rhys to see hundreds of soldiers sleeping in piles as if they had been shot dead and fallen in place. He shuddered to think what battle would really look like when these same men ran into the entire Rebel army.

Rhys walked slowly in a large circle around the camp, trying to keep sight of his belongings by focusing on the silhouette of a large ash tree. Without the formal structure of a camp setting it was easy in the dark to lose track of a soldier's resting place.

The walking calmed him.

He passed two guards who stopped him and whispered, "Sorry, Lieutenant, you ain't supposed to be up. You got to bed down like everyone else."

"I'm going now," he said, and the guards moved on.

Circling back to his temporary bedding Rhys saw a familiar shape walking ahead of him. He caught up and the soldier turned as he heard his steps.

"It happened again?" Rhys said quietly.

"'Fraid so," Sandler said. "I slept right next to him, but he managed to get up without waking me. And I stowed all the laudanum, too. Damn if he doesn't have more stashed away somewhere."

Rhys felt uneasy knowing the doctor was wandering around camp. He debated whether he should move his bedding or even stay up all night.

Suddenly the physical and mental exhaustion of the past twenty-four hours enveloped him. He sagged.

Who cares what happens tonight? he thought. *I can't single-handedly guard the entire regiment.*

"Good luck finding the doctor," Rhys said, walking away.

REVEILLE WAS NOT SOUNDED AT DAYBREAK. INSTEAD GUARDS came through rousing the troops. No campfires were permitted, and soldiers filled their canteens from the creek and ate hardtack and bacon cooked the night before.

With sixty rounds of ammunition in their cartridge boxes, full canteens, and knapsacks the soldier labored in marching order up a dusty road that led through a thick forest into open farm fields with wheat in full, blonde midsummer growth. The supply wagons stayed behind as the blue rows of bobbing caps and rifle barrels swept by.

Titus had spent the night waking and dozing in a cycle. He was called in with the other pickets when the sun was an ugly orange smear in the east.

He found his knapsack and accoutrements in a pile where he had left them, and even though the regiment had already pulled out, he knew he could catch up fast enough.

He noticed that Buster's pack was still on the ground and waited for him. But the longer he waited, the more he fretted about how far he and Buster would need to double-quick in order to catch up to Company I.

After another fifteen minutes, Titus began to worry about his friend. He ticked off the likely reasons why Buster would be tardy: he fell asleep and was too lazy to rush back to camp; he deserted since he was now back in Pennsylvania and closer to home; he was sick.

Or some misfortune had befallen him.

This last possibility gnawed at Titus. He did not think it likely that Seibert and Buster had come into contact with each other during the night. But there was something strange in the air the previous night, and it bothered him.

And yet Buster was one of the most resourceful men Titus had ever met. He was entirely capable of getting himself out of almost any dire situation.

So where was he?

Titus's stomach felt sour and he rubbed it absently.

Finally, he pulled on his knapsack and began to retrace his steps back to the area that he and Buster had sat on picket duty.

It was not easy finding the precise location because the daylight had changed his perspective completely. He looked for landmarks that he might have seen as black silhouettes in the moonlight but was still uncertain of the area they had been directed to guard. Titus was forced to cut across a huge torrent of soldiers moving north like a slow but powerful river.

At one point he was stopped by a marshal who demanded to know why he wasn't with his unit. Perhaps it was Titus's clipped demeanor or fierce intensity, but when Titus answered, "I'm lookin' fer my friend and don't git in my way," the marshal simply snarled and let him pass.

He spent almost thirty minutes moving through the saplings and brush looking for where Buster should have been stationed on picket.

Titus called out Buster's name several times but to no avail. He finally gave up and turned around, sure now that Buster had returned by another route and retrieved his belongings. The thought buoyed him and he moved quickly to rejoin the blue horde streaming north.

Titus stumbled upon a mound of branches freshly broken off and scattered. He had not seen it earlier. The branches seemed to cover something.

He knew instantly what was under the branches because he could see Buster's right boot sticking out. He knew it was Buster's boot because he had sat next to him one night several weeks earlier as Buster had sewn on a new leather sole using a homemade awl.

Titus's face tightened and his mind went blank as the full force of dread fell over him. He tossed back the branches and found Buster staring straight up into the forest canopy with half-closed eyelids, his neck slit neatly underneath his chin. His forehead had been cut somehow, the blood having coagulated so that it distorted the shape of the cut. But Titus didn't need to clean the wound to know what the shape was.

He looked up into sky and made a short yelping sound; it was not a cry nor scream, but something in between. His mind danced furiously between rage and despair, back and forth in an escalating seesaw of emotion.

He sat down next to Buster's body and sighed deeply. Titus half-expected to see Buster sit up yelling, "I fooled you!" Already he noticed that two small black ants were crawling on Buster's cheek and he furiously swiped them away, saying "Get off him you bastards."

Minutes passed as Titus sat back with his hands propping him up; he peered around the forest, out past an opening to a freshly plowed field. Through his hands he could make out the seismic trembling caused by heavy wagons and horses pulling artillery pieces nearby.

He rested like that for twenty minutes, let loose with one final drawn-out sigh, and then searched through Buster's pockets for anything of value to send to his family. Like many soldiers going into battle, Buster had written down his name and unit on a piece of paper and stashed it in his jacket pocket. Titus left the note there so that his body could be identified.

He stood up, removed Buster's bayonet, attached it to his rifle and stabbed it into the ground. He hooked Buster's cap over the rifle butt.

Maybe someone will find him, he thought, *and give this man a proper burial.*

He began to jog, slowly at first, then more rapidly in an effort to catch up to his regiment. His mind, though troubled, was gaining focus. He needed to complete a task. Nothing was going to stop him, he told himself, from settling this thing. Nothing.

TENSION PERMEATED THE ENTIRE BRIGADE AS IT MOVED forward, but Rhys was too fatigued to worry about what lay ahead. The reddish-brown dust was thick and began to coat his throat and nostrils, forcing him and hundreds of others to cough and spit in a cacophony of expectoration.

The brigade stepped out with the 223rd first in line, followed by 239th and the 240th. In typical, heavy-marching order over long distances, the lines of soldiers quickly strung out and became slightly disorganized. This morning, with the sun already blazing, the regiments were kept tight with little room for spreading out.

Titus had nearly run out of energy by the time he found the regiment. He was sweating profusely, and his field jacket was soaked around his neck and lower back, emitting the peculiar cloying smell given off by wet wool. The quick-time pace, the dust, and the heat were making it hard for him to focus on anything more than the knapsack of the man marching in front, a private named James Wolcott.

Every now and then a group of riders would roar by, their clanging swords and the deep rumble of their horses the only evidence the marching soldiers had that they were nearby. Mercifully, after nearly forty-five minutes of fast marching the brigade halted and the soldiers rested in place, taking measured sips of their canteens, unsure of how much they'd need the rest of the day.

Titus only took a small sip from his canteen, betting that he would need the water later. Banging the cork stopper down with his open palm he began to step closer to the front of the regiment looking for members of Company

C. The entire regiment, though depleted, still numbered close to seven hundred soldiers, so it was not going to be easy to find Seibert. But he was confident that before the day was out he'd find him.

"Damn it sure is hot," Wolcott said. "I jest cain't stand all this walkin' in the dust. Coats my nose and throat and even my eyeballs."

"It don't coat yer eyeballs," Blute said. "Maybe it coats yer other tiny balls between yer legs, but not yer eyeballs."

"You some kind of doctor of eyeballs?" Wolcott said. "I know when my eyeballs get clogged with dust and when they don't, and they's clogged right now."

Titus tried not to pay attention to the nervous banter of soldiers about to enter battle. He was fixated on only one person and he strained to find him.

"Hey, Titus," Blute said. "Where do you reckon Buster is? I ain't seen him. Think he skedaddled?"

"No," Titus said. "He ain't skedaddled."

"Well he sure as hell ain't here," Blute said.

"Don't you worry about Buster," Titus said quietly.

Suddenly a deep, concussive boom could be heard echoing off the trees and across fields. Hundreds of small conversations in the brigade stopped as soldiers shifted their gaze, trying to discern the direction of the artillery fire. Eventually the soldiers' gaze synchronized northwest as the booming continued with more regularity.

Titus could see that officers on horseback were clustered at the head of the column. Several junior officers peeled away from the group and raced down the line yelling, "Double-quick now, men. March on the double-quick."

The 223rd started off at a jog, followed by the other two regiments trying to keep up. Titus could barely stay up with the tall and lanky Wolcott in front of him. The Enfield, at nine and a half pounds, felt increasingly heavy as he held it in front of his chest, its barrel bouncing up and down with the thousands of others in a strange syncopated ballet of blue metal.

The brigade halted clumsily after only ten minutes and stood down for yet another break. Then it started off yet again. The column veered from the road and headed across a knee-high cornfield. Titus saw three civilians walking briskly away down the road they had just come from. One was an old man with thick white hair. With each hand he led a young child. Only the little boy looked back at the blue horde going in the opposite direction; his sister kept her face looking forward.

CHAPTER 19

Rhys had followed Capt. Lynch for nearly half a mile, at first paralleling a dirt road thick with marching Union soldiers, then across a field of young cornstalks, and then up a small rise, down into a swale and up again to the top of a ridge, where Lynch suddenly pulled up.

Looking north across a mile of undulating wheat fields, Rhys could barely see a group of gray-clad soldiers and artillery pieces snuggled up against a tree line. The Rebel cannons fired in succession, their thick blue-gray smoke clearly visible for at least a second or two before the sound of the firing caught up to Rhys and Lynch on the ridge.

He could barely trace the trajectory of the balls that flew through the muggy air, each one arching gracefully over the wheat fields and then landing near a farmhouse that stood on another ridge a half mile away.

The farmhouse was flanked by a regiment of blue-coated soldiers. The cannonade was coming at the farmhouse from the right, which was north. But the Union soldiers were actually facing straight ahead to the west. Rhys understood immediately that the Union soldiers at the farmhouse were in an untenable position. They were facing straight ahead to the west because they were being threatened from that direction. But they were easy targets on their right flank from the Rebel artillery a mile away to the north.

Rhys tried to keep Nancy steady, agitated as she was by the surprisingly powerful roar of the artillery.

"Those poor bastards are getting the worst of it," Lynch said. "I think that's the Iron Brigade at the farmhouse. They're preparing to meet a force of Rebels from their front but they're taking a beating from that artillery on their right flank. They'll need support up there."

Lynch turned in his saddle and his voice moved seamlessly from a conversational tone to an official one.

"Lt. Rhys, get back to Rittenhouse and tell him the Rebels are here, west of town at this farmhouse," Lynch said. "Direct him here right away. Do you understand?"

"Yes sir," he said, turning Nancy sharply with a snap of the reins.

Rhys had gone only a quarter of a mile when he came across three men on horseback. He pulled up. "Where is Col. Rittenhouse's command?" he asked, without checking for rank and bothering with decorum.

"His troops are right behind us," a captain said. "Where are the Rebels?"

Rhys directed the three soldiers to the ridge behind him and took off looking for Rittenhouse, returning again through the cornfield. Rhys could see dust from soldiers marching on a road up ahead, and he asked the officers at the head of the column to direct him to the colonel.

By now he and Nancy were breathing heavily and were caked in dust that stuck to their sweaty bodies. As he made his way back past the column of marchers, Rhys was also nervous and giddy with fear. He could feel the powerful forces of battle beginning to congregate, and he was both awed and scared by it.

Rhys found Rittenhouse stern and boiling with anger.

"Where is the enemy?" he asked. "Why can't anyone tell me where the enemy is? Who is in command up there?"

Rhys dismounted and described what he and Lynch had seen, repeating Lynch's order to direct Rittenhouse to the farmhouse.

And just as quickly one of Rittenhouse's adjutants ordered Rhys to return to the farmhouse and report that the Rittenhouse's brigade was en route to support them.

Retracing his path Rhys rode back over the cornfield that now sported a trampled path carved into its stalks by the horse traffic. As he galloped closer to the farmhouse the cannonade was louder. He noticed a Union battery of three Napoleons that had just unlimbered next to the barn and were firing back at the Rebel battery.

He galloped up to the farmhouse looking for Capt. Lynch. He needed to report that the battalion was on its way to support the farmhouse, but there was so much chaos and noise that it was difficult to find who was in charge. Finally he saw the unit's color guard behind the barn and raced up to report to a group of officers, some of whom were on horseback. Others stood in a group around a man sitting on the ground.

Rhys was directed to a Col. Rogers, who was sitting awkwardly on the ground in their midst. Rhys jumped off his horse, tossed the reins to someone, and approached the ring of soldiers.

"Col. Rogers, sir?" Rhys asked.

"Yes, that's me." Col. Rogers was sitting on the ground, his left leg pulled up so that his knee was level with his bearded chin. Six inches above the Colonel's straightened right knee was a piece of rope that had been tied around his thigh with a stick twisted into a tourniquet.

Rogers's right pants leg was cut open below the tourniquet displaying—almost immodestly—the colonel's white-skinned knee smeared in both fresh and coagulating blood. An eruption on the inside of his knee showed where a piece of metal had sheared the kneecap.

Rhys was about to speak when a loud crash caused the group of men to flinch in unison. He arched his back away from the sound and saw a piece of the farmhouse roof fly into the air.

Rhys quickly repeated his orders to the colonel. There was a brief discussion among the officers about what disposition the troops should be in to withstand the expected infantry assault from their front while trying to avoid bombardment from their right flank.

Finally, almost reluctantly, one of the officers said, "Col. Rogers, I'm afraid that you should be moved a field hospital. That leg does not look good, and you've lost a lot of blood."

Rhys slowly removed himself from the group and remounted. He had no specific orders at the moment and was interested in finding Capt. Lynch. Hearing the sound of one, then two exploding shells in the woods behind the farmhouse, Nancy leaped to flee the field under her own volition and had to be forcibly reined into control.

JUST AT THE POINT WHEN TITUS THOUGHT HE could not run any farther, the brigade came to a halt. The three regiments stopped in a heaving, coughing, sweating clump just west of the town in a swale between two ridges. To their right were the outskirts of a town. Running perpendicular in front of them was a gravel-covered road that stretched from the town on their right to the far left, past a farmstead that was crawling with Union soldiers.

The Union soldiers at the farm seemed to be menaced by Rebel soldiers to their front and Rebel cannon fire from their right.

The Rebel artillery battery fired a three-gun salvo into the Union soldiers at the farmstead, exploding on top of them. Titus was not a military strategist, but he could plainly see that the Union force at the farmhouse could not simultaneously fight a battle to their front and withstand a cannonade from their right flank.

Exhausted, sweating profusely, and feeling strangely distracted, Titus took an almost theoretical interest in the situation facing the soldiers at the farm. He guessed that the troops there would soon be ordered to pull back nearer town and join Titus's brigade.

But he was wrong.

Instead, all three regiments of the brigade were suddenly ordered to drop their knapsacks in a heap at the bottom of the small swale. One soldier from each regiment was left behind as a guard.

"You reckon we'll ever see our packs again?" Blute said as they double-quicked toward the farmhouse.

"Nope," Titus said through heavy gulps of air.

"What the hell is the name of this town we're tryin' to defend?" Blute asked. "Some fellar back there said it was Gettysburg, but I reckon it's got to be Hanover."

"I don't care if it's Richmond were defendin'," Titus said, relieved now to have dumped his knapsack. "Sooner we get this damned battle over the happier I'll be."

"Well suit yerself," Blute said. "I'd be just as happy not to get my britches shot off in no battle."

The three new regiments trundled the mile to the farmhouse and took up position in the same direction—facing west away from town—as the Union troops already there. Still, many soldiers were visibly unnerved by the artillery rounds that kept streaking in across the wheat fields on their right.

Titus didn't like the exposed position of the Union troops at the farmhouse when he saw them from afar, and he liked it even less standing with those same soldiers. But it was now obvious why the entire Union force was facing west and trying to ignore the artillery from their right—a Rebel force of perhaps a thousand men were jostling toward the farmhouse from that direction.

Titus heard the well-rehearsed orders, "Prepare to load," "Load," "Handle Cartridge," "Tear Cartridge." With that, hundreds of snowflake-like pieces of light-brown paper were spit out of dry mouths and floated to the ground as the soldiers bit off the tops of the paper packets holding the powder and the lead bullets. Each man withdrew the iron ramrod from underneath the barrel of his gun, turned the rod upside down, and used the flared end to push the Minié rounds down the barrel. Returning the rods, each soldier followed orders to prime his weapons with firing caps.

Titus did not know why they were loading their weapons since there were no Confederate soldiers that he could see in range in front of them.

Company G was ordered out as skirmishers and directed to advance in front of the main force in a long, spread-out line.

Up to this point Titus had not heard a single rifle discharge; the air was filled with the sound of artillery from both sides firing away from long range.

"I ain't likin' this," Blute said to Titus. "They's just got us out here bein' target practice for them Rebs. Maybe we should be gettin' behind that barn there."

Titus ignored Blute and tried to concentrate on the skirmishers out front. If the skirmishers came under fire, then the assault would be underway and there was no telling how that battle would end. He was prepared to stand his ground, fire his weapon when directed, even advance and charge if so directed. But he wanted it to be over, since killing Rebels was not top of his mind any longer.

His only worry was that he would not survive the day and would not be able to settle his score. The entire Rebel army had become a nuisance to him, nothing more or less.

Titus's palms were sweating against the deep-brown walnut stock of the Enfield. He did not want to think about what effect a Minié ball would have on his flesh and bone, or how he'd hold up to the chunks of iron thrown off by the exploding artillery shells.

"Damnit why don't they jest move us behind that barn there," Blute started up again, as three rounds of solid shot crashed down on the soldiers. One ball hit the trunk of the large oak in the front yard of the farmhouse, sending leaves and splinters flying and bringing down a huge branch in a crash.

"Stop yer yappin,'" Titus said. "Nothin' we can do about it."

But Blute continued to talk, mostly to himself, complaining about their exposed position and his desire to move to cover. And Titus was not immune to his friend's complaints: standing in formation without breaking ranks while being fired upon from afar was enough to make a man a nervous wreck. Officers and noncommissioned officers walked behind the ranks exhorting the soldiers to remain vigilant.

"Hang in there, men," Titus heard an officer yell. "Those Rebel gunners hardly know how to fire those pieces, much less find the range. Just stand your ground."

Much of their training in repeated, mindlessly boring drills was premised, Titus knew, on bolstering men's courage in battle when confronted with just this kind of onslaught.

The worst thing soldiers could do in combat, everyone knew, was to turn and simply run to the rear. It had happened so many times already—and its effect so devastating on the outcome of a battle—that Union soldiers were now threatened with charges of desertion and even execution if they collapsed in battle.

The problem was that once the collapse to the rear started, it was nearly impossible to stop. The same herd instinct that kept soldiers fortified as they stood together unbroken during a barrage, also worked in reverse when soldiers began to break for the rear.

CHAPTER 20

They had started to stack the wounded in and around the door of the barn in anticipation of its use as a field hospital. Morse had to step over several groaning soldiers in order to get into the darkened structure. He and Sandler busied themselves by trying to find items around the barn they could use.

Sandler found several rough-hewn sawhorses in a back corner and was startled when a fat black cat with white neck streak hissed and scooted between his legs as its hiding place was disturbed.

"Get out of here, you rascal," Sandler yelled, trying to kick it with his right foot.

Morse was able to yank a small door off its hinges, though not without some intense shoving, yanking, and twisting. It felt strange to destroy the property of someone he had never met and likely never would meet. Regardless, he was driven at this particular moment to do anything in his modest power to save the lives of the wounded. It was the reason he was there, and in a perverse way, it felt much more useful to aid men wounded in battle than men sickened from dysentery.

In the background, as they worked to prepare their field hospital, Morse and Sandler could hear and feel the artillery as the detonations shook the boards holding the barn together. Every now and then an explosion would erupt nearby and Morse would look in that direction, but Sandler seemed not to care.

They put the door flat onto the sawhorses, lit a lantern, and laid out some of Morse's surgical supplies on a small crate they positioned next to their makeshift operating table.

Morse had started to walk to the open barn door when a red flash of light and simultaneous explosion sent him flying backward onto the manure- and hay-strewn barn floor.

"Are you hit, doctor?" Sandler said standing over him. "Are you OK?"

"Yes, I'm fine," Morse said. "Just help me up, please."

He stood in the wide barn doorway and counted seven soldiers lying just outside. Most were ambulatory, but at least one was completely flat on his side facing away from Morse. The doctor walked over to the soldier, kneeled, and gently turned him onto his back.

As he did so, the man mumbled something unintelligible. The wounded soldier held his blood-covered hands tightly against his stomach as if he were protecting a jewel of vast importance. Morse firmly pried the man's hands away from his body but stopped; the wounded soldier held eight inches of his large intestine that were sliding out from a deep gash across his stomach.

The man spoke again but Morse could not understand him.

The doctor quickly glanced around at the other wounded men, some holding their shins or arms, but none apparently as seriously injured as this man.

What am I supposed to do to save this man? he thought. *I could push the intestines back into the body cavity and sew him up, but if the organ is perforated, it will just lead to sickness and a miserable death. And he has lost so much blood already. Damn, damn.*

"Dr. Morse, what should we do?" Sandler said, urging him to action.

Morse sighed. "We can't do anything with this man I'm afraid," he turned to stand up but the wounded soldier reached out with his right hand and wrapped it tightly around Morse's wrist.

The doctor reached down and pried the man's hand off of his wrist, the slippery blood making it hard for the man to maintain his grip.

"Sandler, give this man a good dose of chloroform," he said.

"Chloroform?" Sandler said, perplexed. "Now?"

"Yes, damnit. Give him a few extra drops, if you know what I mean."

Sandler looked at Morse oddly, then turned and headed back into the barn and quickly returned with the copper funnel they used to administer the sedative. Underneath the wide part of the funnel was a small sponge held in place with a piece of wire. Sandler pulled the dropper out of the bottle, and placed three drops onto the sponge.

Morse, looking over as he administered to another soldier, said, "Give him two more drops."

"Sir? That may be too much."

"Just do it, Sandler, for God's sake."

Sandler gave the sponge two more drops. He put the funnel over the man's nose and mouth and said, "Just breathe and count to fifty, fellar. You'll be fine."

AFTER AN HOUR OF REPEATED ARTILLERY SHELLING FROM their right flank, Titus was relieved to see that the brigade was going to be repositioned. In order to cover two fronts at the same time, the 239th and the 223rd were ordered to turn right to face north. Now the entire Union line was bent at ninety degrees like a reversed "L," with one portion facing west and the other line hinged and bent to the right, facing the wheat fields and Rebel artillery to the north.

To Titus, the Union position was still not tenable, but the re-alignment was at least an acknowledgement that something had to be done. And it couldn't have come at a more opportune time. When they repositioned themselves along the gravel road to face the artillery, it was obvious that the cannonade was not their only problem from that direction. Across the ocean-like waves of golden wheat stalks Titus saw a mass of gray soldiers moving toward them. The Rebel soldiers they had originally faced had not advanced after all.

None of these maneuvers made any sense to Titus, but he was content to face one fight at a time. The one stomping toward them across the wheat fields was immediate and in plain view.

"Oh boy, here they come," someone said nearby.

"Shit," Blute said suddenly. "I ain't gonna sit still for this."

Titus turned fast enough to grab Blute's arm.

"Don't you dare take off," he said, looking up the line to see a junior lieutenant and a master sergeant walking their way and exhorting the men to stand steady.

"They'll shoot you dead to rights, you crazy fool," Titus said.

"It's just plum stupid to be standin' here," Blute said.

Titus let go of Blute's arm and swung the butt of his rifle into Blute's stomach as hard as he could, sending his friend to the ground on one knee as he howled in pain.

"Goddamn you!" Blute said gasping for air. "Yer crazy!"

Blute stumbled to his feet, warily taking several steps away from Titus.

Suddenly, up and down the line, orders were barked. Titus strained to hear what Capt. Fetzer was yelling, but it was soon repeated by the junior officers and noncommissioned officers: the entire regiment was being ordered to advance across the gravel road and to occupy a railroad cut that ran parallel to the road.

Titus had seen the cut but he had not paid much attention to it, looking past it into the wheat fields beyond. Already he could see the advancing line of butternut-colored uniforms moving slowly toward them.

Titus shoved Blute ahead of him as he took off running with the rest of the seven hundred men in the regiment across the road and over a small grassy field to the railroad cut. The soldiers were ordered to get into the cut and crawl up the other side of it.

Titus shoved Blute forward and they both slid on their butts down the recently excavated cut. Thin slices of freshly unearthed shale clattered like dinner plates around them as they slid to the bottom in a rush. Because the railroad line was under construction there were no rail tracks at the bottom making it easier for the soldiers to run across and climb up the other side.

As the regiment clawed its way up, many toppled back down or struggled to maintain their balance in the loose shale.

Titus needed three attempts to make it to the top, digging in his toes to gain a hold on the hillside. His head was just above the crest and his elbows rested on the flat ground in front holding his rifle. Titus was relieved to find Blute positioned to his left.

Not all members of the regiment made it to the top of the cut; several had hurt themselves sliding down the steepest part of the gulley and were hobbling down the cut to a more shallow area so they could crawl out and return to where they had started back across the road.

The maneuver seemed stupid to Titus; they had run across an exposed patch of ground to get into the cut and were clinging precariously to loose shale. Their rifles lay straight out on the flat ground facing a split-rail fence about fifty yards ahead at the edge of the wheat field.

With his eyes no higher than a blade of grass Titus could not see anything but the very top of the rail fence and wondered if the Rebels were still advancing. And now in a dizzying reversal of the direction of their earlier bombardment, Titus heard the detonations of several Rebel artillery pieces from the west and looked up the length of the railroad cut to his left. Two balls of solid shot went over their heads.

Titus felt a ripple of fear. In the time that they had taken to set up position in the railroad cut, the Rebel force to the west had quickly positioned a battery of artillery so that they could shoot right down the length of the railroad cut as if they were throwing boulders down a deep gulley.

Titus heard Capt. Fetzer on the floor of the cut behind him arguing with another officer about the Rebel batteries that were going to keep firing down the throat of the cut to tear up the regiment.

Titus suddenly saw movement in front of him across the swaying wheat field. Perhaps it was the angle of his view, which was ground level, but it appeared that the entire army of Robert E. Lee was moving toward the railroad cut.

He heard Fetzer and the other company commanders ordering the regiment to hold their fire until directed.

"Aim low, men; don't waste those shots," Fetzer yelled, who had crawled to the top of the cut.

Titus realized that the advancing Rebels did not even see the Union soldiers whose heads and rifles were barely visible above the lip of the railroad cut. Someone screamed, "Fire!" The roar of hundreds of rifles firing at once split the air.

For just a moment Titus felt a sickening pity for the Rebel soldiers. He saw men falling and stumbling in piles as hats were shot off heads. Pieces of flesh flew into the air mixed with splinters from the wood rails.

The smoke from the massive discharge momentarily clouded his view, and Titus was just as happy not to see so many contorted shapes rolling on the ground.

What he was not prepared for, though, was what he saw next.

Out of the heavy blue-gray fog emerged the remainder of the Rebel force, now with numerous gaps, but still coming forward. They were making a strange, almost feral scream. They fired simultaneously at the Union soldiers. Titus heard the lead slugs whirring over their heads, and out of the corner of his eye he saw several Union soldiers slide on their backs, lifeless, down the dirt wall to the floor of the cut.

And there was yet another problem that had not occurred to anyone in the Union force—it was nearly impossible to reload since everyone was perched precariously on the loose shale sides of the railroad cut and could not keep their balance.

The order to retreat back to the roadside behind them was shouted and the entire force slid down to the bottom and commenced to climb up the other side in a wild scramble. Titus grabbed Blute's arm and ran about thirty feet down the lengthy of the cut to find a shallower exit.

By this time the Rebel infantry had reloaded. They fired again at the retreating Union soldiers. Titus flinched reflexively as he raced back across the open field to the road. Men stumbled and fell all around him.

The regiment reformed in a gutter on the other side of the road where they had started from just twenty minutes earlier.

Titus was stunned to see how many blue shapes were lying on the open field between the gravel road and the railroad cut. There was also the peculiar detritus of battle littered everywhere: campaign caps, rifles, canteens. Pieces of cartridge paper blew like confetti in the warm summer breeze.

They were ordered to fire at will. Titus commenced the process of methodically reloading his weapon and firing at the Rebels, who had now taken up position in the railroad cut the Union soldiers had just abandoned. Behind the Rebels in the cut, Titus could see at least one additional regiment of butternut soldiers running across the wheat field in support of their comrades.

Titus tried to concentrate on each action in the reloading process to keep his mind off the terrible sounds. Soft lead bullets hitting the flesh and bone of his fellow soldiers made a peculiar sound, like a firm slap against a baby's bottom. Soldiers all around him gyrated and fell in heaps. Some yelled as they clutched a part of their body. Others simply collapsed without a sound.

He was surprised to see Blute eagerly firing at the Rebel horde in front of them.

Periodically Titus would hazard a quick glance around, looking for Seibert. The advance and retreat from the railroad cut had inadvertently mixed companies together so that Titus was standing next to a very tall soldier he had never seen before.

At one point, caught up in the murderous volley and stained from gunpowder, smoke, and sweat, Titus surprised himself by yelling at the top of lungs, "Come on, you Rebel bastards!"

After several back-and-forth volleys, the air between the two opposing forces became opaque with smoke. Titus did not know what he was aiming at and started to slow his rate of firing.

"Damn, I think I been shot," Blute said suddenly, looking puzzled. Titus stared as his friend wavered, then fell into an awkward sitting position, and finally slid quietly onto his side.

RHYS FOLLOWED RITTENHOUSE'S ENTOURAGE AS IT CRISSCROSSED THE area around the farmhouse—to the woods on the south, back to the barn, out to the gravel road, and then back to the farmhouse. He had completely lost contact with Capt. Lynch and was getting worried about him. There were wounded and dead men in great numbers near the gravel road, but there were also dead horses strewn across the landscape. He wondered if Capt. Lynch was underneath one of those horses.

Listening to the debate taking place, Rhys understood that Rittenhouse wanted to retake the railroad cut. Other officers thought it was unwise to risk so many men, especially since the Rebel artillery had situated itself at the western edge of the cut and could fire endlessly down the length of it.

Several officers were now more concerned about the original enemy force that faced the Union soldiers to the west. Even though they had put out skirmishers in that direction earlier in the day, the Rebels had never advanced. Instead the Union soldiers were forced to pivot to confront the Rebel group advancing across the wheat fields to their right.

If the original Rebel force advanced from the west, the three Union regiments would have to fight infantry on two fronts simultaneously.

"I'm not going to order a retreat, if that's what you're suggesting," Rittenhouse shouted.

"Sir, why don't we regroup back near the town, where we'll be supported by the artillery there?" an officer shot back. "We'll be aligned on top of that ridge there and the Rebels will have to straighten out and fight us on one front, not two. It's our only hope, sir. We can't stay here much longer."

Rittenhouse did not answer. His horse danced nervously underneath him as an artillery round burst in the tree line behind the farmhouse. Rittenhouse suddenly took off toward the farmhouse fifty yards away. His small entourage, including Rhys, followed. The colonel halted, grabbed the binoculars hanging around his neck, and looked west at the original Rebel force.

Rhys did not have binoculars but he could easily see Rebel infantry units assembling in that new direction. In twenty minutes, the brigade would be either forced to retreat or fight on two flanks simultaneously.

Rittenhouse dropped his binoculars and they swung back and forth briefly from the thin leather strap around his neck. "We're in perfect position here on the high ground to hold them off but we have no reinforcements!"

"Sir," someone said, "we need to move soon. We can't stay out here by ourselves."

"Damnit, damnit, damnit," Rittenhouse said. "Give the order to regroup on the ridge at the edge of town."

An officer Rhys did not recognize directed two men to relay the order to retreat to the commanding officers of the 240th and 239th.

"You," the officer said, pointing to Rhys. "Relay the order to the 223rd. They're to retire in order to that ridge, with the 223rd setting off first. Do you understand?"

"Yes, sir," Rhys said, turning his horse toward the road two hundred yards away. Dodging dead and wounded soldiers and horses, destroyed artillery limbers, and downed tree limbs, he quickly came up behind the 223rd, their color guard almost directly in front of him. The air was heavy with smoke and there appeared to be a stream of soldiers either limping back from the line, or being helped by someone looking for an excuse to leave the line.

"I have orders for the commander of the 223rd!" Rhys yelled.

"He's up there," a lieutenant said, pointing fifty yards away. "You see him?"

"Yes, thank you," Rhys responded above the roar of rifle fire.

He spotted the commander and raced toward him. But Nancy shuddered to a halt after several steps. She started to run again and then slowed to an awkward canter. Rhys dug his heels into the animal's side and yelled, "Nancy, come on now! Get, girl!"

She started up again and then, as if a trap door had been pulled open underneath, Nancy fell forward onto her knees sending Rhys head first into the ground. He felt a pain in his left shoulder as he hit the ground and rolled over several times, his sword handle digging awkwardly into his stomach.

Rhys stood up quickly. Nancy tried to regain her footing, reminding him of a foal trying to stand for the first time. The horse was only ten yards behind the line of infantrymen furiously exchanging volleys with Rebels in the cut, and as Nancy fought to stand, her legs flailed wildly, nearly kicking a Union captain nearby.

Rhys, conscious of his mission to deliver an important order, spotted the regimental commander close by. He was tempted to go back to comfort Nancy but that gesture seemed out of place at the moment. He knew he must deliver the order. The officer who had nearly been kicked by Nancy walked over to the struggling animal, raised his pistol to her head, and fired.

CHAPTER 21

He was shocked at the damage the Minié balls inflicted on human appendages, shattering arms, shins, and thigh bones like they were porcelain.

But worse were the wounds to the stomach and chest. Morse did not know what to do with men who had gaping holes in their stomach and perforated internal organs. These types of wounds to the trunk of a man caused terrible pain. He could sedate them and search for the lead, but more often than not the ball had sliced the man's liver or kidneys, releasing fluids that should not see the light of day. He had operated on at least ten men with stomach wounds and wondered if he should have bothered.

Mercifully, the two other regimental surgeons had joined him in the barn. Morse marveled at how fast and efficient Dr. Calloway was in removing a limb. In fact a mound of arms and legs were piled high behind Calloway, many legs with their boots still on.

Morse noticed that Sandler tried to calm some of the more agitated patients, often reciting Biblical verse as if it were a salve. The doctor was not a student of the Bible and did not recognize any of it. At one point he heard Sandler telling a horribly mutilated soldier, "For the day of their calamity is at hand, and the things that shall come upon them make haste."

But of all the challenges Morse faced, none was more upsetting than the wounded soldiers who begged, pleaded, threatened, and even pathetically offered bribes to Morse to let them keep a leg or an arm.

Sandler was forced to come to his aid at one point when a corporal from the 240th grabbed the front of Morse's blood-stained tunic and held on with all his might threatening him if he dared cut off his left leg.

"Damn you, doctor, if you cut my leg off I'm goin' to hunt you down after this here war and kill you and yer childrens, and if you gots no childrens I'll kill yer parents and everyone you knows. You hear me? Goddamn you, you hear me, you fiend?"

Morse promised not to remove his leg and ordered Sandler to sedate him. When the soldier was unconscious Morse probed around the wound with his bloody fingers, the man's shin was shattered in at least a half-dozen pieces. He used tweezers to remove some of the bigger pieces of bone, then stopped and eyed the large saw he had used that afternoon many times before. There was dried blood on the wooden handle and bits of flesh and bone stuck to the teeth of the saw.

Morse looked up at an exhausted Sandler, who just shrugged.

After several seconds of thought, Morse said, "He can keep his damned leg, for all I care."

Morse poured some water over the wound and then made quick work with the silk sutures to close the wound.

They had retreated a mile back toward the town. Rittenhouse halted the battalion and turned it around on a small ridge facing west where they had just retreated from.

Titus lost sight of Blute back near the gravel road and wondered how badly wounded he was. He felt sorry for his friend but was powerless to stop from being swept along in the current of combat. The three regiments had regrouped and turned to face the advancing Rebels, but the line of command had broken down as companies intermingled. Titus did not recognize anyone nearby but commenced to turn with the hundreds of other soldiers and prepared to fight once again.

He was comforted by the fact that two Union artillery batteries had unlimbered nearby and were firing into Rebel infantry, which was now converging from the west and north into a single powerful force.

An officer raced up and down behind his section and yelled to the soldiers that reinforcements were on the way.

Titus didn't believe a word, not because he thought the officer was lying but because it didn't matter. Right now in front of him was an enormous force of Rebel infantry, six or more regiments coming right toward them astride the gravel road they had just used to scamper toward the town. It did not matter if the entire Union Army was on its way to this ridge in Pennsylvania, Titus knew. In fifteen minutes he would be in the thick of battle. There was no time for reinforcements now.

He was suddenly aware of an intense thirst and he reached for his canteen on his hip, uncorked the top, and viciously guzzled the warm water. It did not slake his thirst one iota.

Titus was shocked at the fierceness of the Rebel soldiers and did not like the way they screamed at the top of their lungs when they charged the railroad cut. The sound was unnatural, and it unnerved him. And the gray-clad soldiers didn't stop advancing, no matter how badly shredded their regiments were. It was folly to think the three Union regiments and the artillery batteries next to them could survive the next Rebel advance.

Already the Rebel artillery batteries had retargeted the new Union position and there was mass flinching as the shells exploded over their heads in an awful crash, raining chunks of iron in search of a shoulder, calf, or rib to smash. At other times the solid balls remained intact and did their work by rolling through rows of men and horses dismembering and decapitating as they bounced.

With the brief respite afforded by the Rebels' regrouping in front of them, Titus searched for Seibert. He was calm and steady as he walked around looking at the soot-stained faces of the battalion's survivors.

A passing officer ordered Titus to get back into line, and he complied briefly until the officer moved on. Then he began his search again, stepping backward down the length of the force arrayed on the hill.

So focused was he on his mission that he did not hear the dreaded whistling of Whitworth artillery rounds that were tearing into the massed soldiers. The Whitworth, a British-made artillery piece used by Confederate units, produced a strange, shrieking sound as the shell arced overhead.

Titus grew calm and purposeful. His breathing slowed and he paced casually through the surviving members of the three regiments, carefully looking into the faces of weary men. He was seeking a single soldier and was confident he would find him, Rebel or no Rebels.

It finally occurred to Titus that Seibert might have been killed or wounded and that his search was in vain. The thought of not settling with Seibert caught Titus off guard, and he felt a sudden draining of emotion.

Damnit, he berated himself. *Why didn't you find that man earlier? You coulda rooted him out at the railroad cut.*

The thought of Buster lying under the brush, half-closed eyes staring into the blue Pennsylvania sky, sparked a cascade of emotion that he had suppressed all day. But again, he forced his emotions down quickly as he concentrated on the here and the now.

A Whitworth round screamed overhead and exploded fifty yards to the rear of the line.

And then he saw him.

Behind the main line of soldiers a second, ragged line of Union infantry had settled partway up a slight incline. Seibert was standing forty feet away to Titus's left.

He felt a perverse thrill at having found his quarry.

Seibert stood with his rifle half-cocked, awaiting orders. Titus noticed that although Seibert was standing with a group of soldiers, he also seemed apart from them in some imperceptible way. Seibert made no small talk. He didn't look around or do anything except stare straight ahead at the Rebel infantry moving toward them. He did not seem scared. Nor did he appear to notice Titus looking at him.

Titus slid directly backward up the incline to join the group of soldiers there. Then he began to work his way down the line toward Seibert. He was not certain what he was going to say, if anything, when he found himself standing next to Seibert. Nor did he have a plan in mind for how he intended to settle the issue.

But he was certain of one thing—he knew what the outcome was going to be. He was not going to leave the issue up to legal authorities, the provost marshals, or a Rebel ball for that matter. The army had larger issues on its hands, and he would not trouble them with this bit of justice.

As he inched closer to Seibert, he felt along the left side of his waist with his right hand and found the handle of his knife, pulled it out of its sheath, and put it blade first into his right pants pocket so that it was reachable in an instant.

He stepped backward several times and came up behind Seibert. Titus stood there staring into the back of the man's tanned, almost black neck. He thought briefly of Buster, and then he casually glanced around to see who was nearby. No one was behind him directly except a sergeant who kept yelling hoarsely to make sure the soldiers had loaded and primed their rifles.

Titus felt the blade of the knife pressing on his thigh through his wool pants and considered how he might use it. It occurred to him almost as an afterthought that he could take several steps backward, raise his rifle when ordered and simply let the barrel's aim drop at the last minute. No one would notice and Seibert would be dead before his body hit the ground.

While he mulled this plan, the sergeant pulled up behind Titus, shouted "What the hell are you doin' back here?" and shoved him forward into line directly to Seibert's left. For several seconds Titus stood looking forward. He slowly swiveled to look; Seibert was staring at him.

Titus was not prepared for Seibert's response; he showed no recognition, nor betrayed fear, anxiety, or concern of any kind. His face was blank. Titus kept staring at him in a manner that he meant to be threatening; he did not care that Seibert knew he was here to settle this thing. It made no difference, because Titus was certain he would prevail.

Still, when Seibert turned away to face forward again it bothered Titus that the man showed not slightest hint of fear.

"I found him," Titus said, still facing Seibert.

Seibert seemed not to hear; or he was not interested. He kept staring forward.

"I told you I found him," Titus said, this time taking a small step toward Seibert.

Seibert pursed his lips in concentration as the orders were shouted up and down the line to aim their weapons.

"Good," Seibert said.

Titus snarled at Seibert, but Seibert did not seem to care. Titus reached down with his right hand and gripped the knife handle.

In other circumstances and with less on his mind, Titus would have heard the round screeching toward his position. He might have flinched or turned away reflexively. Instead it exploded almost directly overhead at the same time the order to fire was given. The concussion shook every particle in his body, from the follicles of hair on his head to his toenails.

He found himself sitting on the ground, his rifle lying across his lap as if he were on picket duty somewhere alone next to a tree.

He tried to stand up but faltered, feeling weak and confused. He saw soldiers all around him lying on the ground; some were motionless while others were crawling on all fours dragging themselves away in odd directions, some even toward the Rebel lines.

Titus stood up and regained his balance. He looked for Seibert, half expecting him to be sprawled on the ground next to him. At that moment a volley of Rebel lead balls tore through the Union ranks sending pieces of flesh and splatters of blood into the air. He felt a ball roar past his cheek like an angry hornet and flinched.

Titus noticed that the Union soldiers who had been arrayed in a line facing the Rebel attack were now moving slowly backward. No one had called a retreat that he heard but the contagion had started, and the survivors started to evaporate to the rear like a slow but determined ooze of blue tar.

Titus's hat had been blown off his head and for a moment he considered reaching down for it but was quickly pressed by the troops moving to the rear. He moved back with the soldiers and instantly spied Seibert only ten feet away. Titus tried to close the distance between the two men but the crush of soldiers slowed his progress.

Titus was suddenly overcome with a premonition that he was going to die. It settled upon him like religious conviction or a truth that was unassailable. It did not bother him as much as he had feared. He accepted it.

What did it matter? he told himself. *I just need to get to Seibert first.*

He dropped his rifle, pulled the knife out of his pocket, and shoved his way in the direction that he had last seen Seibert.

He managed to make lateral progress, keeping an eye on the strained, furtive faces of the men he encountered. His diligence paid off as he sidled up next to Seibert. He grabbed him with his left hand and turned Seibert so that they faced each other. And with all the energy he could muster, he swung his right hand forward, preparing to bury the blade in Seibert's stomach.

A powerful white light enshrouded Titus and he shook violently, as if a thousand horses had materialized and were trampling him. For a moment—a fraction of a moment—he wondered if this event was of a religious nature, since he was now blind and felt utterly powerless. Blackness quickly replaced the white light, repressing all sound and tactile feeling. It was not an unpleasant sensation, and he marveled briefly at the quiet and solitude it presented him. And before fading completely, he felt a sad, remorseful disappointment that he was not able to complete his task.

CHAPTER 22

Rhys was not adept at firing a rifle, but he could load and shoot if pressed. After losing Nancy he delivered his orders on foot and was confronted with two choices: stay and fight with the infantry, or retire on foot to find Col. Rittenhouse. He would not be blamed for leaving the battle if that's what he chose to do, but Rhys had always felt his participation as a second lieutenant was peripheral at best. Standing behind a regiment of engaged infantry felt better somehow.

His mind was made up for him by a stray Minié ball that clipped his right ear and knocked his hat off. His ear bled so profusely that he wondered if he was more seriously injured, but another soldier assured him it was not serious. He picked up a discarded rifle, took a cartridge box off another wounded soldier, and clumsily entered the fray. He got off each round at the painfully slow rate of one every thirty seconds or so, much slower than the average infantryman who could fire three times a minute.

Joining the battle was the easy part; leaving it was nearly impossible.

Caught up in the swirling chaos, he was stunned by its raw, visceral nature. As a mounted officer and messenger he typically flitted about like a dragonfly, rushing from one stop to another, above and past the real action taking place. He was aware that men could be torn asunder by solid cannon balls and pieces of iron and lead, and he had already witnessed some of this action as he rode by on horseback. But standing in place and firing blindly into what looked like a thick blue fog seemed strange, yet invigorating.

Stranger and more frightening still was what came *out* of the fog: lead pellets the size of a man's thumb capable of extraordinary destruction. The constant flow of lead wreaked havoc with the flesh it came into contact with. At one point the top of a soldier's head disintegrated in front of Rhys, splattering him with a pinkish material that he guessed was the poor man's brain.

Still, he tried not to waver and continued to fire, withdrawing toward town when they were ordered to do so along with the shattered brigade. Their last stand on the ridge was the most terrifying twenty minutes in his life. They tried to re-form the retreating regiments on the top of the ridge, and while most soldiers turned to face the approaching enemy, a fair number just kept walking rapidly away from battle.

The Rebels closed to within firing distance and their first volley created such devastation that Rhys was sure he was about to die. At one point he reached for the ramrod to reload, only to find the rod missing. In his haste he realized he had left the rod in the barrel and shot it harmlessly toward the Rebel line. He found another rod easily enough.

Rhys's clothes were soaked with sweat. Dust and small bits of grass and debris clung to his face and hands. His mouth felt drier than the inside of a smoldering stone fireplace. He reached for his canteen only to find it had been punctured by a ball and was nearly empty.

The Union line held up reasonably well in the face of the onslaught, but the effect of the Rebel artillery on the Union forces was appalling. Entire groups of men were shredded with pieces of iron from exploding shells. Rhys himself was knocked down by an explosion at one point but was unharmed.

In fact his only injury—besides his nicked ear that afternoon—came when a Union soldier standing to his right suddenly turned to run rearward and accidentally raked Rhys's thigh with his bayonet. The soldier didn't wait for Rhys to protest, he simply dropped his weapon and ran.

When the order came to retreat Rhys took off limping with the rest of the horde, though a Union artillery limber almost ran him over in the process. He looked back and saw bodies strewn across acres of land in a ghastly display of the art of killing with gunpowder and metal.

He was sitting down on a bale of hay when the first of their officers entered the barn. Morse could barely lift his right arm to scratch his nose; the muscles were so devoid of energy. He tried to stand up in deference to the senior officer—a colonel—but he could not even muster that bit of decorum.

Morse looked at his hands and arms; they were coated in dried blood that had caked into a thin reddish-brown crust. His fingernails were still slightly translucent but showed thin black crescents underneath the nails where the blood had coagulated.

The barn was full of wounded men recovering from surgery. Some were still unconscious, but many had woken with incredible pain after having an arm or leg sawed off. An extraordinary number of men called out for their mothers.

Why not call for your father? he thought.

The heat in the barn was nearly intolerable, and at one point Dr. Calloway fainted. They revived him with a splash of warm water from a bucket and a stiff jigger of whiskey.

But when the colonel walked in, it was just as well, because the three surgeons and their aides were incapable of any additional medical treatment.

Morse was stunned by how debonair the Confederate colonel appeared; he wore a gray shell jacket with two rows of equally spaced brass buttons. His gold-colored embroidered neck collar and sleeve braids gave him a bit of flash that the doctor found regal.

"Good evening, sir," the colonel said to Morse. He did not extend his hand, Morse thought, to avoid being smeared.

"Good evening," Morse replied.

"As you are aware, we have taken this ground in today's battle and will be settling in for the night," he said. "You and the other surgeons here will not be interfered with in any way. We know you have tended to some of our soldiers and presume you will continue to do so. Gray or blue, you can see that God has given us the same red blood. Your lack of discrimination is appreciated and duly noted. May we get you anything? Food? Water? Or bourbon, even, for the parched throat?"

"Bourbon, you say?" Morse said.

"Indeed, made with the best Tennessee sour mash," the officer said.

Morse looked up at the officer. He was dashing in his uniform along with his fashionable V-shaped salt-and-pepper beard, but his eyes were shockingly rimmed in black from sleeplessness and perhaps sadness from too much killing.

"Myself, I could partake of a bit of bourbon if so offered," Morse said. "Dr. Calloway and Dr. Smythe, do either of you gentlemen wish to taste some of Tennessee's finest bourbon?"

"Not I," Smythe responded wearily. "I believe sleep is called for at this particular moment."

"I must decline as well," Calloway said. "But I appreciate the offer. My fear is that if I consumed a bit of the elixir I would find myself unable to stop, desiring as I do to forget the details of this day."

"Ah, yes," the officer sighed deeply. "This killing and maiming is so taxing on a man's body and soul."

Morse looked up at the officer and could see out past the barn door into the gathering darkness. He could smell fires as soldiers on both sides tried to eat themselves out of the tragedy they witnessed that day.

"Perhaps I should sleep, too," Morse said. "I doubt I could walk more than ten paces out of this barn without collapsing."

"You remain here, my good man. I will return in a few minutes with a bottle and a glass," the officer said. "It would be my honor."

"I will be offended if you do not bring two glasses, one for me and one for you to join me," Morse said. In a corner of the barn a soldier suddenly cried out, "My God help me. Please, Lord, this is too much to bear!"

He heard voices that manifested themselves as floating images, sliding across a muddled, barely discernible landscape. There was a laugh, and another voice emerged trying to quiet the first voice.

The voices continued to come at him as whispers that sometimes spiked into an expression of surprise or laughter. He could see nothing except a limitless expanse of darkness, sprinkled with star-like pinpricks of light. There was no sense of menace; he was simply confused and began to consider the likelihood that he was experiencing death.

But his idle curiosity did not last. Suddenly the voices that kept intruding on his peace took shape in his imagination as two giant crows. He envisioned the crows stooping over him, their wet black eyes sizing him up. He grimaced as the crows used their long spiked black beaks as bayonets to pick at his body.

Titus tried to say something to chase the birds away, but he could not speak. His tongue was heavy and solid, as if it were a piece of cast iron. His hands were paralyzed when he tried to move them. A wave of fear and revulsion came over him, and he moaned—or at least he tried to moan—to scare the birds away. If he was indeed dead then this must be hell, he thought.

The crows disappeared, and Titus found himself alone again in the inky, almost palpable darkness. But something had changed. He was aware of a struggle that was taking place within him. And he was suddenly overcome with a pervasive feeling of gut-wrenching nausea. The intensity of the sickness jolted him, and he could feel some part of his body move.

Titus realized after several seconds that he had just opened his eyes. His senses told him that he had crossed the threshold from the unconscious world to the waking world. With each passing second he became aware of a profound sickness in his body.

He opened and closed his eyes several times in rapid succession, trying to lubricate his dry eyelids.

My God, he thought. *I'm alive.*

Titus turned his head from side to side and felt an excruciating pain run across his head and neck. He closed his eyes as he fought a sudden urge to vomit. He opened his eyes again, this time more slowly. The sky was dark and there were no stars visible. He wiggled the fingers on his hands, and then with great effort moved his feet, pausing afterward to regain his strength.

His head throbbed, triggering another excruciating stab of nausea. He hyperventilated as he struggled with the pain.

It was at this point that he heard what sounded like the mewing of cats. The sound was all around him, like peeper frogs in a vernal pond. Titus moved his head slowly so as not to arouse the thing that was causing him so much pain. The mewing sounds came again and he tried to concentrate on its cause but he could not comprehend where it was coming from or who was making it.

He heard voices and slowly turned his head and strained to see in the darkness. Thirty feet away he could make out the shapes of two men. They appeared to be holding a candle as they bent down to the ground. One of the men sounded excited, but his partner told him to quiet down. Titus could see items being tossed aside in the candlelight.

He realized they were scavenging items from the dead and wounded, taking pocket watches, rings, currency, anything of value. It was a common practice, he knew, and it comforted him strangely that witnessing this darker side of war meant that he had survived.

Helpless and sick, Titus turned away and closed his eyes again, listening to the mewing. He finally understood that the feline-like sounds were coming from the wounded soldiers lying all around him.

Some were crying in exhausted murmurs, others were praying and repeating phrases over and over again. Some called out for help, but their voices were so worn down by the hours lying in the field and the severity of their wounds that they could barely push air past their vocal chords. Men with less serious wounds had crawled away hours ago. Titus guessed it was perhaps early morning, in which case the wounded and dead had been lying in place for as long as six hours, perhaps longer.

An unearthly desire began to creep over Titus like nothing he had ever experienced. The desire permeated every single molecule in his dusty, inert body. He needed *water*. The desire to drink water overcame every other impulse, including fear and pain.

He began a painful, slow search for his canteen. He found it lying underneath the small of his back. Titus was willing to tolerate the searing pain in his head in order to get at the canteen, and he made small controlled movements to dig it out. The strap around his shoulder was tangled in his arm and he struggled for what seemed like ten minutes to inch it closer to his face.

When he had wrestled it to his chest, he realized the cork stopper was dislodged. He tilted the vessel to his lips and was rewarded with a thimbleful of warm water. He dropped the canteen in disgust on his chest and rested, gathering strength.

He needed water so badly that he was prepared to do something he'd felt incapable of just minutes beforehand: move to search for canteens. Before setting out, he decided to investigate his body for wounds, starting at his thighs and progressing to his arms, chest, and neck. He reluctantly raised his right hand to his head, knowing somehow that it was the origin of his sickness. On his chin he felt the caked sheen of dried blood and his fingers followed the dried rivulet like an inquisitive spider up past his ear.

Above his right ear his hair hardened to the stiffness of aged hickory and several inches higher his fingers found a gash that parted his hair like the work of a barber's greased comb. The gash was about six inches long, running diagonally from his right temple toward his ear.

Titus dropped his hand and rested, but urged on by his need for water, he turned himself onto his stomach and raised his head to see in front of him. In the distance numerous campfires were visible, and in their eerie, flickering light he saw lumps of crumpled men. He dropped his chin onto the grass and its oily, sharp smell invigorated him.

He dug his elbows into the ground and pulled himself forward. Progress was slow at first as he slithered over rifles, cartridge boxes and shoes. Each object he crawled over was painful since their edges creased his ribs. The first body he came across did not have a canteen, and he pressed on. The second body did have a half-full canteen but its shoulder strap was tight against the dead man's body and Titus did not have the strength to either turn the dead man over or break the strap. So he positioned his face against the man's stomach and drank the warm water from the canteen, some of it running down his chin into the soil.

Buoyed by this success, Titus moved on to yet another body, but this one was still alive. The wounded soldier was a Rebel, and he moaned softly, almost musically. Titus was able to wrestle the canteen off the man's shoulder and took a long pull from it. Then he positioned the canteen over the wounded soldier's mouth and gently poured the remaining water into it. The soldier did not seem to recognize the water, and most of it ran out the side of his mouth into the warm grass.

Exhausted, Titus rolled onto his back and looked up into the starless night. He thought now of just two people: a man named Buster and a man named Seibert. When Titus thought of Seibert, an overpowering rage took hold of him. It was so strong that he opened his eyes into the darkness to rid himself of Seibert's face.

Damn that man, Titus thought. *God protect him from me.*

Titus closed his eyes again and tried to sleep, but the mewing from the Rebel right next to him was too upsetting. He tried to crawl away but he was exhausted, so he lay there listening to the barely audible moaning.

"Mother, please help me," the man seemed to be saying.

But Titus could not be sure.

Sam had never seen Col. Rittenhouse so spent. There was not enough time and the field of battle was so fluid and uncertain that Sam had not put up the Colonel's tent.

But Rittenhouse did not mind any inconvenience at this late hour, which Sam estimated to be two a.m. The evening was relatively warm with a soft wind from the south. The colonel had just returned from yet another meeting, and he could barely stand up from fatigue.

When Sam gave him his meal he just nodded and picked at the food. Sam noticed he was more interested in the whiskey than the food, and at one point Rittenhouse dropped his fork onto the Pennsylvania soil and simply stared at it, unwilling or unable to pick it up.

Sam retrieved it and put it back in his hand.

"How ya feelin' there, Colonel?" Sam asked. "You all right?"

Rittenhouse nodded.

"I don't have a brigade any longer," Rittenhouse said, staring at his tin plate. "They act like I have a brigade but I can't find half of them. I'm supposed to have them aligned in the morning next to Hancock's brigade but most of my men are missing. Or dead. How the hell am I supposed to put my brigade in line when I don't have it? Answer that, would you, Sam? How can they expect me to do that?"

Sam shrugged, having never seen this despondent side of the colonel before. Intuitively he stepped away from Rittenhouse into the lantern's shadows. Time and time again he had learned to stay clear of men who showed signs of immense stress.

"And look at this," Rittenhouse said to Sam, though his servant was at least ten feet away. "Look how close this one came."

The colonel raised his left arm to show a tear in the blue wool jacket near his armpit. Sam stepped forward into the light again to look at the near miss.

"Just an inch or two closer to my body and I wouldn't be here right now, Sam," Rittenhouse said. "That's how razor thin the difference is between life and death out here. One inch, one second, one step, and you're gone. Explain that to me, Sam, would you? I don't understand it. It's just insane. Makes no sense."

Sam did not dispute the colonel's logic that life and death were so narrowly distanced, since every slave was well aware of that basic truth. He slowly stepped backward again into the shadows, since there was nothing he could do for Rittenhouse now. In the distance rifle fire erupted suddenly, as it had sporadically all night, only to stop just as suddenly.

THE REBEL STRETCHER BEARERS WORKED THE FIELD THE next morning, picking through the bodies and removing their wounded. Titus watched them idly, as they crisscrossed the field. He was surprised at how many soldiers they took away who were still alive, including the Rebel next to him who had moaned all night.

As the day progressed Titus crawled around on his elbows in search of more water. At one point he hazarded to sit up and nearly fainted as the pain and nausea overcame him. Lying on his side, the left side of his face pressed against the flattened grass, Titus fought to remain conscious. He eagerly smelled the grass blades that protruded into his nostrils, focusing on the only signs of life and vitality he could find in that field.

Sometime in the late morning, with the sun shielded by a thick cover of clouds, Titus simply gave in and fell into a deep, strange sleep. His dream was a kaleidoscope of images that softly floated by, unthreatening and entirely peaceful. He enjoyed the respite and tried to stay in this place for as long as possible, but later in the day Titus awoke to a huge roar of gunfire and artillery about a mile away.

The sun was low but still shrouded by clouds, and he turned his body to look into the direction of the gunfire. It was impossible to guess what might be happening. The field he lay in was occupied by Rebels, so the Union had obviously given up ground the day before. But were they winning the battle, or losing as they had so many others against Lee and his army of screamers?

The sounds of the battle continued for more than an hour then petered out as the daylight began to wane. And to his amazement, as the sun began to set, he saw Union stretcher bearers working their way through the field of blue and gray humps.

"You alive there, fellar?" he heard someone say.

He nodded vigorously, or what he thought was vigor because he could not speak.

"He's gone," the voice said.

For the first time since waking Titus panicked; if they left him there he would not survive. Using every scintilla of energy remaining in his wracked body Titus moaned and raised his right hand.

"No, wait," he heard someone say. "This one here is still goin.'"

Titus felt his body being lifted and placed onto a canvas stretcher, and while he was relieved to be taken from the field the jostling hurt his head immensely.

But nothing prepared him for the cart ride, which bounced and bumped its way for what seemed like hours. At one point he turned on his left side and squeezed his flattened hands as if in prayer under his head as a cushion, only to find himself looking into the eyes of another wounded soldier staring back at him twelve inches away.

Neither man spoke in the darkness, but through the mysterious communicative powers of suffering they shared their misery. In the wagon's lantern light Titus saw dried blood stains emanating from the man's nostrils that had coagulated in maroon crystals on his brown mustache. He heard him wheezing and every now and then when the cart hit a big rock or imperfection in the path the soldier would close his eyes in pain.

Sometime during the cart ride Titus passed out, which he was grateful for since he could not bear his cart mate's suffering any longer.

When he woke Titus noticed that the sun had risen. He had been moved to a larger ambulance that held a half-dozen wounded men. He and one other soldier were lying down, while the other patients sat on attached benches on either side.

Titus tried not to look around because it took nearly every ounce of his energy to remain composed due to the painful jostling of the wagon. Having lost all sense of dignity, Titus would groan loudly whenever the wagon hit a rock or hole in the road. He did not care who heard him now, and besides, he felt a perverse satisfaction in venting his discomfort in such a public manner.

Titus eventually fell into a sort of numbed semi-consciousness, barely able to feel his body yet alert enough to hear the talk of the wounded soldiers. At one point he thought someone was speaking to him.

He opened his eyes slowly and found himself staring at the well-worn shoes of an infantryman.

"You think you could git away?" the soldier said, leaning down off the bench, but still too far for Titus to see him.

Convinced it was a dream, Titus dozed again, but the man's voice grew louder.

"You reckon you could jest git away?" the soldier repeated.

Titus tried to turn his head upward but was startled to see the man had kneeled next to him, and had pushed his face only inches from Titus's.

"Yer nothin' but vermin," the man whispered.

Titus felt a powerful mixture of confusion and alarm as he stared at Seibert's shoes in order to avoid the intense glare.

"Yer gonna die," Seibert said. "You know that?"

"No," Titus said, or he thought he said. It was difficult to know what was happening since his senses were a jumble and his emotions were being stretched to their limit.

"Go away," Titus said feebly.

"Got something fer yer head," Seibert said, grabbing Titus' face and turning it sharply toward him. Titus felt Seibert's finger trace something on his forehead. Then Seibert let his head drop back harshly onto the boards of the wagon sending bright yellow stars careening across his vision.

CHAPTER 23

While he was hungry beyond belief, Dr. Morse could not tolerate the sight of food and had pushed his plate of ham and boiled greens away. He nibbled at the corner of a piece of hardtack. Drs. Calloway and Smythe sat with him on top of crates around a small fire. Smythe had tried earlier to engage the other two surgeons in conversation but Morse and Calloway did not rise to the bait.

The prior two days were so unspeakably bad that Morse could not bear to do anything except take his laudanum and whiskey and find someplace to sleep. The pile of sawed-off limbs chest high outside the barn was so profoundly disturbing that the Confederate commander in charge of the area had ordered his troops to bury them.

The renewed fighting they heard late that day had depressed the surgeons and their small staffs even further; they were nearly out of supplies and the wounded from both sides were still lined up haphazardly outside the barn waiting patiently for attention. Many had died simply waiting in line and Morse refused to even step outside to triage those waiting, instead directing Sandler to pick and choose as he wished.

At one point earlier in the day, a Confederate captain had been brought in and moved to the front of the line. The officer had taken a Minié ball to the jaw; it smashed his teeth and exited through the other cheek.

Perhaps it was the fact that he was being given preferential treatment—like all officers on either side—or maybe it was just his fatigue and disgust at the sight of so many damaged and suffering humans, but Morse grew hostile at having to attend the captain.

Two of the captain's junior officers had brought him in and stood nearby while Morse attended to him, giving him some of the last drops of chloroform that they had in the barn.

"Do you think he'll be all right?" one of the lieutenants asked. "He weren't talkin' much."

"You wouldn't talk much if you lost all your teeth, would you now?" Morse snapped.

"He done lost all his teeth?" the other lieutenant asked. "How is he supposed to eat then?"

"How the hell do I know?" Morse said.

Morse poured some water into the unconscious man's mouth and picked out several larger tooth fragments. The man's tongue had been lacerated, and his breath was especially foul.

Morse sewed up the two sides of the captain's face using the horsehair sutures, now that the silk was gone.

"You reckon' he'll be fine?" one of the lieutenants asked as they moved him back outside to recover.

"I believe he will be just fine," Morse said curtly, but he knew—he already had developed a strange sense for who would live and who wouldn't—that the captain would die soon, either from suppuration or inability to eat.

It's not that Morse cared about the captain, or any other person who came through the last two days. Though every now and then he would see something that triggered a profound sense of pity, like the Rebel soldier they brought in who was not more than sixteen years old, if even that. The boy had not a wisp of facial hair and looked almost angelic, with his shock of unkempt blond hair and sky-blue eyes. The boy's small delicate left wrist had nearly snapped off from a Minié ball, and it just hung there like a screen door flapping back and forth. The boy had cried earlier, his tear streaks dried to a milky white on his cheeks.

"Will you tell my father I'm OK?" the boy asked Morse. "Can yer do that fer me, sir?"

"Of course I can," Morse lied.

"I know'd he's worried sick about me," the boy said. "You'll tell him?"

"Yes, but you need to sleep for a while," Morse said putting two drops of chloroform onto the funnel's sponge. "Just start breathing this medicine and count up to fifty."

"I cain't count," the boy said. "Will the medicine still work then, sir?"

"Yes, it will work, just start breathing until you fall asleep," he said. "Please, you need to breathe this medicine. Now start."

"Yes, sir," the boy said.

After he was unconscious Morse took more time than he should have, sawing slowly through the ulnae and radius bones, and delicately clipping away the tendons and connective tissue.

He picked up the boy's hand and was about to toss it into the pile of appendages, but stopped and inspected it, turning it around, looking at the palm that had a small scar in the middle of it. The boy's tiny fingers had already curled and his fingernails almost seemed feminine in their daintiness.

"Doctor?" Sandler said.

Morse looked up and realized that his aide was telling him to stop dawdling and get to work, since at least a hundred men were strewn throughout the barn, waiting to be attended to.

The doctor turned and tossed the little hand into the pile of arms and legs. Later when he obsessively stole a glance at the pile to look for the child's hand, it was gone, indistinguishable from the other items congregating there.

TITUS DOES NOT REMEMBER THE INTERVENING DAYS; HE seemed to be shuttled from one temporary hospital to another, but he was not sure. Perhaps he did not move at all, or maybe he was moved ten times, he could not remember nor care to remember.

He kept complaining to the orderlies and nurses about a soldier named Seibert who was threatening him, but they assured him that there was no one named Seibert there.

He began to regain his strength as he convalesced at a large military hospital near Harrisburg. There were women nurses in this hospital, and Titus liked the attention they gave him, especially a young brown-haired nurse with large freckles all over her face named Valerie.

Perhaps it was because Titus needed no serious medical interventions and was not in constant pain, or perhaps it was just that she liked Titus, but Valerie seemed to flit about him regularly.

One day she said, "Titus, I have something for you."

"What could that be?" he asked. "Nobody knows where I am. Must be a mistake."

"No I don't believe it is a mistake," she said. "Here it is."

She held up a dirty knapsack with his name clearly visible on its side.

"I was told the army found all these packs after the battle and is returning them to their owners," she said. "You and two other soldiers here received these today. Aren't you pleased about that? It must have all your belongings in there."

Titus looked at the worn canvas and leather knapsack.

"I wonder what they did with the packs of all the dead soldiers?" Titus asked sharply. "Sell them?"

Valerie's light hazel eyes dropped to the floor. "I don't reckon I know what they did with them."

Titus was instantly sorry. "I'm sure they'll send them back to their families," he said, though he knew the army often did not do that for simple enlisted soldiers.

"Yes, I'm certain that's what they've done," she said, setting the pack onto the floor next to his bed.

After she left he reached over and pulled it up into bed, the creosote smell of too much wood smoke still permeating the canvas. He also smiled when he saw the black stain created in the front that Buster caused when he distractedly tossed it aside once onto a pile of smoldering charcoal. At the time Titus had given his tentmate hell for something so foolish, but now, he flashed a sad smile at the recollection.

Opening the straps he looked inside both amused and repelled by the accoutrements of his life as a foot soldier in the service of Abraham Lincoln and the Republic. Near the bottom he noticed the twine-encumbered parcel that Buster had given him to hold.

Titus quickly closed the pack and dropped it onto the floor in a thud.

HE WAS ALLOWED TO GO HOME ON LEAVE, but Titus turned it down and asked to return to Company I with the 239th. After eleven weeks of recuperation, his head wound had improved to the point that he only suffered the occasional migraine. The hair had started to grow back into the crease in his hairline left by the exploding shell fragment.

One physician had even recommended Titus be discharged for medical reasons, but Titus disagreed and demanded to be returned to his regiment.

During his stay in the Harrisburg hospital he had befriended a young cavalryman named Arnold Wilseck from the Fifth Michigan. Wilseck lost his left leg below the knee when his horse was shot out from underneath him and crushed it when the animal toppled.

Wilseck fell in and out of despondency about the amputation and what it meant for his future as an apprentice railroad engineer. Titus had listened sympathetically as the twenty-two-year-old said he was humiliated by the fact that he lost his leg due to a horse and not a Rebel ball or shell. He even confided to Titus that he considered killing himself with the cavalry revolver he still had in his belongings.

That night Titus woke up when one of the other convalescing soldiers started screaming in his sleep. Nightmares and violent miasmic eruptions occurred nearly every night. The nurses tried their best to calm the disturbed men. That night Titus tossed and turned for more than an hour after waking.

And right before he was about to pass off to sleep, the thought came to him with such searing clarity that he sat up in bed. He continued to process the idea for so long that he could not remember when he eventually fell asleep. But after breakfast the following morning he found Wilseck playing cards with two other convalescents and waited for the game to break up before he approached the cavalryman.

"How you feelin' there, Arnold?" Titus asked, sitting down next to him, the white wicker chair squeaking as it took his weight.

"Today is a mighty good day for me," Wilseck said. "Just won me some money and got two letters from home. Couldn't be more pleased, except if the good lord gave me back my leg, in which case I'd gladly give back all my poker winnin's and repent all the sinful things I done in Washington with them whores. Did you ever visit with them whores in Washington?"

"Cain't say I did," Titus said.

"Let me tell you somethin', thems womens were so pretty, but boy, did they end up takin' nearly all my money, after liquorin' me up and such. Bet they'd still take on a man without a leg, jest as long as they'd have money, wouldn't you think?"

"I reckon they would," Titus said.

Wilseck put his playing cards into the pocket of his hospital shirt and was starting to stand using his new crutches when Titus stopped him.

"Hold on there, Arnold," he said. "I've been thinkin' about somethin' you said that's mighty troublesome to me."

"What are you talkin' about?" Wilseck said.

"You said the other day that you was feelin' so low that you considered killin' yerself with that revolver of yours," Titus said. "You remember that?"

"Oh, that," Arnold said. "I jest say things like that when I'm feelin' low. Don't pay no attention to my sayin's."

"Well it's too late now, you got my attention," Titus said. "I'd never forgive myself if I let you kill yerself. There's enough killin' goin' on out there without a man killin' hisself."

"I appreciate yer thinkin' about me like that, but I was just low that day," Wilseck said, starting to stand again.

"Now wait there a minute, Arnold," Titus said. "I'd feel a whole lot better if you let me buy that pistol from you, the Colt you have next to yer bed. Us fellars in the infantry don't get pistols; it's just officers and you cavalrymen that gets to carry them. I got plenty of money and would sleep a whole lot better if you let me take it off yer hands for thirty dollars."

"What!" Wilseck said. "That's more'n what two of them pistols is worth. Maybe that shell there knocked you silly in the head. I don't reckon you know what yer sayin'."

Titus reached into his pocket and pulled out a combination of silver dollars and paper currency that equaled thirty dollars and put it on the wicker table in front of them.

"Just give me that pistol of yours and that money's all yours," he said.

"Damn," Wilseck said. "I cain't do that. Yer brain ain't workin' so well right now. I'd feel like I was robbin' a baby if I took that."

"Then take what's you want of it, and give me that pistol so's to get it away from you and those black thoughts of yers," Titus said. Titus could see that his protestations aside, Wilseck could not keep his eyes off of the money and after going back and forth for ten minutes more the cavalryman took the thirty dollars and Titus followed him back to his bed.

Wilseck kept asking Titus if he realized how much he was paying, but Titus hushed him several times since weapons were not allowed in the hospital, and he did not want it confiscated by a hypervigilant nurse.

Wilseck gave him the pistol, the powder flask, a small box of lead balls, percussion caps and cotton wads. Titus rushed the pistol and ancillary items back to his bed and packed them at the bottom of his knapsack.

TITUS FELT A REASSURANCE ABOUT THE FAMILIAR SMELLS around the camp and he reported to the company commander's tent as soon as he arrived. Capt. Fetzer, the former commander, had been promoted and was replaced by David Massey, the only company officer to have survived the battle in Pennsylvania.

"Well, we're just as pleased to get some veterans back," Massey told Titus as he took his papers and turned them over to his aide Sgt. Hunter. "They come straggling in from being exchanged, or from hospitals, or God knows where, but it's a relief. Welcome back, Pvt. Mott."

Sgt. Hunter took his time writing up Titus's return, adding his name to the rolls, fussing with a pile of muster cards, then directing him to the area where Company I was tented.

"Oh, and yer a corporal now," Hunter said.

"I am?"

"You lasted this long so yer a corporal," he said. "You keep this up you'll be a general in about six months, I reckon."

"I don't want to be no corporal," Titus said.

"You got no choice; yer a corporal, so just take the extra money and don't get in a huff. And who did you share a tent with?" Hunter asked.

"Buster Sturger," Titus said.

"Oh, yeah, that's right," Hunter said, "I remember that fellar. He sure was a wild one. And funny, too. But I reckon you know'd he didn't make it?"

"I think I know'd that," Titus said.

"They found bodies all over the countryside near Gettysburg and he was found somewheres nearby. He must a got wounded and crawled away to die. It's too bad."

"Yep," Titus said quickly.

"We got a few new fellars that don't got no tentmates so you're welcome to tent with them or live by yerself, whichever you want," Hunter said. "You know'd most of the ones that survived, they're still here."

"By the way Sergeant, do you happen to know where I can find Lt. Rhys?" Titus asked. "Did he get through all right?"

"You mean Capt. Rhys?"

"Well, he was a second lieutenant when I last seen him, but I reckon things change quickly here," Titus said.

"If it's Capt. Rhys yer lookin' fer, he's commanding Company B now," Hunter said.

"Tell me, did a Pvt. Seibert from Company C make it through all right?" Titus asked.

"I don't know about that man in particular, but I can tell you that Company C is right full of conscripts now, so there ain't many of the original men left. Was he a friend of yours?"

"Yep," Titus said. "A right special friend."

———

THE NIGHT WAS ALIVE WITH THE RUSTLING OF leaves and branches in the warm southwesterly breeze. Titus found the captain sitting outside his tent by himself writing something by lantern light.

"Sir," he said. "Do you have a moment?"

Rhys looked up and squinted in the dark.

"Who is there? I can't see," Rhys said.

"It's Cpl. Mott from Company I."

"How can I help you, Corporal?"

"I have a kinda crazy question to ask you," Titus said.

"You do?" Rhys said putting down his notebook. "What kind of crazy question?"

"It has to do with somethin' I thought you was investigatin' before," Titus said. "At least I thought you was."

Rhys shielded his eyes briefly with his right hand to block the glare from the lantern, taking a longer look at the man standing in front of him.

"What might you be referring to?" he said.

"It's about them killin's that went on in the regiment when we was in Virginia before, do you remember that?"

Rhys stared at the man, and absently shooed away several large gray moths that pinged the lantern glass in suicidal forays.

"What do you want to talk about?" Rhys said.

"I was just wonderin' sir, whether you and the good doctor were able to get some suspects on yer list? We was told the doctor was helpin' you."

Rhys continued to stare at Titus for longer than Titus found comfortable.

"I just got released from the hospital," Titus said. "Got me a head wound but I'm all better now. And I was just wonderin' if you and the doctor had a list of suspects that you was lookin' at?"

"To be honest with you – did you say your name was Mott?"

"Yes sir."

"Well, Cpl. Mott, I have to tell you that you're the first person to bring that subject up in quite a while," he said. "We did have an investigation going but it basically stopped after the battle there at Gettysburg. There was so much carnage and confusion that when we reorganized the regiment we just dropped the investigation."

"Did them killin's stop?" Titus asked.

"Yes, they did. And since they stopped we figured that the killer didn't make it through the battle. Or he was wounded and returned home, or maybe he just deserted."

"Mmm," Titus said.

"Tell me, Corporal, why are you raising the subject now? To be honest, I don't understand your interest in this subject."

"Well, I was just wonderin' if a particular soldier was on yer list of suspects?" Titus said.

"But why would you be interested in who was or wasn't on the list? Do you know something about the killer? Do you know who he was?"

"I reckon I have a good idea who he was, and I was just checkin' to see if you had him on yer list."

"Our list was pretty small, and I don't have it in front of me, but why don't you give me his name?"

"His name was Loren Seibert," Titus said. "He was a private in Company C."

"What makes you think this man Seibert was the killer? And if you thought he was the killer, why didn't you come tell me back then?"

"When I started suspectin' him," Titus said, "we was already movin' into Pennsylvania and then before I know'd it I was lyin' in a hospital. This is my first day back in the regiment."

Rhys studied the man in the lantern light closely.

"So you think the killer was this man Seibert. But you didn't tell me why you thought it was him."

"I seen the way he reacted to some situations," Titus said.

"That's all? You just observed him and decided he was a killer?"

"Well, that and what happened in Pennsylvania outside that damn town," Titus said, shifting on his feet and brushing away a mosquito that was haunting his earlobe.

"Sit down here," Rhys said. "I'm having trouble seeing you. Go on, sit right there."

Titus sat down in a wood folding chair facing Rhys.

"What happened in Pennsylvania?" the Captain asked.

"I knowed this man Seibert was an odd fellar who always carried a knife and had already threatened my friend," Titus said. "In one argument he damn near sliced my friend's throat. This Seibert fellar was a strange fellar. He sure carried a grudge."

Titus could not believe he was talking like this to Capt. Rhys, a man he did not know, and about a subject that was unsettling. But it just came tumbling out, and Titus needed to share his thinking with someone. Every now and then, though, he had a notion that maybe that Rebel artillery shell had knocked something loose from him. He did not understand why he spent so much energy thinking about Seibert.

"So what happened in Pennsylvania?" Rhys asked again.

"It was Seibert that killed my friend Buster Sturger," Titus said. "He cut his throat when he was on picket duty the night before the battle."

"Are you sure of this?" Rhys said, sitting up in his chair.

"Well, I didn't see Seibert do it, but I found my friend the next mornin' with his throat cut. And that fellar Seibert was also on picket duty nearby."

"But that's the only evidence you have?" Rhys said.

"Ain't that enough?" Titus said.

"No, not really," he said. "Have you filed official charges against this man Seibert?"

"Nope," Titus said.

"Well, if you feel strongly about this then I suggest you bring it up with your company commander," Rhys said. "To be honest, though, and I mean no disrespect, Cpl. Mott, but I don't think this will go very far. With all the troubles this army is facing, the desertions, the dead and wounded, the draft riots we've been reading about, well, I just don't think that they're going to focus on your charges against this soldier."

Rhys looked at his visitor and did not know what to say. There were so many strange things that occurred to men after battle. Some soldiers seemed nearly immune to the carnage, while others were deeply troubled. One sergeant from his company who survived Gettysburg unscathed had killed himself the prior week in camp. Rhys was not even aware that the sergeant was troubled.

Mott was sitting on the front of the chair and was clearly agitated.

"Do you think you might be confused on what you saw?" Rhys asked. "Don't you think that you might be overreaching here about the intentions of this man Seibert?"

"No, sir, I ain't confused at all," Titus said firmly. "And this fellar Seibert come up to me when I was wounded in an ambulance."

"He did?" Rhys said. "What happened?"

"He told me I was vermin and that I wasn't goin' to git away," Titus said.

"Seibert said that to you?"

"Yes, sir, he did," Titus said. "And he did one other thing; he bent down and put a mark on my forehead, just like them other fellars that were kilt."

"You mean he cut a cross in your forehead?" Rhys said.

"No, he jest poked his bloody finger onto my head and made a mark," Titus said.

Rhys thought about this for a second. "But you're still alive, and if he was the murderer don't you think he'd have killed you?"

"He thought I was a goner," Titus said. "So to get his satisfaction, he jest wanted me to know I was gonna die. But I showed him. I survived."

Rhys sighed, looked around the camp absently and then returned his gaze to his visitor. "Isn't it possible that you imagined all this stuff with Pvt. Seibert?" Rhys said.

"No, sir," Titus said.

"Are you swearing out a charge of murder on Seibert then? Is that what you're intending to do? Have you approached Seibert yet?"

"No, sir, Seibert's gone," Titus said.

"Gone?"

"I went lookin' for him right away, but he's discharged. Took a ball in the gut and they said he survived and got discharged home."

"So what is it you're looking for, then?" Rhys said. "You want us to send the marshals and bring him back?"

"Maybe," Rhys said.

"But surely you know that no one—even in this crazy world of killing we're in right now—will issue a warrant based upon the evidence you claim to have. I think you need to give this idea some time to settle. Perhaps you need more rest. How long did you say you were hospitalized?"

"I don't need no rest," Titus said. "I was just askin' if this man was on yer list."

"What if he was?" Rhys said. "Or what if he wasn't? What difference does it make? I think you need to let this thing go away. I'm sorry about the death of your friend, but that battle left thousands and thousand of dead and wounded men. Hell, they're still trying to get rid of several thousand horses that were killed in that battle."

"I don't care about no horses," Titus said. "But my friend Buster didn't need to die that way, at the hands of a murderer. If he'd a taken a ball from a Rebel, then so be it. But from one of his own? And an evil man, at that, who already was killin' soldiers."

"But you don't know that for sure," Rhys said. "There's not enough evidence. Surely you can see that?"

"You said yerself the murderin' stopped after the battle," Titus said. "I seen what I seen. You cain't talk that out of me. No words you got can take away the sight I had that day when I found my friend all cut up. And I know who did it. And he came to me when I was wounded and he was wounded, and he sure as hell made my mind up right there. He was thinkin' he could get away with it, that there's no earthly way anyone would know. But I seen it. Yer words cain't take that away."

"You need more rest," Rhys said standing up and grabbing the lantern. "You should see the surgeon. He's a new one—Dr. Morse has been taken prisoner and hasn't been paroled yet."

CHAPTER 24

Titus bided his time as the brigade moved south, across the Potomac and back into Virginia, chasing the remnants of Lee's army. He was forced to take on some duties as corporal but still slept by himself and stayed to himself.

Three weeks later he approached Capt. Massey after a particularly long drawn-out drill.

"Sir, can I speak to you about somethin'?" Titus said.

"Of course, Cpl. Mott. What is it?"

"Well, sir, when I was released from the hospital some of them doctors wanted me to take a discharge out of the service, but I said I wanted to return to my regiment," Titus said. "And they told me that I should at least go home and see my family. But I said I had to get back to fightin' them Secessionists."

"That was a mighty brave thing to do, Mott, and we appreciate your fervor. I just wish we had more men like you with that kind of devotion."

"Well, the thing is Captain, that now I'm wishin' I had gone home," Titus said. "I'm feelin' homesick and was wonderin' if you might give me leave for just a short time?"

"Hell, of course I can, Mott," Massey said. "The more rested you are the better it'll be for our side. I'll get some papers cut for you."

"Thank you kindly, sir," Titus said. "I'll be back all rested fer sure."

———————————

TITUS DIDN'T KNOW WHETHER IT WAS THE WOUND to the head or just the fact that he was not as strong as before the injury, but he could not walk far without taking a rest. This was upsetting to him since at one time he could easily march twenty miles in a single day without so much as a moan, but now, walking by himself down country roads with just his knapsack was exhausting.

Twice sympathetic farmers gave him wagon rides, asking where he was going and if they could help.

In each case he told them he was going to visit his brother in Cumberland, but of course he did not have a brother. He mostly slept on the side of the road tucked into the woods nearby, used as he was to the Spartan living of a foot soldier.

When he got closer to his destination he asked directions, now changing his story about visiting a brother and instead was going to visit a pal from the army.

On the night before reaching the farm, Titus slept farther back in a patch of second-growth oak and maple trees. Even though the October night was cold, with a clear sky and almost no breeze, he did not start a fire and ate some hard tack and bacon he had cooked two days before.

The following morning he walked at least five miles before he came to the property he was looking for; a small, ramshackle farmhouse that stood back at least a quarter mile from the dirt road.

The farm was nestled up against a hill that was only partially cleared of timber. A small herd of cattle was busy browsing through the remnants of a tilled field. Titus stopped at the muddy lane leading up to the farmhouse and debated for the thousandth time whether he should go through with it.

He reached around to the small of his back and felt the pistol that was tucked in at his britches, his blue field jacket covering the weapon. He sighed, took off his cap, and wiped his forehead, being careful not to touch the scar on his head since it was still tender.

Titus turned when he heard the sound of a horse approaching from behind on the road. He saw a boy riding bareback on a thick-shouldered work horse. He waited for the boy to pass him, but like everyone out this way people were inquisitive and friendly. The boy pulled up.

"You a soldier?" he said.

"Yep," Titus said.

"You been in some big battles?"

"I guess so."

"You kill a lot of them Rebs?"

"Not many, I reckon," Titus said.

"Wish I was old enough to join the army," the boy said. "I was thinkin' they needed drummer boys, but my pop said they don't need 'em as much as they need soldiers. What do you reckon? Do they need drummers?"

"Yer pop is right, they don't need no drummers. Got plenty of them. You stay right here. Wait to yer old enough. There's plenty of Rebs to kill if that's what yer hankerin' fer."

"I bet I could get me a couple of them if I was given the chance," the boy said.

"But you got to remember one thing," Titus said.

"What's that?"

"Thems Rebels is tryin' to kill you as much as you'se tryin' to kill them."

"I ain't afraid of them," the boy said.

"I don't reckon you are," Titus said taking off his cap again and wiping his brow.

"Is that a scar on yer head?"

"It is," Titus said replacing the cap.

"You got shot?"

"I did."

"By a bullet?"

"No, by an artillery shell."

"Did it hurt?

"A bit."

"You better now?"

"I am."

The two stared at each other for several seconds.

"Where you goin'?" the boy asked.

"Goin' to see a friend of mine from the army," Titus said. "You know a fellar named Loren Seibert?"

"Well yer lookin' at his farm right before yer eyes," the boy said. "That's his farm right there." He pointed to the little farmhouse.

"You know'd Seibert in the army?" the boy asked.

"Yep," Titus said.

"He took a Rebel ball to his belly, but I guess you know'd that," the boy said.

"I reckon I heard that," Titus said. "I'm just gonna go over there right now and say my hellos."

"Well he ain't there," the boy said. "He's over at Will Jenkins' farm. Ol' Will needed another hand gettin' a mighty big boulder dragged away. Seibert asked me to keep an eye on them cattle over there. Said I would if he'd tell me stories about the fightin' he was in, but he never wants to talk about it."

"When do you reckon he'll be back?" Titus asked.

"I don't know," the boy said. "Probably after supper. Mr. Jenkins will surely feed him fer his work."

Titus rehearsed what he intended to do so many times that it had become a kind of ritualized ceremony. It was an abstraction that stood outside of time and place, residing solely in his rage-fed imagination.

But talking to this eager and trusting boy on a dusty road in central Pennsylvania kicked off an unexpected cascade of doubt. In a panic Titus wondered if he really was prepared for this act.

He looked up at the boy in his faded overalls and bare feet, took a sideways glance at the forlorn farmhouse, and then looked back at the boy. Titus sighed, as if releasing pressure from a long-simmering steam kettle.

"Well, can you do a favor for me then?" Titus said, pulling the knapsack off his shoulder and putting it on the ground. He unstrapped it and pulled out a wad of paper tied together with a piece of string. Tight under the string was a pencil.

"When you see him next, can you just give Seibert this note that has my name on it?" Titus said. "Too bad I cain't stay. Only got a few more days on leave. You be sure to hand him this paper, would you, son?"

Titus licked the end of the pencil stub and wrote in block letters: "Buster Sturger, Company I, 239th PA Vols. We played cards. Yer lucky you ain't here today."

"Course I would," the boy said. "But he'll be mighty sore if you don't wait fer him to return."

"I really got to get goin," Titus said, handing the boy the piece of paper. "You be sure to give it to him. I reckon that'll be enough."

"You bet," the boy said.

CHAPTER 25

The farther Titus got from Seibert's farm the better he felt, as if a couple of twelve-pound artillery rounds had been lifted from his knapsack. His pace was quick now, as if he was on a hard march with the entire regiment, the imaginary cadence of thousands of steps mesmerizing him into a walking trance.

He was relieved that he had not seen Seibert, and had not done what he had come to do. Originally it had made perfect sense that he would travel this far into the Pennsylvania hill country in search of this man, to right the wrong and to set the ledger even on this man's deeds. He had steeled himself with what he was going to do to honor Buster and the other men dispatched at this man's hands. He had rehearsed the deed over and over again until it seemed so natural and right.

But Seibert was not home when Titus arrived and it was a signal that he was not going to follow through with his plan. It was not going to be his role; it would be someone else's job. Surely this Satan of a man would cross someone or kill someone else, and they would eventually find him and string him up.

But it would not be Titus's job; he was done with the whole mess. Maybe Capt. Rhys was right, Titus thought. Maybe that shell knocked some good sense out of his poor stupid head.

The air cooled dramatically after the sun slipped below the hills to the west and it was not long before he found a stretch of forest away from any farmhouses. He walked into a stand of trees about fifty feet from the road and started a fire immediately. He cooked his last stash of bacon in his skillet, wiping up the grease with a piece of hard tack. Titus then made a bed for himself, using the half-tent as a cover and his gum cloth to ward off the dampness seeping up through the forest floor.

He worried that he put too much wood on the fire but its warmth was welcome as the damp fall night took hold. For the first time in many nights Titus fell asleep almost instantly.

Sometime in the night, he could not remember when, he got up and threw more scrap wood on the fire to keep him warm and promptly fell asleep. The next sound he heard was a snap, it was dull and muffled, but it was still a sound that alerted him. He opened his eyes to see that the fire was barely alive and would soon be burned out. The snap was not from the wood burning, he realized.

The forest was full of deer, black bears, possums and raccoons, but Titus was not taking any chances and he reached into his knapsack and pulled out the pistol. Putting his free hand over the hammer to absorb the sound he pulled it back to its full cock.

He strained to hear what might be going on around him. After nearly five minutes of lying absolutely still and hearing nothing, Titus relaxed and was about to release the hammer when he heard the unmistakable sound of something large moving around behind the lean-to.

"Who is it out there?" Titus demanded.

"Who the hell do you think it is?" came the reply.

Titus closed his eyes briefly in despair; why had he not kept on walking? Why was this night turning into something awful after he had made the decision to let it go? How can this be happening? His head began to ache as he collected his thoughts.

"Well, whoever you are, you should come out so I can see you," Titus said. "It ain't right to be sneakin' behind a man like that."

Titus heard footsteps rustling around behind the lean-to on his left, and the steps continued circling farther away so that eventually he could see someone standing at least twenty feet on the other side of the fire.

"What can I do fer you?" Titus said. "Am I on yer land? If so, I'm sorry. I'm just a Union soldier returnin' home and don't want no trouble. I'll gladly leave, if that's what yer askin' me to do."

"How big a fool do you reckon I am?" the man said, still indistinguishable in the glare of the fire. "You leave a note with that boy announcin' to me that you're someone that I know'd is dead. Buster Sturger got kilt at Gettysburg. Question is, why the hell are you comin' this far to leave me a note sayin' yer him. What kind of man does that?"

Titus sat forward on his elbow, the pistol in front of his chest pointing in the general direction of Seibert. He wanted his visitor to see the weapon.

"I wrote you that note to remind you of what you done to Buster that night before the battle," Titus said. "But I don't care no more. I'm tired out thinkin' of that day, and I'm wishin' you a good night. Just leave me be."

"What do you mean, 'what I done to Buster that night'? Them Rebels smote yer cheatin' friend. I'm just glad someone did it."

"You tryin' to tell me that you didn't cut Buster up?" Titus said, being tugged into a discussion he was determined earlier not to have.

Seibert took several steps closer to Titus, the fire between them. Titus could see Seibert was not carrying a weapon.

"I know'd who you are," Seibert said. "Yer that friend of Buster's that jumped me in that card game, aren't you?"

"If I hadn't got that knife away from you, you woulda cut his head off like you did to them other soldiers," Titus said.

"A man that cheats like that deserves scarin'," he said. "Bible says 'whoever knows the right thing to do and fails to do it, for him it is sin.'"

"I was watchin' that card game, and I didn't see no cheatin'," Titus said, sitting up cross-legged, his right hand on the pistol as it rested in his lap.

"Well, I guess you don't play much cards then. It ain't my fault yer a stupid fellar. Yer friend marked the cards, if I recollect properly."

"No he didn't," Titus said. "Yer a liar and murderer. Now just git and leave me be. I don't want nothin' to do with you. I don't care if you go out and kill everyone in this here valley. I'm through thinkin' about you and yer evil ways."

"You think you can just come around my home here and talk about me bein' a killer? Who else you been talkin' to in the valley beside the boy? You talk to that old man Parker? I bet you told ol' Parker some of your crazy ideas. Damn you, you pack up right now and get out of here. Go on, git packed up."

"We ain't in the army right now, Seibert," Titus said, anger boiling up rapidly inside him. It started in his stomach and spread out in a burning hot flash across his chest and into his face. "You cain't be bossin' a man around. I ain't on yer property and you got no cause to order me around."

"When a man comes around and talks behind another man's back, sayin' things that ain't true just to have his neighbors turn against him, well I can do whatever I need to do to protect myself. You best git out right now."

"I only talked to that boy, so quit yer complainin' about me talkin' to yer neighbors," Titus said. "And stop orderin' me around like you was a captain." Titus found that his teeth were clenched so tightly that his words were barely intelligible. "You cain't be forcin' me to do nothin'. You got that, you murderin' thief?"

"Stop callin' me that!" Seibert said, reaching into his pocket and pulling out long, thin-bladed knife.

Titus raised his pistol. "You stop right there."

"You bastard," Seibert said, stepping toward him. "Yer turnin' my neighbors against me with yer talkin'. They's all against me and now I seen why!"

"Stop, right there," Titus said.

Titus could now see Seibert's eyes sparkling in the firelight between them as he began to rush at him; it was the same cold, steady, penetrating gaze he saw on the ridge west of town in Pennsylvania that day.

The flash from Titus' pistol was so bright that he was blinded as the recoil rocked him backward on his haunches. He looked at Seibert but he was not there. Startled, Titus jumped up scanning left and right, re-cocking the hammer of the pistol as the cylinder rotated to expose the next primed round.

When he stood, he saw the soles of Seibert's shoes, beaten and worn down to tattered pieces of leather. Seibert had fallen backward away from Titus; he was not able to see his body because the fire's glow between them had hidden him.

Titus slowly walked over stood looking down at Seibert. Miraculously Titus had shot Seibert directly above his heart and killed him instantly. Titus collapsed in a heap next to Seibert and sat there, looking at the fire. He felt a strange mixture of satisfaction, fear and, oddly, sadness.

He had joined the army to save the Union but was suddenly confused about what he was doing sitting next to a dead man in the Pennsylvania countryside, hundreds of miles from the nearest Rebel soldier.

After twenty minutes of staring into the embers, and with a sharp headache coming on, Titus got up and put more wood on the fire. He packed his half-tent away and all his belongings. Then, using his skillet as a shovel, he dug a shallow grave and rolled Seibert's body and his knife into the depression. He stamped on the mound to keep the soil tight, then dragged several large downed branches and piled them over the grave.

Finally, he took his canteen and poured as much water as he could spare to extinguish the fire. Afterward he scattered the wet coals with his shoes and dragged even more leaves and branches over the area.

Before he left he stood over the mound in the darkness, the only sound was that of the trees swaying slightly in the cold wind.

"I got him, Buster," Titus said up through the nearly bare branches into the starlit sky. "I got the bastard. Don't feel nothin' inside me except maybe relief. Hope yer restin' easier now."

He made his way out of the stand of trees and found Seibert's horse tied up to a sapling.

Titus unhooked him, slapped him mightily on his haunch, and yelled "Git! Go on. Git back home!"

And then he started walking down the dirt road, his breath barely visible in the night as a ghostlike vapor. Darkened farmhouses were visible as he marched by, set back from the road. Occasionally a dog barked as he marched, but mostly the only sound he heard was that of his soles slapping the dirt road.

At first his headache grew worse as the pain seared across his temple and down his neck. But after a while his body temperature rose, and he discovered a marching cadence that pushed him quickly and decisively to the east, where he knew the sun rises each day.

EPILOGUE

Clive Rhys commanded Company B until the Battle of the Wilderness in May 1864, when he was promoted to major and assigned to the headquarters staff of the First Corps. In January 1865 he contracted variola and was hospitalized in Alexandria, Virginia. After four weeks in the hospital he was released and rejoined the First Corps in Petersburg, Virginia. In March 1865 he asked for and was given a transfer to the Second Cavalry regiment. In a skirmish in the Shenandoah Valley, Rhys was lightly wounded in the arm and was convalescing in a hospital when the war ended. He returned to civilian life in Schenectady, New York, and took up a position with the family business manufacturing wheels for railroad cars. In 1868, citing boredom—and against the wishes of his father—Rhys reenlisted in the Army and joined the Second Cavalry as a captain. In 1876, in a battle with the Oglala Sioux near the Rosebud River in Montana, Rhys was killed. He is buried near Butte in a military cemetery.

Stanley Rittenhouse was promoted to general in October 1863 and given command of the First Corps under Major General Burns. At the Battle of the Wilderness the First Corps performed poorly and Rittenhouse was transferred to the Quartermaster Corps, where he finished out the war stationed in Baltimore, Maryland. He returned to his hometown of Media, Pennsylvania, and went into business with his father-in-law, a shopkeeper. Using his talents from the Quartermaster Corps, Rittenhouse grew the store into a chain of stores throughout Eastern Pennsylvania. In 1878, he ran for US Congress as a Republican and won a close general election. He won reelection 12 times before retiring in 1902. He was a regular participant in reunions at Gettysburg and was instrumental in raising funds for the Pennsylvania monument at the battlefield. He died in 1913 from heart failure, leaving his wife and two grown children.

Dr. Grayson Morse was captured at Gettysburg and taken to Richmond and incarcerated in Libby Prison where he attended the prisoners there, mostly Union officers. In October he was paroled at Camp Parole in Alexandria, Virginia, and exchanged later that month. He rejoined the regiment as its surgeon. In May 1864, Morse's field hospital was overrun in the Battle of the Wilderness, and he was captured again but released almost immediately to return to Union lines. He continued to serve the regiment until the end of the war, when he returned to the small rural community of Newburg, Pennsylvania. In 1870, he accepted a teaching position at Johns Hopkins School of Medicine, and remained a popular, if eccentric, teacher at the school until he died suddenly in 1875. He never married and lived alone in a townhouse on Beech Street near the campus. After his death, his lone surviving sister from Boston cleaned out his townhouse. They found thousands of books and magazines throughout the house, as well as hundreds of empty vials of laudanum in the basement.

Titus Mott remained with the 239th for the remainder of the war, rising to the rank of sergeant. During the Battle of the Wilderness in May 1864, he was shot through his left hand, recuperated at a hospital in Washington,

DC, and returned to service later that fall. In February 1865, he was wounded in his left calf at the Battle of Hatcher's Run. He was given a medical discharge and returned to Shippensburg, Pennsylvania. In 1867, he married Eleanor McPherson and moved to Harrisburg, Pennsylvania, where he went to work at a steel mill, later rising to plant manager. He and Eleanor had four children over a span of seven years. In 1876, a man named Peter Sandler was arrested in Philadelphia, Pennsylvania, for the gruesome murder of the pastor of an Episcopal Church on East Street. The pastor was discovered in the rectory with his head nearly severed from the attack and a mark on his forehead. After his arrest, Sandler confessed to Philadelphia police that he had murdered more than thirty people over a span of twenty years. At first police did not believe Sandler's boasts, but he gave investigators the approximate dates and circumstances of the killings, nearly all of which he said involved either a fatal stabbing or the slitting of the victim's throat. Sandler said he always marked the foreheads of his victims with a cross. Asked why he killed his victims, Sandler said that God had chosen him to sacrifice individuals who had blasphemed. He chose his victims, he told the investigators, through his sense of smell. The police corroborated many of the recent killings that had taken place in Virginia, Maryland and Western Pennsylvania. Sensational media reports of the "Philadelphia Butcher" shocked and titillated readers up and down the East Coast. One part of Sandler's confession that gained attention in Washington, DC, was his claim that he started his killing spree while serving as a surgeon's aide in the Union Army during the Civil War. Federal records showed that Sandler had served in the 239th Pennsylvania Volunteers as a medical aide and was captured, paroled and exchanged after the battle of Gettysburg. There were no official records detailing murders in the 239th and Philadelphia police dismissed those claims. Titus became obsessed by the news surrounding Sandler's arrest. When Sandler was put on trial for the murder of the pastor, Titus took a brief leave of absence from the Harrisburg Steel Manufacturing Co., and moved to a hotel in Philadelphia to attend the proceedings daily. Sandler was convicted and sentenced to death by hanging. The day the trial ended Titus returned home and immediately brushed past his wife Eleanor and children to enter the attic. He found his old Army knapsack and removed a package wrapped in brown paper and string. He found a deck of worn playing cards inside and took them downstairs to his writing desk. He spread the cards design-side up on his desktop and took a magnifying glass to the cards as Eleanor stood in the doorway. Titus noticed that each of the aces had a blue mark in the very center of the swirling design; the ace of spades had one tick, the ace of diamonds had two, the ace of clubs had three, and the ace of hearts had four. The magnifying glass suggested the marks had been done by hand using blue ink. When he found similar marks on two other face cards he dropped the magnifying glass and left the room, telling Eleanor to remove the cards and to burn them. Titus returned to work at the mill and retired as president in 1910 at age sixty-four. In 1914 Titus's picture was published on the front page of the *New York Herald Tribune*, along with a half-dozen other surviving veterans of the Civil War, leading an antiwar march in New York City. He died in 1917 of heart disease and is buried in Harrisburg's main public cemetery.

AUTHOR'S NOTE

THE IDEA OF WRITING *TITUS* WAS BORN OUT of an article I wrote for the *Boston Sunday Globe Magazine* that was published Nov. 22, 1992. The article was a first-person narrative of a visit to Gettysburg with my then eight-year-old son Michael to retrace the steps of my great-grandfather John W. Yocum, a private in Company I of the 149th Pennsylvania Volunteers. The 149th Pennsylvania Volunteers was involved in a pivotal engagement on the first day of the Battle of Gettysburg on July 1, 1863. The engagement roamed over McPherson's Farm, an adjacent unfinished railroad cut west of town, and finally the streets of Gettysburg itself. Pvt. Yocum was captured that day, but he was paroled and rejoined his regiment later that summer and remained with the 149th until the end of the war.

Weaving fiction into historic events is a delicate exercise, especially when the subject is the US Civil War. Reenactors, hobbyists, and historians are experts in many aspects of this conflict and understandably take great umbrage at inaccuracies.

I have taken the liberty of creating three fictional Union regiments in this novel – the 223rd, the 239th, and 240th Pennsylvania Volunteers. These fictional regiments are loosely based upon the real 143rd, 149th, and 150th Pennsylvania regiments immediately before and during the Battle of Gettysburg. Those actual regiments suffered heavy losses at the railroad cut west of town and in a retreat later through the town of Gettysburg.

Any resemblance to actual individuals in those three regiments is purely coincidental. The characters at the heart of this story and the murders described are fictional and do not refer to actual people or incidents.

A special thanks to the individuals who have kindly offered advice and direction for this novel, including Denise, Michael, Nicole, Robert, Joe, Lynne, Margaret, and several other volunteer "readers."

I'd also like to thank author and historian Patrick Schroeder for reviewing sections of this novel for historical accuracy. Schroeder is currently the full-time Historian of Appomattox Court House National Historical Park, and the owner of Schroeder Publications, which focuses on the Civil War. If the reader finds any inaccuracies in this novel, it is safe to assume those errors occurred in sections of the novel that Schroeder was not asked to review.

SELECTED BIBLIOGRAPHY

There are thousands of books written about every conceivable aspect of the US Civil War, ranging from self-published memoirs to finely researched manuscripts from noted historians. There are also numerous websites, both amateur and academic, that document every nuance of the war. I have chosen to highlight four books and two websites that were particularly helpful to me.

Billings, John Davis. *Hardtack and Coffee; Or, The Unwritten Story of Army Life*. Boston, MA: G. M. Smith & Company, 1887.

Matthews, Richard. *The 149th Pennsylvania Volunteer Infantry Unit in the Civil War*. Jefferson, NC: McFarland & Company Inc., 1994.

Morse, Charles Fessenden. *Letters Written During the Civil War 1861–1865*. Boston, MA: T. R. Marvin & Son, Printers, 1898.

Wiley, Bell Irvin. *The Life of Billy Yank: The Common Soldier of the Union*. Baton Rouge, LA: Louisiana State University Press, 2008 (updated).

WEBSITES:

http://www.nps.gov/history/museum/exhibits/gettex/index.htm
http://www.archives.gov/research/military/civil-war/photos/index.html